D0228696

BUT FOR BUNTER

BOOKS BY DAVID HUGHES

Fiction
A Feeling in the Air
Sealed with a Loving Kiss
The Horsehair Sofa
The Major
The Man Who Invented Tomorrow
Memories of Dying
A Genoese Fancy
The Imperial German Dinner Service
The Pork Butcher

Non-fiction
J. B. Priestley: An Informal Study
The Road to Stockholm
The Seven Ages of England
The Rosewater Revolution
Evergreens

BUT FOR
BUNTER

DAVID HUGHES

HEINEMANN · LONDON

LANCASHIRE LIBRARY

00799163

William Heinemann Ltd
10 Upper Grosvenor Street, London W1X 9PA
LONDON   MELBOURNE   TORONTO
JOHANNESBURG   AUCKLAND

First published 1985
Copyright © David Hughes 1985
SBN 434 35410 4

18544325

Typeset by Richard Clay (The Chaucer Press) Ltd,
Bungay, Suffolk
Printed in Great Britain by St Edmundsbury Press,
Bury St Edmunds, Suffolk

To the Famous Five

Jeremy Bullmore
Giles Gordon
Michael Gough
Miles Huddleston
Godfrey Smith

with thanks and love

I

It was my ex-wife, on one of the rare meetings she fixed to see for herself how much I had deteriorated, who told me that Billy Bunter was still alive.

We were sitting side by side on stools at a wine-bar in Mayfair. I had just pointed out that one of her black stockings was laddered above the knee, then tit-for-tat her skinny fingers had tapped my paunch, so it was fair to suppose that her remark about Bunter was crudely personal. When we were first married she often behaved as if the great Bunter were a potential rival, because my friends and I spent afternoons testing one another's memory of goings-on at Greyfriars and chortling over fatuities that excluded her. I had been unable to explain an addiction buried in my childhood.

I pulled in my stomach. 'Rubbish,' I said.

'No, no,' she insisted. 'I mean it. You never believe me, do you? He's still alive, your hero. Only just, mind you. If you hurry you might catch him as he drops off the perch. Or have you grown out of him at last? But you'd be wrong again,' she added unexpectedly. 'He's a wonderful old bird.'

These occasions were never easy. Lesley had the knack of interpreting slips of her own as betrayals on my part. It took

LANCASHIRE LIBRARY

her affair with a landscape gardener to persuade her that I had
broken up our marriage. Since her view of things had built-in
rectitude, any effort to correct the facts, even for the record,
brought me only humiliation. For no reason better than to
foment the quarrel which she considered I lost no opportunity
to pick with her, Lesley had now decided that Billy Bunter was
fact, not fiction, and that by failing to accept her vision of the
truth, I was not only manufacturing an insult to her but blinding myself to my own best interests which she had all along had
at heart.

Plying her with drink sometimes blunted her attack, but
more often seduced her into reliving her love for me. With a
glum sense of risk I ordered two more glasses of Rioja and she
said, 'Are you trying to get me pissed?'

'Bunter,' I said, steeling my mind against contradiction, 'was
a character in a schoolboy paper called *The Magnet*. He came
on the scene in 1908 when he was fourteen and vanished from
it, having added not a year to his age, when the paper ceased
publication in 1940. Nowadays I hardly give him a thought.
But he was a living legend to those of us who attended the
same kind of school, and the only way he survives is as our
affectionate tribute to a number of the deadly sins which a lot
of us commit but don't admit, namely, greed, pride, sloth, envy
and avarice, none of which happens to be a fault of yours.'

'How about lust?' said Lesley with a coy gleam.

'Bunter never suffered from it.'

'He does now,' she said, combining a wink with a good go
at her glass. 'The old devil made a gargantuan pass at me and
he's not fourteen, he's eighty-nine. What are you doing next
weekend?'

I knew better than to suppose this an invitation, if only
because Lesley knew better than to think I would accept it.
'It's a busy one,' I said, adding mendacity to the list of deadly
sins. 'I have several engagements, a drinks thing with some
people, the odd dinner . . .'

Quite false. I was already looking forward to holing up in my Pimlico house, losing a pound or two at the gym round the corner, and putting my psyche in order after buying Lesley too many drinks.

'And I've a paper to prepare for the office,' I added. 'A report for the Minister about the state of culture now, what children are reading if anything, public money going down the comprehensive drain, you know the kind of stuff.'

Quite true. But I had no intention of ruining my days of rest, or the rest of my days, with such guff, when I could dictate a lot of it on Monday afternoon to Joanna Feathers before taking her out for a glass or two of something not unlike Rioja.

Lesley gave me the fond stare of patronage she reserved for surveying my hollow life, then guzzled an inch of wine. 'Oh, I'm not suggesting a damned thing about your precious week-end,' she said, scratching her thigh above the ladder. 'Only I do think you owe it to yourself – for the sake of your past if you like, though I think it might also improve your present – to pop down and see Archibald.'

'Archibald?'

'Culture!' she said at an apparent tangent, but only to lose no chance of reviling my profession. 'What's that? The state of culture now! Archibald knows more about the twentieth century than you've had hot dinners.'

I grimaced, and not only at her vulgarity – the phrase sounded too much like an invitation to invite her to dine. She favoured Wheeler's, a branch of which was almost next door. All I wanted, if anything, was the haddock and chips they doled out at Seafresh in the Wilton Road near home, and a couple of cups of their strong tea, and a good book.

'Can his name really be Archibald?' I said, trying to echo the very contempt she had conferred on both culture and me.

'Billy Bunter,' she said. 'One and the same. You won't accept it. You never do, do you? But there he is, down there in Kent, and if you miss him you'll never forgive me, I know you. Don't you think it's fairly touching that I'm still interested in your hobbies? I've got my own life to lead, you know, it's very exciting what's going on, more of that anon, but I do want you to fulfil yourself and be happy, darling, you know that even if you can't admit it – it's a question of maturity really, isn't it?'

She looked grave. Her fingers, gesticulating in search of the truth she always found elusive, again hovered near my belly. I felt guiltily hungry for the fish and chips.

'I actually think, listen now, do,' Lesley said, 'that it's time you got Billy Bunter out of your system. That's why you're still in the Government or on the fringes of it – you can't get beyond the self who died all those years ago, can you? *The real you.* So why not meet the original of the hero you used to go on about? Don't be a coward. I couldn't bear that.' As if anaesthetising her sensibilities against ultimate disappointment in me, Lesley tossed back the rest of her wine. 'Ring him up,' she wheedled. 'Ring up Archibald.'

'What's his actual name and address?' I asked, with a stir of interest that shamed me even as I spoke.

'Let's see . . .'

Lesley's fingers plunged into the manic chaos of her handbag. A scuffed cheque-book flapped on to the bar like a reproach for my inability to support her. Various cosmetics churned inside the bag to vouch for her continuing desirability. And then an address book stuffed with unopened bills – I felt a flash of the old agony that I might have to pay them – surfaced, and she was trying to make out her own illegible writing without re-course to the reading-glasses that lurked among the other threats at the bottom of her holdall.

'Ah,' she said with myopic slowness, 'I think this is it. Read it out. I want you to tell me what it says, so I know it's sunk in.'

I looked where her finger dithered, an inch beyond the cracked polish on the nail which had dug into my back night after night from the Suez crisis to the decline of the Beatles. I had to blink to grasp the name, just as I had to think to remember what making love to her was like. Nor were my eye exercises, practised at weekends as religiously as the jogging, working too well as yet.

'Archibald Aitken,' I said,

'Write it down at once.'

'My memory's still all right.'

'I talked him into it,' Lesley said. 'He's expecting you. I think he wants people to know the story before he dies. Wouldn't you like to be famous, darling? But I suppose you can't be, stuck where you are. I always said you could do better, go further – and become yourself. Perhaps it's not too late for your Billy Bunter to teach you a thing or two even now. What did you say his phone number was?'

I narrowed my glance at her blurred page of addresses and read out New Romney 771.

'Exactly!' cried Lesley. 'Don't mope in your pad all weekend long, darling. Go to Archibald, embrace him from me, let yourself go for once, wallow in the nostalgia of it all, learn from his experience, pit your wits against a man twice your size, and don't come running back to me saying I didn't warn you.'

She looked me sadly in the eye with triumph, then a smile of complicity formed. 'Another glass of wine? A toast to your Mr Bunter?'

'Alas, I must go,' I said, feeling wretched, sliding my belly sideways off the stool.

'I wish you'd never gone,' she said, stuffing her addresses back in the bag. 'But you have, haven't you? You're not really there any more.'

It was to be my secretary Joanna, hardly one to favour my ex-wife's efforts to revitalise my routine, who at length per-suaded me that it might be amusing to set out on a quest for this phantom Bunter. But that didn't happen quite yet for the simple reason that when the taxi dropped me at home she wasn't there. I hadn't asked her. And I had sabotaged Friday evening, the most secret time of my week, by brooding on Lesley's power to suggest that the life we once shared had been granted entirely to her as part of the settlement, leaving none left over for me. It had always felt like a miscarriage of justice. It felt no less like it after a number of whiskies alone in my drawing-room.

I thought of telephoning Joanna for consultation, but it was a wet night and Hampstead was in another world. Though real enough, my secretary Joanna retained for me the smack of pure fantasy. So discreet was her nature that she only showed any sign that we were having an affair when actually in bed with me. As I saw it, she no more wanted me to overwhelm her nights with random passion or her day with unofficial innuendo than I wanted her smalls festooning my bathroom. She left no tokens of possession; we sought no commitment. In the dark, perhaps once or twice a week, we were different people, while our relations in the office, also never discussed, were based on cool respect. In other words, I hardly knew her.

The next morning, to spite Lesley, I did no work on the report. My hangover had less to do with alcohol than with the brain damage her descents always seemed to inflict. She simply sapped my identity. The sunlight in Tachbrook Street bit into my eyes as I shopped in the market, and I only started feeling healthier when I decided not to footle around in the gymnasium with other chaps trying to catch up their lost youth, but instead to ask Joanna to share the sea-trout with me over a working lunch. Working? Even at weekends we kept up pretences, as though our affair were fiction, a tawdry novel we picked up to read for an instant before dropping off.

For reasons of her own – one never enquired why – Joanna wasn't available, but she could manage the evening. This was only a partial disappointment. I had my anticipation to keep me warm. So after a dozen oysters at Overton's in Victoria and as many minutes in the station watching ill-matched couples nag their way abroad on the afternoon boat-train, I made my way to the reference library and looked up Archibald Aitken in *Who's Who*. He was not there. Nor was Frank Richards, author of the Bunter stories; not surprising, for he was not only dead, but a pseudonym. I vaguely wondered why he had thought fit to conceal his identity. It obviously wasn't for the same reason as George Eliot. No woman in a thousand years could have given birth to William George Bunter, the Fat Owl of the Remove.

It was by no means impossible, however, that Lesley had invented Archibald Aitken. She was never short of schemes for mocking my existence. For instance, she had often evinced a mournful glee in pointing out the triviality of my interests – school, university, job – in comparison with hers: buildings, gardens, life. Yesterday she could have been attempting a subtle coup, as she viewed it, at the expense of my profession, one she considered childish. Though not in elective office, I served politicians, pulled strings for them behind the scenes, while she had always hoped to play hostess to names that rang bells. More blatantly perhaps, and I returned to this suspicion, she was turning her knife in my physical vanity.

She needn't have bothered. It was in tatters. Much of my work, say a quarter, two hours out of a daily eight, consisted of lunching. And it showed. Unlike T. S. Eliot's old man, it was the tops of my trousers that I wore rolled, because I had no choice: my belly sagged over my waistline, crumpling the cut of a decent suit, and also filled out good shirts from Jermyn Street, straining the downward stripes into gaudy parabolas of self-indulgence. All those lunches had gone to my face too. The cheeks had swollen into rugose cushions that concealed the bone structure which Lesley had once eyed with desire. Jowls hung in slack upholstery above my tightening collars. I couldn't say that my luncheons had much to do with my hair, but the diminishing quantity of the latter had kept pace with the increasing quality of the former. I still felt youthful enough. But mirrors, as I stared into them through glasses that bit into my nose, had become my enemies of promise. In point of fact I was a fattening, balding, ageing man – considered alluring by Joanna, I suppose, though maybe she had refused lunch only to avoid going to bed in daylight.

I mooned into the lending library and consulted the catalogue for references to Bunter. There was none under fiction. Had the hapless Owl quite vanished from the ken of our distracted times? Was I even more old-fashioned than I pretended? Out of touch? No, for under *Magnet* (*The*) I found a mass of volumes listed. They were all bound sets of the dear old paper in facsimile, published over the last couple of decades by someone who evidently felt that the appetite for adventure, as catered for by high jinks at Greyfriars, was not lost.

I was quite taken aback by the extent of Bunter's harmless crimes against humanity on offer in that library. It seemed that the entire building must be full of the fellow, crowding out such minor figures as Eliot (T. S. or George). I felt a growing elation, as if about to embrace the best, or the funniest, of my youth again. I searched the shelves. The volumes were not under fiction, and that pleased me. Biography? Surely not. And then, curiously late, I thought: yes, of course, the children's section, and that gave me a slight shock – I realised that I no longer thought of Bunter as suitable fare for children, though a child myself when my father introduced me to the flawed hero whom he, in his own boyhood, had looked up to and down on. It seemed a calculated insult on the part of the library service to let this great character loose among the kids of all those liberated parents doing up their Pimlico homes at cost to save cash for country cottages, while the said offspring went native in the local comprehensives.

Yet there was nothing of Bunter or *The Magnet* in the junior area of the library. I wandered up to the desk. An elderly woman, probably about my age, was making a fuss about a Harold Robbins she had ordered. I waited while she rejected a Forsyth after staring at the first paragraph as if it were a locked door. I watched her tack away to the shelves grumbling loosely between her teeth in search of a Cartland romance. Then, trying to exert charm, I asked about the books whose reference numbers I had noted on a slip of card.

'If they're not in they're out,' said the youngish lady.

'All of them?'

'However many there are they're out if they're not there,' she explained.

'That's a bit unlikely, isn't it?'

'If not published pre-1900 or of special interest, meaning not for children, in which case apply to the chief librarian in writing, the books you want are out.' She simpered fiercely. 'You're not the only borrower.'

'Is he really still that popular?' I mused. It was a mistake to attempt mounting a discussion. Her face hardened under threat. I suddenly saw myself as a frustrated boor imposing on the patience of this bridling drudge – who now gave my list of numbers a last glance.

'Oh, it's Billy Bunter,' she sniffed, as though recognising me. 'What do you expect?'

I no longer knew what I expected. But as I strolled out of that stuffy interior into a sun that was fading to orange on the stucco terraces, I at once grasped a ridiculous fact: I believed Lesley. I had spent that entire day, even while shopping for food and scoffing oysters instead of going into training, while envying those people off to the continent rather than drafting my report, while marking time in the library as though doing compulsive research on a subject that mattered, I had passed all those hours believing that Bunter was still alive.

Alive? Certainly I myself felt more alive as a result of this farcical proposition. At one moment I had even contemplated telephoning Bunter or whoever he was in his senile retreat at

New Romney, which just showed how strong was my longing
that he should exist. He was like a set of awkward facts on which
I had been commissioned to report. Yet so vividly had Bunter's
presence taken hold of my mind that emerging into the sunlit
streets also had the freedom of toddling along inside a story –
not precisely as the hero, more of a minor character – towards
a doom or dénouement chosen by someone else. I felt distinctly
piqued by all this, but help was on her way.

Joanna Feathers arrived in pink slacks on the dot of eight. We
shared an unspoken admiration for punctuality as well as each
other. It was a beautiful dusk and her appearance righted my
thoughts: what a wicked way for a grown man to have
squandered his afternoon. She was carrying a notebook to lend
conviction to her role.

I settled Joanna down with a vodka and tonic and a heaped
saucer of cashew nuts. As usual – much of our leisure being
conducted with the formality we observed at the office – I gave
her a subject to chew over while I prepared our meal.

'I want you to think very carefully,' I began.

'Don't I always?'

'No, but this time I require your views on a subject that
will challenge all your powers – Billy Bunter.'

'Billy Bunter?' she said with a short laugh. 'You must be
joking.'

'No prejudgments,' I said. 'I want a plain account of your
knowledge, not a typically feminine response to the idea of a
fat boy.'

'Is this something to do with our work?'

'It might be.'

'What has Billy Bunter got to do with the state of culture
now?'

'There you go again,' I said, leaving her to calm down and
get her material in order.

My cooking was more intuitive than informed, the only act

I could usually perform without thinking. Joanna, on the other hand, needed time to dredge up her haul of polytechnic prejudices, her first-year psychology spiced with scraps of general knowledge; unfinished courses lay beached on the shores of her ignorance, poor girl. She was also very bright, so by the time the sea-trout was poached, the cabbage blanched, the cucumber sharpened with vinegar, she was just about ready for me.

We sat down at the round table under the window. We smiled. Joanna bit on a new potato and swallowed hard. She coughed; tears trembled on her eyelids.

'Billy Bunter,' she said with a lump in her throat.

'Wait a tick,' I sighed. I put the potatoes on to boil for another minute. 'Let's start all over again.'

'The fish is delicious,' Joanna said, dabbing her eyes.

'Mind the bones.'

'Did you put any sugar in with the cucumber?'

'No, but it won't take long.' With slight irritation I sprinkled sugar on the salad, then said, 'Let's try once more.'

'What can I tell you?' she said modestly. 'I saw a TV series about Billy Bunter when I was a little girl, and all I remember is this big bottom, which teachers in black gowns kept on caning, and now, of course, with hindsight, it's pretty obvious that this answered to certain sado-masochistic tendencies in modern society.'

'Did it?'

'In a male-dominated society,' said Joanna, getting into her stride, 'crime and punishment are a *sine qua non*, but then so is guilt – you know how guilty we're made to feel about everything we do . . .'

'Are we?'

'So, you see, Billy Bunter is a sort of focus, as I see it, for this guilt we all feel, and he's getting on his fat bottom all the comeuppance we think we deserve for the terrible things we do to each other, like in wars and one-night stands and you name it.'

I looked at her plump lips spouting this pabulum and my interest stirred vaguely. 'Do you personally feel you deserve such retribution?' I asked.

Joanna gazed at me, then lowered her eyes becomingly as the point struck home.

'I'm not a man,' she said, shifting uneasily in her chair.

'Do only men feel this guilt?'

'Ask yourself,' she replied. 'You're a public official having a fling with his secretary. How does that make you feel?'

In fact I almost blushed. Never before had Joanna addressed me with such pert intimacy, yet I was hardly to blame for the image of taut posteriors which she had lodged in my mind. Her own, though not on the scale of those mentioned in her sociological outburst, were ample. I had never had the discourtesy to watch them in the office atop her equally satisfactory legs, but that was thanks to the sharp division I made – a moral one, I liked to think – between public duty and private indulgence. Now that she had dragged the latter into the open, I did indeed feel guilty, as well as faintly annoyed.

'But I'm not a married man,' I expostulated.

'You were.'

'There's a difference between past and present.'

'There isn't,' she said. 'Here we are sitting in the present talking about your past. It's all one, isn't it? And you do rather behave like a married man. I've never known anyone so keen on keeping the illicit bit alive and kicking. You hardly let me even suspect we're having an affair. It only happens when you turn off the light. Are you afraid I'll notice you're molesting me and run off and tell the beaks, so that you'll get the cane?'

I stared at her very nearly aghast. It was time to take matters in hand. Luckily it was also time to take off the potatoes. They were overdone, but so were Joanna's strictures. We ate the rest of the meal in silence, as though both of us were trying hard to digest my faults as well as the food. We reached the cheese. She smiled forgivingly.

'So tell me what's this all of a sudden about Billy Bunter,' she said.

Putting aside the fear that I was really too old and gross to merit familiarity with anyone, let alone an abruptly outspoken girl of twenty-seven, I told Joanna what had happened. With a show of guilt I admitted that I had met my ex-wife for a drink, which now enabled me with a clear conscience to apply my mind to the subject that mattered. 'Since it's possible that Billy Bunter is still alive,' I said, 'I'll begin by giving you the necessary background.'

'And then throw the meeting open to questions?'

'If there's time.'

We exchanged a smile that verged on complicity. Crossing her legs, Joanna stared out at other windows where dinner parties similar to ours were in progress, while I outlined the early history of Greyfriars School for her benefit. Old memories of *The Magnet* quickened as I recalled the dates – a monastery in the Dark Ages, a foundation for poor scholars in 1551, a public school when George I granted a charter in 1716 – which, when they cropped up in my father's expert reminiscence, had made the place seem so very real to me, a venerable pile sunk in a corner of the Kent countryside blowing with apple-blossom and sprouting oast-houses. It had sounded like paradise to a boy about to fail common entrance.

'It sounds like hell,' interrupted Joanna.

'Do be quiet. I'm just putting the centuries in perspective for you.'

I then moved into that period closer to our own times when in a single year Greyfriars achieved the prominence which for thousands of twentieth-century boys, many of them now in positions of power, the school had never surrendered. The moment that thus made history occurred in 1908, when the name of W. G. Bunter was entered on the books. Why did it make history? Because never in the entire span of privileged education in this country had a lad so representative of its values, yet so humorously hostile to them, been allowed to run riot without getting expelled.

'He sounds awful,' Joanna said.

'No worse than most of us.'

'Speak for yourself.' She drew a deep breath as if to plunge our chat into even deeper waters. 'I mean, men aren't the only fish in the sea. Have you spared a thought for us women? We . . .'

'Wait,' I snapped. The point was, I continued, that in each of his activities Bunter came close to being thrown out. But skulking behind all his offences, his theft of other people's tuck, his unflagging efforts to outwit the staff, the out-of-bounds adventures that cruelly implicated innocent boys, behind the cunning and tale-telling and treachery, the image of an English gentleman was never quite obscured. Here in Bunter was a boy, learning even the easy lessons of life the hard way, avoiding any chance of improving himself but always paying the price, who was later destined to make a distinguished contribution to the well-being of the British Empire or its aftermath. He would fight with grit if not courage in any wars which others might declare on us, survive those conflicts against the odds, fail tests of character as abysmally as exams, but in the end profit from the friendships forged at school to swing his way up the ladder of preferment to the highest appointments in the land.

I paused. It was an error. Joanna looked at me eagerly.

'What, is he now Prime Minister or something?'

'He might be, but he isn't,' I explained rattily. 'I'm talking in hypothetical terms.'

'That's part of your trouble.'

'The point you're missing is that Bunter never grew up,' I said. 'He was always fourteen in the stories. That's why Lesley's absurd insistence on his still being alive is so disconcerting.'

Joanna's brow creased. 'What might have happened to him then, even if nothing did?' she asked, transferring her gaze to other diners across the gardens.

I was quite clear on this issue. What at school had been horrifying in Bunter's behaviour would later, in the drawing-rooms where he flaunted the ambitions of young manhood, be thought amusingly individual. Hostesses would have adored his very monstrosity. Clubs, at least those whose unwritten rules condoned the effects of wine on men with their way to make, would not only welcome him to membership but, like the school, never expel him for insulting a servant or indulging in horseplay on the premises. Indeed, I concluded, Bunter's genius was to show that the standards of a civilised nation needed no stretching to accommodate the invariably rotten conduct of those who took that nation's helm. 'The century that gave Bunter birth has become just like him,' I said. 'Idle, vain, smug, overweight, snobbish, vulgar and thoroughly interesting. You don't have to look far to see that.'

I glanced up to see how far Joanna was looking. Her eyes, gazing into the window's distant prospect of people like ourselves sorting out their differences over indifferent meals, had the slight glaze of the late-night viewer.

'So, you see,' I finished, in a lame effort to recapture her attention, 'Billy Bunter is everyman writ large.'

'What you're saying to me,' Joanna said, 'is that you're still a naughty little boy with a hilarious future in front of you.' She paused. 'May I please use your bathroom?'

Against my will – I hadn't finished, indeed had hardly started – my ears pricked up at this request. It was the agreed signal. But why so early? Our convention, preparatory to discovering that we were in bed together, was that Joanna should elect to spend ten minutes in the bathroom while I, absent-mindedly behaving as if she had gone home, undressed without due haste, pretended to read a page, yawned and turned off the light – and within seconds I would be alone no more.

I was aware of this stratagem's absurdity, but somehow we had done it too many times to break the spell. It was moreover quite exciting that at the ocular level our bodies remained a mystery. Making love to her – as one began to do now – was inevitably to imagine her in clothes, the naked body in my arms a mere fantasy compared with the shapely figure which in theory was now being carried home to Hampstead in a taxi. Meanwhile the skin I never saw, the contours I normally glimpsed only through wool or silk, were exquisite to the blind touch, and it had never occurred to me until this evening, as my hand itched to slap her bottom in the run-up to our climax, that there was something awfully dirty about it. As I fell away from her, I was just that naughty little boy Joanna had posited in her final remark before making off to the bathroom.

As if only too ready to prove how right she was about my immaturity, I fell asleep in her arms, head nestling at her breast, and not for many moons – perhaps since childhood – had I slept so soundly, with a sixth sense of rain driving like dreams against the window in the small hours.

For once Joanna was there in the morning. Fully dressed, of course. She brought me tea in bed. This was – well, extra-ordinary: comforting – how could it fail to be comforting after such a night? – but also obscene. This was Sunday, my day alone, the sacred day for wondering how I had got where I was, whether there was anywhere further to go, and which parts of my life were worth it, if any.

'Sorry to be still here, Patrick,' she said, 'but you're not through yet. I switched off in the middle like that because I couldn't bear what you were telling me.'

'Why not?' I muttered. 'It was all perfectly straightforward, rather boring in fact.'

'You had your heart in it,' she said simply.

Careful not to slop, I put my cup down on the bedside table.

'What's wrong with that?'

'Nothing,' she said, looking miserable. 'I didn't know you had a heart, that's all.'

To this I had no spontaneous reaction. It was hard to know whether to be affronted by her earlier doubt or flattered by her discovery of inner depths or depressed by her ignorance of anatomy. So I said, concerned to tread with delicacy, conscious of being in the presence of, and possibly causing, loads of emotion, 'Surely I wouldn't, would I, let the evenings we share end as they do if I had no feelings?'

'It's difficult to tell,' she said. 'You're not the world's best lover, you know.'

'Am I not?'

'I suppose it's your training,' Joanna said. 'Everything has to be so correct. Those stately manners of yours are quite scary, really, it's like being ravished by a robot. I don't know why you don't just snatch what you want and to hell with your good opinion of yourself and then try again harder and shout something rude or amorous to me, and I truly wish you had slapped my bottom when you wanted to last night, but now I know you have some feelings I suppose it's all right, isn't it?'

Drinking the dregs of the tea, I racked my brains for some recollection of the hint I had given her that I was a man inflamed by inner passions.

'What was I actually talking about at the time you got this impression?'

'Billy Bunter,' she said.

I looked wildly round for something. What was it? Oh, yes, cigarettes, there were no cigarettes in the house. And I had a longing to slosh something potent in my teacup. And hers. Why on earth should the sudden revival of Bunter as a subject be making us both so sorrowful? We were gawping at each other like bad actors. Whereas actually Bunter was supposed to be fun! And so was love! I felt a glow in the various extremes of my body that were still aching for a cigarette. I had an audacious vision of the day that might stretch before us, no day ever like it, our day, drawing the curtains on the morning after the champagne that was already on the ice, and much

later dining out. We had all this and more; it was lodged in the
future. But it stuck in my throat.

Then Joanna said, 'That man your wife mentioned, why
shouldn't he exist?'

'He probably does, poor fellow.'

'Why are you resisting him?'

'I just don't like my legends spurned and spat on.'

'Why don't you ring him up?'

'Why would he want to see me?'

'You're behaving quite nuttily, you know,' Joanna said.
'You're saying that if Billy Bunter has a real-life model who
happens to be alive still, this somehow turns the whole of you
into a fiction. How dare you, sir? I don't want to be served this
afternoon by a man who thinks he doesn't exist.'

I swallowed slightly, feeling again the twinge of erotic disgust
in the words she had chosen to illumine an area best kept dark.
But I had my conventional escape: asking her kindly to leave
the room, I set about dressing for the day – brown cords,
tweed jacket, silk scarf – and I gazed into the bathroom mirror
half hoping she would have left when I emerged in clothes, so
that I wouldn't have to answer any more questions that weren't
worth asking.

But Joanna was still there. She didn't blink at my holiday
looks. In fact she had a glass in her hand.

'I found some bubbly in your fridge,' she said festively. 'It
looked lonely. Let's have it for breakfast. And then call him up.'

And that seemed the last straw – not that she had thieved
champagne or taken my hospitality for granted or impugned
my techniques in my own bed, but that like Lesley, like all
women, she could grasp only one point and then never leave it
alone: in this case, that all life's ills would be converted into
marvels and I would spring forth a man glowing with achievement, if only, if only I picked up the telephone and placed a
unique visionary call to the old bugger who was supposed to be
young Bunter. It was all too much.

'Look, you stupid thing,' I shouted with surprising ease, 'I don't want to, I won't, I can't.'

'Steady,' she said.

'It's not in me,' I said. 'I haven't got any reason to do it, you twit. If this Archibald is real, and there he is in Kent, dribbling over his broth and wondering why he's not in intensive care, and resting on the ludicrous laurels that being Bunter has brought down on his head, it means that the whole fabric of my childhood comes crashing around my ears.'

'You called me stupid,' said Joanna pensively.

'But don't you see, how can I explain?' I went on. 'He and his chums were my imagination, they fed it, made it grow. They were the figures I lapped up or the examples I knew I had to avoid. It could have been Shakespeare or Beethoven, but it wasn't. It was Bunter and his crew. I could always see them in my mind's eye, planning all kinds of capers that I would like to have cut, and whenever I did something wrong or silly or got into trouble, I could compare it with their efforts, as if I were appealing to the gods.'

'A twit, am I?' she murmured.

'They were on my side, you see,' I replied. 'They were everlasting youth, before the ghastly business of being adult set in. And they've remained in my imagination ever since, as touchstones – ridiculous, isn't it? But they're there, unravaged by time, unflapped by all the anxieties and rages I've suffered since. A reality that never changes, burnt into the back of my mind like a pokerwork definition of good and evil. To find that Bunter of all people were real – Christ, it would be like discovering that Jesus really had contrived a second coming and was getting ready somewhere in Israel or Glastonbury to spoil every damn thing he did the first time. I don't want my imagination pushed off the edge of the cliff by reality. It'll kill me.'

There was a dragging pause. The champagne in Joanna's glass fizzed bravely. To judge by the weight of the silence I was dead already by her standards, but a flush of rude excitement convinced me that some sort of resurrection was at hand. I was glad to have been so insulting. It seemed to free me. I didn't care what I destroyed. It was life.

'You called me names,' she said.

'The heat of the moment.'

'It wasn't very polite.'

'Nor would telephoning Archibald be.'

'I didn't like it,' Joanna said in blurred tones.

'I don't give a tinker's.'

Her hand moved involuntarily to the glass of flat fizz, then withdrew. For some reason I noticed her knees as they straightened. A stocking wrinkled. By now she was standing up, a person who had recently been naked. She was once a little girl. She had a job that kept her in the same room with me for much of the day. She had often been in tears at times when I never knew her. She had accused me of being a child. And now she did it again.

'You want to go on being a small boy,' said Joanna lightly, halfway to the door, picking up her notebook. 'Okay, okay. Let's confine our business to the office. Here's the first time I've seen you want to do something, and you don't dare give it a whirl. Nice champers. Who were you keeping it for? Someone more real than me, I bet. Bunter, I shouldn't wonder, from the way you go all soppy when anyone mentions his name.'

I didn't stop her leaving. I hadn't the heart – or, rather, my habitual defences, in the nick of time, reared up: expenditure of emotion left only pain in its wake, so it was better to rein it in, wait till it passed. Yet I couldn't fathom why she had to go, just when I was starting to talk sense. Her behaviour was quite irrational. I wished she had gone to the bathroom instead. It would have shut her up. On the other hand it was hardly yet noon. Not even the pubs were open.

I spent the morning finishing her champagne and drafting a cross note to Lesley telling her not to interfere. Luckily I had no stamps.

2

As was to be expected Joanna conducted herself at the office on Monday with decorum, and we got through a tidy bit of work before the afternoon post delivered the bombshell.

We had started the day with one or two instances of arguably deliberate misunderstanding.

'I still have several weeks of grace before the Minister expects the first draft of my report,' I began.

'Oh, really?' Joanna said.

'Excuse me, you're supposed to be taking this down, Miss Feathers, not commenting upon it.'

'Why, is it part of the report?'

'I'm warming up,' I said. 'We can cut it later. Sometimes it helps to have one's words typed out, if only to discover what one thinks.' I paused, my eyes on the blouse she was wearing. 'Here we go then. The aim of this report is a large one.'

Upright, bottom positioned firmly on the chair, she settled down to shorthand.

'That aim is to pin down exactly where and how and why English culture, how I detest that word, has taken the wrong turn,' I continued. 'Look at England, just look at her folly. Nothing but a fertile field for the fostering of false values.'

Joanna sniffed and gurgled, as if I had mentioned sex. I glanced up from my thought.

'All those effs,' she explained modestly.

'It's not funny at all, Miss Feathers,' I said. 'Please continue. Harsh words are needed and it's up to me to provide them without distorting the facts. My one anxiety is to reveal how the fruits of twentieth-century effort in the arts, capital A for Arts, can and must nourish the future, and that is dependent on a shift of emphasis in the schools which will permit the humanities to triumph over the deadly aim of the sciences, stop. As yet my superiors know nothing of this cunning intention to produce less a formal document, for them to patronise and set aside, than a revolutionary pamphlet, to make the media sit up and shout. New paragraph. The teachers, of course, are at the root of the trouble. The standard of literacy in primary schools is little short of appalling. The type and paucity of reading matter offered to children of both sexes at the age of puberty can hardly be underestimated. The teachers have succeeded in . . . in . . .'

'Substituting chaos for discipline and technology for imagination,' Joanna said, as though quoting an authority.

'Why do you say that?'

'Because you said it in bed the other night.'

'Substituting computers for culture,' I went on with a frown, 'and videos for vitality.'

All morning we slaved at our dictation. I was just striking form when it turned out that Joanna had a lunch date. With whom? One never asked. Instead, eating some sandwiches from the canteen washed down by some claret from Berry Bros, I spent the hour gazing with smug pleasure at the amenities which the Government, on securing my services from the college where I enjoyed a fellowship in history, had placed at my disposal.

These were not bad. It was a nice little empire I ruled. The office overlooked Green Park in a building that had once been the home of a statesman and later a club. Elements of both grace and space had survived, and to support the atmosphere of a distinguished past the Arts Council had lent me pictures and items of furniture that would normally have been touring the provinces. My desk was a set-piece of domestic sculpture designed by a pupil of William Morris. Dornford Yates had worked at it, as had Sir Henry Campbell-Bannerman. The whole room dropped names. I had much of Conan Doyle's library stacked up on shelves borrowed from the Wallace Collection, while excellent facilities for listening to music or the spoken word had been installed at my request. Rather amusingly two channels of the quadrophonic sound emerged from the holes in a Henry Moore that would otherwise be adorning a small park in a suburb. This room of mine, I often felt, contained the best of England protected by noble windows from the polluted heart of the capital. The stuff was in public ownership, of course, but at least for the nonce I was steward of all I surveyed.

Well, almost all. Not of Joanna, who came back from lunch looking flushed; nor of my peace of mind, which was shattered by the letter she handed me. It was marked personal, posted in Ashford, and addressed from The Dunes, Littlestone-on-Sea, Kent. It read as follows:

My dear Mr Weymouth,

I am informed by your charming wife not only of your existence, of which I had been to my shame unaware, but of your sterling work in attempting to raise the tone of our times and correct some of the so-called 'facts' which in my humble opinion have done lasting damage to this country. Pray God, I say, it is not too late for change! I have long thought I had a part to play, however modest, in clearing up some of the misapprehensions that have made our century what it is, and to that end it would give me the utmost pleasure to make your acquaintance and to see if the old adage that great minds think alike can be proved to have some truth in it. These days, alas, my stamina not being what it was (I am eighty-nine, but a long way from senile!), I am not in the habit of motoring to the metropolis, but you will be very welcome to partake of my hospitality if next weekend would suit you. A breath of fresh air will do you the world of good.

Yours sincerely,
Archibald Aitken.

Actually, on recovering from the shock, my response was one of intense relief. I hadn't had to lift a finger. I was simply being pushed by fate in a direction that had tempted me but made me feel foolish.

The fact of the letter too – here it solidly lay on Dornford Yates's old desk – rendered it inconceivable that Aitken had any direct connection with Billy Bunter. He was doubtless just a fat old relic who, like an earlier version of myself, had been brought up on *The Magnet* and needed a sympathetic audience for a last giggle over Greyfriars before he expired. It would be a kindness to visit him. I would listen with avid nostalgia to his recitals from a faraway childhood that echoed my own, as I pushed his wheelchair along the promenade and took deep breaths of the fresh air of youth.

'Are you ready to carry on?' enquired Joanna.

I fluttered an impatient hand at her.

'I'm thinking,' I said.

My next reaction to the letter was to feel briefly pleased with Lesley for poking her nose into my life as much as she had when married. I had a slight right to blame her for betraying an official secret in blabbing to the old boy about the nature of my work for the Government. Yet wasn't there a rather touching aspect to her concern to bring together two men who might have much in common? Perhaps I had always misjudged her, just as until my current researches started I had misjudged, or taken for granted on its own terms, the whole of contemporary civilisation in Britain.

That was pitching it a bit high. But I now felt almost grateful to Lesley for a favour which Aitken's letter had transformed into an opportunity.

'Have you stopped thinking yet?' said Joanna impertinently, pencil poised.

I looked out at Green Park beyond the double glazing. Trees were waving in the wind. Rain drummed in bursts much as it had in my dreams the night before last. I heard the far-off grumble of traffic in Piccadilly below, and it sounded like a rumour that was happening inside me, a promise, a murmur of the future. Out there among the leaves the air was fresh, the mystery hidden. Here in the routine of the room there was only the past.

I stood up and stretched. The papers on Campbell-Bannerman's desk had an outmoded look.

'That'll be enough for now,' I said, consigning the illiteracy of British children to the pending tray while I slipped Aitken's letter into my pocket.

'But it's only three o'clock.'

'Have an early night, Miss Feathers. You look as though you need it. Oh, and by the way,' I added, 'I've decided to pop down at the weekend and see that chap I mentioned earlier. He might be able to help us – as I think you were good enough to suggest. I may be wasting our time. But it's worth "giving it a whirl".'

'Well done!' she said in a whisper, easing her bottom from the chair.

Within twenty minutes I had walked in a breeze of fine rain across Green Park and was enquiring at Charing Cross about the times of trains to Kent on Fridays.

The Dunes seemed a long way from Piccadilly. First the train clanked over viaducts past veteran warehouses, then quickened into a waste of tower-blocks, then sped through a string of suburbs aping country, and at last entered a muffled landscape of orchards rolling away towards the oast-houses that in memory hid Greyfriars.

At Ashford I took a taxi that wended along narrow lanes into a land so flat that it resembled a lost green sea with waves of hedges now and then breaking aimlessly across the distances: Romney Marsh, of course, with churches rearing at intervals out of banks of trees to remind me that history had once passed this way. I knew nothing of these parts, except that they had been out of bounds to Bunter.

As we reached without warning the real sea, a tanker etched on the dusk, my driver turned into a long curve of promenade where pre-war bungalows alternated with tall boarding-houses. It all looked as shut as a memory. Up a short track, with the swells of a golf-course behind it, we entered a drive that meandered in and out of low-slung trees. I began regretting the whole enterprise.

I stepped out in front of a large house of uncertain age that rambled back into further windblown shrubberies. Weather had pitted the pebbledash, vegetation cloaked the windows, unseen sea gurgled on shingle close at hand. As the climax to my trip into an England I had never visited, the whole place wore an air of pitiable decrepitude. The taxi spurted away off the gravel as if abandoning me for ever.

On the steps stood an emaciated figure with a narrow head in a suit a lot too large, as if dressed up for a charade. His age was anyone's guess. Forty perhaps. His manner suggested the furtive urgency of a small boy dying for a widdle.

He had small prim lips. He said nothing.

'Patrick Weymouth. Mr Aitken asked me for the week-end.'

'I know. I wrote the letter. He's beyond it. Edgar Smedley's the name.' He tested the weight of my bag with thin white fingers. 'We tried to get A. J. P. Taylor, you know, for this,' he said in a throttled way, as if a bone were stuck in his throat.

'For what?'

He writhed slightly. 'To judge for himself. To judge the historical evidence.'

'Why him?'

'The alterations,' Smedley said, 'need a careful hand.'

'What did he say?'

'I have my letter to show you if you don't believe me,' Smedley said, picking up my suitcase. 'A polite letter. Very flattering in tone. Typed out.'

'And he didn't answer?'

With a dull snigger Smedley led the way indoors. There was a lofty hall with one candle lit. 'Economy,' said Smedley. 'You play your part in all this and it'll be a blaze of light.' The roof beams were in darkness, as was I. In the shadows lurked a mass of unwieldy furniture.

We climbed a staircase into the gloom, Smedley's trousers tramping voluminously ahead of me. 'No, he didn't reply.' His voice threw back a strangled echo. 'That stamped the man. Scared, you see – scared of having to change his mind. Blinding himself to history. Mr Aitken doesn't have to interpret our times. He's not some scholar sitting in a college. Mr Aitken is a source.'

We passed down a dim corridor that seemed to lead nowhere.

'What am I doing here then?' I asked.

'We spare no trouble in looking for the right man,' he said. 'A. J. P. Taylor didn't respond to our pleas. You did. He could have taken all the credit for the alterations. Made his name.'

'But what exactly are these alterations?'

Smedley unlocked a door. The bedroom felt damp, but a coal fire was laid in a black grate. 'You'll find out,' he said, depositing my suitcase on the narrow bed. I still found it impossible to tell from Smedley's glottal delivery whether he had mentioned a noted historian of the day to pay me the compliment of equality or to put me in my place. By now I wished only that I shared A. J. P. Taylor's knack of ignoring lunatic letters. Only the lure of Bunter, reverberating in my spirit from long ago, had led me into this indignity, this quicksand of false pretences. How on earth had I succumbed to the vanity of supposing that life owed me a revelation? At this point Smedley began a sidelong exit.

'One moment, Mr Smedley,' I said. 'I think I must insist on knowing what you expect of me?'

'Nothing,' he replied at the door. 'My first choice was Hugh Trevor-Roper. You weren't my idea. It was Mr Aitken in one of his takings. Thinks he's in love with some gardening woman – your wife, is it? Now and then we must allow him his little whims. That's old age for you.'

'Where is Mr Aitken?'

'I never bring him down before eight,' said Smedley. 'You have time for a bath. Help yourself to a drink, if you can find one. We're testing you out, you see.'

In the gloomy room I forced my mind to relax. It wasn't easy. The hot tap produced a trickle of water that was tepid before there was enough to relax in, and I got muddled in the ill-lit corridors while trying to aim for the stairs. Annoyance crept into my bones. At length I ended up in the lofty hall, in which now hung a dense silence that made me feel watched.

But at least the drink I badly needed was on offer. At first sight a lavish display: lots of glasses, a jug of water, the better brands of spirits. I picked up the whisky with a slight jerk that betokened emptiness. If drained, it might have yielded a pub single. Of gin there was little trace. A dark bottle that looked full turned out to smell of distant sherry. And then I abruptly realised that I was crouched over this table, tension in every muscle, behaving like an alcoholic sorting through a dustbin.

Trying to appear normal in a silence that discouraged it, I gazed into the obscurity in the hope of locating more solid evidence of my host; his tastes or interests, the kind of things he collected. Only bad furniture loomed in the hall. I wondered how much further I could explore without affronting Smedley. Not a sound broke the deadlock. My spine bristled disagreeably. I felt my way back to the generous array of empties intending to make do with the drop of whisky when I saw a door. It was ajar. A light gleamed through the crack. I had a sense that somebody was behind it.

But it was just as empty as the bottles. Except for a pair of leather armchairs and books by the hundred. Books? Surely they, if anything, would divulge the truth about their owner. Anyway, in the absence of drink, nothing could have prevented my looking at them; I ached for some prop that would make me feel busy. Entering a room full of books was like stumbling on sanity again.

One glance at the shelves told me how little I needed to ask Archibald Aitken whether or not he was the original, at least in his own mind, of William George Bunter. For here, rising from floor to picture-rail, was a fine collection of one of the delights of the twentieth century. One of the obsessions too? Perhaps. But if I say that bound copies of *The Magnet*, without a single number missing, formed the heart of this noble library, any schoolboy over fifty, and many younger, will thrill with the pleasure that swamped me on merely surveying such trove. I knew quite well, as we all did, that these magazines were a monument to repetitive triviality long dead, however much larger than life they might look when viewed as a whole. I knew that the doings of pimpled lads were so much rubbish compared with the wider culture it was my professional duty to assess. But the happiness! What happiness in just gazing at this rare assemblage of the best of boyhood, what joy in contemplating a round-up of my past! It was a draught of the very freedom I had been invited here to taste.

I opened a volume. The pages were frayed at the edges. A
smudged image of a cricketer in a soft cap caught my eye:
a hero. The fields inside me opened out into full summer. An
inside left's leg lifted into the sky: another hero. The cheers
inside me unfroze. A fat bottom was being ejected at speed
from a third-class carriage, a fat face yelled silently out of the
past. Bunter! Just to glimpse these narrow columns of type
placed me at once in the spring of 1940, when my father
descended on me from London one glorious weekend and
brought me his tattered collection of *Magnet*s to show me for
the first time. He had often spoken of Bunter before the war,
lightly, as if fearing scorn. Only now did he judge me old
enough, at eleven or so, to be entrusted with the physical proof
that Greyfriars, and so many traditions inexplicable to infants
or foreigners or women, really existed. 'This'll make you laugh,
boy,' he said.

Squatting in a hot field behind the bungalow where I was
billeted as an evacuee, father showed me my way about that
world as he turned the faded page, told me to guard the papers
with my life, sat on his haunches to smile at the silly way I
laughed, and hurried back by an evening train to his hush-hush
war-work in threatened London. 'Don't cry, boy,' he said,
shaking his head as the whistle blew and the carriages moved
off.

That night in bed I started reading out of duty and soon
perked up and my elbow ached and the bulb in the torch started
flickering. And thereafter for weeks on end I read back and
forth over the territory as it grew familiar, and I learnt with
what passion a page of print seized hold of my mind, and how
completely a world of which I had no experience not only
established dominion over me, but intensified my longings for
an equal excitement in the world outside it. Fiction was a rush
of truth; facts just got muddled in.

Thus I became aware of Dunkirk, but only as a prank.
The Famous Five, risking punishment by going out of bounds

to meet a national crisis, were rushing to the rescue in tugs and steamers and having the time of their lives. Norway fell to the invader, and it was snowing over the playing-fields, and the game against a neighbouring school was cancelled. France gave in, and poor Charpentier, the French master, his homeland ravaged by hordes of Huns, was dying in defence of liberty. Day after day, as that spring ripened into a summer that never rained, I poured into the friendless Sussex village all the heroes and villains who kept me company by night. Bunter and his bullying, the boys and their japes, were my bulwark against the invasion that never came.

Meanwhile – fact, but fact with an edge, so it felt like fiction – I was taking nature apart too. I looked for nests in hedges billowing with blossom as fighters traced smoke in the sky. I fed cows over gates with torn tufts from the ditches. I was putting a world of my own together at just the point in history when its destruction had a daily imminence, but there was something so magic and undoomed about that extra reality in my reading about Greyfriars, a microcosm in which horror always hovered but turned out to be a misunderstanding, that I knew every bad situation would end up all smiles because it always did on paper.

Here at The Dunes all this cheered me immensely. I shut the book on Bunter's fat features contorting with fury as yet another plan misfired and walked back into the hall, to address myself to the spot of whisky they had been keeping for A. J. P. Taylor. To hell with my dubious welcome, I felt like celebrating. Forget the glasses, the water, the etiquette. I lifted the bottle and swigged.

At that moment, caught in the act, I heard the pad of slippered footsteps. I looked up, bottle in hand, and there, descending the stairs in stiff-legged slow march, fingers tight on the rail, exuding a blind awareness of the humour of his age and condition, a very bulky man with tiny feet moved shiftily towards me. A hand lifted in warning.

'Ssssh,' he said.

He had almost no hair on his dome. A long fringe of white spumed at the collar of a black velvet jacket. His eyes were watery and benign above a pair of gold-rimmed glasses that perched on a blunt nose. His mouth was splayed out in a rictus of concentration, or pain, as if will-power alone were propelling his body into the room. But the stomach! The stomach bulged behind a tight waistcoat, a convexity tacked into place by buttons, a hemisphere that wobbled at every step, a globe that mapped decades of application to pantry and cellar. Between neck and waist nothing but this belly had any say. Its demands had long since overwhelmed his chest. His ribs were buried under decades of fat. Yet his mien had bravura, even bravado. Every slow move suggested an outrageous pride in the fact that his survival into advanced age had been at the expense of every known method of securing a long life.

'Ssssh,' he puffed again as he neared me. 'Edgar's looking into our dinner. Won't be any cop. But I've got a plan. Charming wife said you were rolling in it. Have you brought money?'

Without a second thought I patted my wallet.

'Yes. Well, credit cards. A bit of cash.'

'Good, good, good,' he panted. 'Whatever happens this evening, don't go off the deep end. I've got masses to tell you. Can you stand the strain?'

'Yes,' I whispered back.

'You need an iron nerve.'

'I can manage that.'

'Good man. I took to you on sight.'

At which point the diminutive figure of Edgar Smedley came dashing down the stairs.

'This is dreadful, Archie,' he cried feebly. 'You are not in your room.'

'Here I am instead,' said Aitken with an uneasy smirk.

'You know you must never leave your quarters until everything is made ready for you. You know that.' Smedley stood quivering in his outsize suit, kneading the folds of his trousers with those white hands, his cold eyes overheated by rage. 'Have you been talking to our visitor?'

'No, no, heavens, no,' Aitken said, flopping about on the sofa as if beached.

'Is that the truth?'

'Cross my heart,' said Aitken, fumbling at his chest.

'Very well then,' Smedley said, somewhat mollified. 'You know how it upsets me. It'll be all my fault if you fall downstairs and have a fit.' He turned to me in genuine appeal. 'Mr Weymouth, be my witness.'

'I . . .'

'You saw him overstress himself. The doctors will blame me. He might have died in front of your very eyes.'

'I probably will unless I get something to eat,' Aitken said.

'Soames is seeing to all that,' said Smedley.

'What treats await us?'

'It isn't the thing to talk about food in front of strangers.'

'Oh, dear, manners!' Aitken said. 'Perhaps our guest could do with a drink while he waits?'

'I . . .'

'Oh, we're not all like you, Archie,' said Smedley with a thin smile. 'In any case Mr Weymouth helped himself to the whisky before we came down. You mustn't let him get you into bad habits.'

'Well, I don't think . . .' I began.

'Wait till you've been here a little longer, Mr Weymouth, before you –'

Venture an opinion? Steal drinks? I was never to know, for Smedley's remark was swamped by a mighty clang that sent echoes humming through the house. It was the gong. With an alert tenderness Smedley bent over his master and with an effort levered him upright, uttering fond gasps of encouragement to the old invalid. It was foolishly touching, if only because the little fellow altogether lacked the strength for what he thought he was achieving. He laboured on with a splutter, but it was Aitken, graciously pretending feebleness, who did all the work. He staggered to his feet under the burden of Smedley's help. He allowed his body to be edged, a step at a time, towards the dining-room, where at a mahogany table three places were laid. With alacrity he let himself be lowered slowly into place.

A gaunt figure with florid cheekbones stood lazily in waiting with a grubby napkin over his sleeve.

'Evening, gentlemen,' he said. 'It's pie, no potatoes, spoonful of spinach apiece, with to follow boiled bananas, no cheese, thanks very much.'

'Soames,' said Aitken, subsiding in his chair, 'you do me far too well.'

'Doctor's orders, sir,' said Soames, tucking a corner of the napkin into the old man's collar with a flourish.

Aitken stretched a hand to the carafe. 'What's this white stuff?'

'Water, sir.'

'Fetch my guest some wine.'

'He's had quite enough to drink already, Archie,' said Smedley with a covert wink at me.

'Wine, Mr Weymouth?' said Aitken grandly.

'Well, if you . . .'

'Archie,' interrupted Smedley in wheedling tones. 'You remember what happened to all that wine. Surely you don't want the whole story to come out just yet. It might get into the papers. Tell Mr Weymouth all about Bunter instead. He's not here on a bender at our expense.'

There was a slight pause.

'God damn it,' whispered Aitken.

No more was said, though Smedley whistled a tuneless bar or two, until Soames produced the pie. It was a portly object presented with ceremony. For a moment I studied its outward aspect with a suspicion born of recent events, then made the mistake of looking forward to its savoury interior. With a professional sniff, clearing his throat, Soames aimed a knife at the crust and broke it open. A soggy glittering mess of what looked like opaque spawn spued over the plate. My nostrils were filled with the unlikely reek of seaweed.

'Ah,' said Smedley, rubbing his hands.

'Ugh,' said Aitken, his face briefly obscured by steam.

'Wait till you taste it, sir,' said Soames, serving me a portion.

We all sat very still while Soames tipped some spinach out of a spoon into the soft sputum of the filling. He then retired to start boiling his bananas.

'I'm not Bunter,' Aitken said in abrupt rebellion. 'I can't be Bunter. Bunter would never have responded to such magnificent fare.'

Smedley put a hand to his mouth and tittered.

'You may think me a wag,' he said, 'but it's oysters, Archie – your favourite treat. I picked them up cheaply. Our fishmonger friend didn't know what to do with them. I could see they were good.'

'How?' growled Aitken.

'They were just open enough. I know a good oyster when I see one. I wanted to please our guest.'

Was it possible that he didn't know what he was saying? I put my fork into a fishy fragment of crust. This could kill me. Smedley gazed at me with a shy hostile ache in the back of his eyes, waiting for praise. With a heavy jaw I chewed the crust. It was as lukewarm as my bathwater.

'It,' said Aitken, as to a child, 'is – very good – Edgar.'

'Mmm,' I said.

Smedley relaxed with a fixed grin. The grin remained while he chewed at the stringy spinach. 'As for me,' he said after taking a swill of water, 'I don't go much on oysters. Give me meat any day. When you can afford it.'

With a lavish burp Aitken pushed his plate aside. 'You're a

man of patience, Mr Weymouth,' he said. 'We're asking you to put up with a lot.'

'Far from it.'

'Edgar here tries his best. Not easy for him. He's had to scrimp. He knows I haven't long to go and he's determined to make all he can of it.' Aitken eyed me with force, looking suddenly younger. In a dogged silence Smedley was lapping up every word. 'That was a pie to remember, Edgar, if I survive long enough to remember anything. So at this festive moment I'll retract what I said about not being Bunter. I am in fact Bunter, William George Bunter, no shred of doubt, an even fatter owl and bigger fool than you recall from your early reading.'

'Of course you are,' whispered Smedley, wiping a shred of spinach from his lips.

My hand kept drifting out for wine and finding only water. An unsettling perception of what the verge of insanity must be like had taken hold of my mind. I vaguely wondered when to expect the bananas.

'I was a fat boy at school,' said Aitken, easing comfortably into reminiscence. 'There's always a fat boy.'

'Public schools,' Smedley said, 'have to have a fat boy to take the blame for everyone else being thin.'

Aitken cast him a tired glance. 'So I never regarded my size as of any weight, as it were,' he said. 'I decided then that it was the only fact I need ever accept. Everything else was to be questioned. I have made a career of being fat and asking questions.'

'Life,' Smedley interrupted with complacency, 'is too stupid to answer most of them.'

A slight frown formed between Aitken's bushy eyebrows. 'I recognised in myself a fat boy of more than average ability. I was good at maths, the classics, history . . .'

'Subjects,' Smedley said, 'that make a public school the worst possible foundation for private life.'

'But bad at sport –'

'You couldn't run fast enough.'

'And bad at defying authority –'

'You still couldn't run fast enough!'

'I might have gone on to become a decent enough citizen –'

'A victim,' Smedley said, pursuing his mastery of the tedious aside. 'A dupe of the system we have perfected to set little boys on the road to death and damnation.'

There was a generous pause, which allowed Soames plenty of time to enter with a bubbling dish of bananas and slither them on to our plates. Meanwhile Aitken quietly bulged; he was holding on to his temper in the presence of staff. Soames made an exit. Then, with a peppery air of apology, Aitken said, 'I am telling a story, Edgar. It needs no footnotes. A critical apparatus is out of place. It's just a story. My story. Not yours.'

The thin man stared vengefully at the fat man. It was a sight, to an outsider, as chilling as the bananas. 'I won't listen then,' Smedley said, and to my astonishment he crumpled, hand to brow, a lapel of his ample suit brushing the juices on his plate. 'I'm not listening. It's all lies.'

'There, there,' Aitken said with casual sympathy. 'Now where was I, Mr Weymouth? One day in 1907, yes, the Headmaster ushered in a guest, a famous author, and asked for volunteers to show him round the school. Hands shot up and I was chosen. Only afterwards did I discover that Frank Richards was looking for a character who would breathe life into his piffling stories of adventure in a public school. He wanted his tales not only to contain every facet of the big grown-up world, but to show what a hollow mockery adults always made of that world when they got there.

'So it was no accident, he felt, that a fellow of my size had loomed up on his literary horizon. Here was I, a godsend to a scribbler who needed a handy microcosm. His opinion of me grew by the second as we walked the rounds – form-room, gym, dorm, san, tuckshop, lavs. Somehow I had the gift of making them all seem funny.

'I remember his words to this day. "Archie," he said, "you are exactly what I, as a creative artist, have been waiting for. You are gross. You are unlike your fellow men. You choose to wear, for reasons of eccentricity which I lack the hardihood to invent, check trousers that do nothing to conceal the amplitude of your backside, a bow-tie that only emphasises the repulsive thickness of your neck, and glasses that make you look blind. Neither in fact nor fiction have I encountered any-one so difficult to imagine, for the very reason that you are so totally yourself. Needless to say, I wish to put you into my stories, if only to give them that final touch of verisimilitude which all authors seek. But I fear you will expect rewards that are beyond my means."

'And it was at that moment – looking, yes, at piles of jam tarts on the tuckshop counter – that I was overwhelmed by a brand-new feeling.'

He gazed briefly at Smedley, who was still slumped in a sulk over his bananas.

'An intoxicating sense of power,' he said with satisfaction. 'I had been reading *The Magnet*, of course, we all had, at night, under the sheets, with a torch. Most of us thought the stories average fun, but lacking in something, not quite capturing the essence. In 1907 – and they'd been running a few years – they had so far just missed catching the spirit of the new century.

'But now I was being asked to join it – to improve, immeasur-ably, a society already in existence. I was to provide the humorous element, the touch of farce that alone makes sense of life. My task was to keep looking as though I were the embodiment of evil, then at the last minute to turn out good. Well, not very good perhaps, but a lot better than some. I was to be everyone's butt, even if the principles that guided me – lying, cheating, prevaricating, eating, drinking, all to splendid excess – were victorious in the end. I was to be the touchstone of the twentieth century, harbinger of the disasters that were soon to overtake us, the big fat fly in history's ointment, the mighty symbol of mankind's worst fears.'

What a tale! I was enchanted by it, true or false. I made no judgment. I simply fell for the manner of the telling. It was as if all freedom sprang from a story, wherever it chose to lead me. Homer himself, if he existed, had never worried about facts, but he had liberated the western world. These moments, booming out of old age, had for me an oracular authority that brooked no denial. As Aitken sat back, I probed my reactions. They were too dense for words. I plunged clumsily into the silence with: 'Did Richards, I mean, did he give you anything?' It sounded vulgar.

'Nothing,' Aitken said. 'He told me in so many words that he was going to call me Billy Bunter, and if boys at Eton had already agreed to appear in his stories, he saw no reason to expect any trouble from me.'

'Eton?'

'The school of that name,' said Aitken helpfully.

'What boys at Eton?'

'Oh, don't you know?' Aitken said, as if I had missed that morning's papers. 'I thought everyone knew. The Famous Five really are quite famous, you see – or became so as a result of being put into the stories. I often wonder what would have become of Anthony Eden if he hadn't made his début in *The Magnet* and thus turned into a hero for a generation of school-boys who wanted to grow up just like him.'

'Are you sure about all this?'

'Well, naturally Richards went first to Eton when the idea for a school story that spoke for the new century struck him – only later did he start scraping the bottom of the educational barrel and end up with me – and this lad Eden showed him round. He seemed pleasant enough to Richards for a hero of a sort – eager, you know, and traditional, but with a stubborn streak. So he asked the boy what he'd want to have his name

changed to Harry Wharton and be a leader of the school élite,
and Eden just glassily assumed he was one already, so there
was no arguing. He wasn't crude enough to ask for payment.
In any case his people had money.'

My mind widened involuntarily. A television picture of that
glassy superior Eden at the time of the Suez Crisis merged in
a completely natural way with a remembered drawing of Harry
Wharton in *The Magnet*. He was presiding not over a cabinet
meeting but at a tea in his study. At the same moment I was
gaping at the screen in our Haslemere house, listening to Lesley
rail at the statesman's arrogance, and I was gawping at the
penny weekly under a hedge in Sussex, while enemy fighters
zoomed down to shoot up a neighbouring airfield. Wharton, his
heroics, his headstrong honesty, shimmered in the heat of the
afternoon.

This montage was sharp for a second, then faded. But it
was enough to establish the truth of the improbable. It had
turned Archibald Aitken from a crustily amiable fantastic into
a piece of history. I was even amazed – no logic here – that I
had missed for so long a source of pleasure so obvious as the
link between a study tea at Greyfriars, a brave wave to the
crowds outside No. 10, myself ignoring the drone of planes to
read about my hero, myself years later unable to ignore the
homely nag of Lesley's political views. Of course, I didn't yet
know what to make of these connections. I just snatched at
them. They felt good. Even if the rest of Aitken's autobiography
proved false, I had all this to take away with me. Never had I
experienced such a thrill of proximity to a fresh view of
things.

I had noticed no events at table during the short pause when
all the above shot through my mind. I thought I had heard a
clatter. It might have been my memory of aircraft. I had a
faint impression of Smedley, for whom I now felt only a dazed
amity, jumping to his feet in shock. Perhaps he had stopped a
stray bullet in the dog-fight. But now I realised in this room

that Aitken's head had fallen forward, narrowly missing the mush of uneaten bananas on his plate, coming baldly to rest on the table, where the candlelight shone off it with the refulgence of a halo.

My stomach, which had suffered enough for one evening, surged into my throat. The old man had looked so spry. Now he was obviously dead. Smedley's shriek, also seeming to come to me late, surely proved this assumption. Soames loomed at the vague door to the kitchen.

'Oh, deary me,' he said. 'Not again.'

Urgent wheels squeaked on parquet as the invalid chair I had dreaded all along came into play. As if handling a corpse, none too gently, more persuasive as undertakers than when acting the parts of butler or companion, the two men eased the crumpled balloon of their employer from the jaws of death into the relative life of the wheelchair, where he began a fitful snore at the back of his throat.

'Has he been at it?' Soames hissed, trying to set the lolling head upright on the shoulders.

'Keep your place,' snapped Smedley, and with a final squeak, as the rubber wheels slewed round, the unconscious man was borne away.

The deadly quiet of a nursing-home fell on the dining-room. I waited for Smedley to return with some specious explanation or, even less likely, for Soames to offer me a drink. Of course nothing happened. I sipped some water. I contemplated the limp bananas guttering in the candlelight. The rain drove in from the sea and started lashing the windows.

When I at last lost patience all the lights were off. I had been left to my own resources. I could find no switches. I pretended it was cosy to be on one's own in vile weather. It wasn't. Whose bathroom was Joanna in now? Remembering that spot of whisky, I tiptoed through the dark to the table where the empties were kept, only to find that an aquarium had been substituted. A struck match revealed a goldfish.

Moving away, I kicked an object on the floor. It tinkled. A piece attached to a wire fell off it with a plastic clack. A secretive buzz filled my ears. I bent down and righted the telephone, then thought: why not? I need a word of comfort, I need a whisper with someone. It took three or four more matches to dial the nine digits to connect me to Hampstead, then in total darkness I heard the clamour of the bell in her bedsitter, somehow knowing at the first ring that nobody would answer, least of all Joanna, and that soon I must ring off in case my subterfuge woke up the whole of Kent. Never before had I felt such an edge to a loneliness I hardly knew I suffered.

I rang off, stood up, went dizzy. In the intense gloom there was nothing to hang on to. Slowly, striking more matches that made a loud noise in the corridors like petty protest, I felt my way to my room and stumbled out of my trousers like a drunk. The electricity – Edgar had spoken of economy – must have been turned off at the mains.

Lying there in the dark, I thought of *The Magnet*, of Anthony Eden, of other public figures known to me by repute scurrying along the corridors of Greyfriars with the rain pouring out-side. Listening to this rain, backed by the uneasiness of the sea, I found my mind suffused with the light of that summer when I had first gained access to events at the school which I attended only by proxy.

If England hung in the balance in 1940, so did I. I saw that my whole young life, caught at its moment of least resist-ance by something as simple as a few old magazines, must have set up for itself a viewpoint, if not a vision, that would last, unless I were bloody careful, unto death.

The phoney war was over. I was now in the thick of things. It wasn't that I actually wanted to be all or any of the Famous Five. Nor did I just identify with Billy Bunter in all his cunning energy, his convenient untruths, his escapes so narrow that I squirmed with fear as the dog-fights multiplied in the over-head blue. I simply was them, one and all. I had an eggshell vulnerability to anything done to me. There I lay under my hedge, filling my brains with comical rubbish, yet participating in one of those sparky moments in human history that charged the very atmosphere – the look of a big sky, the sweat of summer heat – with emotion. At such times legends levitated out of the muddle of being a boy, myths swam in the distance among the trees. And dreams beckoned.

3

The weather had hardly improved by morning; nor, it seemed, had Archibald Aitken. When to my surprise Soames brought up a cup of tea he reported that the old man was still weak, but Smedley was trying to dress him. When I came downstairs to the hall Smedley, who was scattering ants' eggs into the small aquarium where a big goldfish hung near an outlet of bubbles, said that Soames was serving the old man a light breakfast in his room. These items of information were published with the gravity of medical bulletins pinned up on death's door.

An hour passed while I drank thin coffee, ate the biscuits provided and, feeling a bit weak myself, ran through one or two further instalments of Bunter's adventures in the bound volumes. Instead of settling to work on his famous history of the school, Mr Quelch was fuming in his study over some as yet unsolved outrage to do with a stolen fruit-cake. Canes swished through the damp air in sadistic rehearsal for the moment of exposure, and I thought morosely of Joanna licking her fingers as she breakfasted off a lot of buttered toast in Hampstead.

Entering to take my tray, Soames announced that in due

course Mr Aitken was to be allowed to make the long journey downstairs. I awaited the cortège with solemn impatience. There were so many questions to ask, if only Smedley could be got out of the way. Who on earth was the little twerp? I opened a window for a glimpse of the beach, whereupon the twerp himself strutted in to shut it, mutter an insult veiled as apology about the effect of draughts on the elderly, and confirm that my host was sacrificing personal comfort to accompany me on an expedition. We were to visit one or two marshland churches within a short drive of Littlestone. In my lack of refreshment I wondered how many shops or pubs we would pass.

'Will you be coming along, Mr Smedley?' I asked, in an effort to assess my chances.

'I'm always there,' he said. 'You've seen what happens when he over-excites himself.'

'Perhaps he isn't getting quite enough to eat,' I hazarded.

'We know best, Mr Weymouth.'

Shortly after ten Aitken, muffled in an ulster almost to his ankles, slowly appeared at the front door, inhibited as usual from normal progress by Smedley's help. He peered at fresh air as if wondering how palatable it was, then drew in several mouthfuls with appetite. In a peaked cap Soames was holding open the rear door of an old grey Wolseley. Wrapping his arms round the huge midriff, Smedley manoeuvred his master down the steps as carefully as a hogshead. Aitken halted in the drive looking vaguely at trees. Easing a shoulder to his armpit, Smedley gave him a push. He didn't budge.

'Feeling dicky, Archie?' enquired Smedley, almost with hope.

'Fetch an umbrella.'

'It won't rain. It said so on the wireless.'

'Or a stick. I need a stick. From my room. The ivory one. Oswald Mosley's stick.'

With a brisk sigh Smedley turned at a trot into the house.

At once Aitken grasped my arm. 'You have the money, my friend?' he whispered. I nodded. 'Then into the motor with all speed.' And without a trace of distress he waddled forward several yards and launched his body on to the leather upholstery. I followed with a stab of excitement. The interior smelt of holidays.

'On, on, Soames!' said Aitken, blinking back at the porch. 'Edgar's had a nasty turn, won't be joining us.'

'Oh, don't try that one again, sir,' Soames said miserably.

'Make haste, man, or you'll never get a reference, let alone a cut in the proceeds.'

With a groan Soames set the vehicle moving gradually down the drive, spitting gravel in our wake. What proceeds? It had criminal overtones, as did our escape. I gazed back. The little man was performing on the steps, as in a silent film, waving the stick (Mosley's?) and mouthing rage. Then he was wiped out by bushes as the car swung into the road and the whole Channel lay for a moment in front of us fretted by sunlight pouring through a shift in the clouds. After one glance at this phenomenon Aitken settled back with a look of imperturbable health.

'Now, old chum, we are off to feast our spirits on a triumph of civilisation.' His voice trembled over a giggle. He vouchsafed an inexplicable wink. 'New Romney church, you know,' he added.

Soames drove glumly on. Not far ahead a church tower threatened against a backdrop of thunderous sky. I foresaw a classical array of memorials whose compliments to death I would have to parse. I imagined nodding, legs aching, over a guided tour of the choir-stalls. Pevsner would be sure to have commended the font. It was now or never.

'I wonder if we have time to stop at that little shop for a moment, Mr Aitken,' I said. 'I need some, yes, well, cigarettes.'

He stared at me in wonder. 'Good idea,' he enunciated without making a sound. His lips moved in rubbery emphasis.

'Wish I'd thought of it myself.' Then, resuming a normal tone that sounded at once deceitful, Aitken said, 'Soames, stop at once, enter that shop, purchase at our expense one packet of costly cigarettes for Mr Weymouth.'

For a moment I thought that my ruse to rustle up a bun or bar of chocolate for myself had been defeated. But it had merely been outclassed. Aitken was after bigger game. The second Soames had padded off to the shop, he cried, 'Take the wheel, quick, thank heavens we think alike,' and within a few more seconds, as we soared away, Soames danced on to the screen of the driving mirror, in the same silent film as had featured Smedley, and mimed a receding comedy of despair. I was so busy watching for him to hurl his peaked cap into the gutter that I almost crashed into the church wall.

'Well done, sir!'

'Where to?'

'Folkestone.'

'No churches?'

'Not on your life,' said Aitken. 'And don't worry yourself. The old Bunter's not dead yet. I told you we were going to feast on civilisation.' He paused. 'We're off to have luncheon.' He paused. 'In France!'

How had I done it? This reckless speed was surely out of character. I was behaving as if the Cinque Ports were the gangster districts of Chicago. Yet I did it with mindless elation. I never gave a thought to the chance that this ancient rascal might die on my hands in mid-Channel or that I was defying the guardians he had set up in authority over his health, his fatness, his age. I took the risk without caution. I took a risk! In retrospect, when I came to pay for it, my conduct would seem unbelievably childish. Now it appeared to be my nature brimming over.

The drive was short and fast. Aitken crowed with pleasure as we took bends. In the mirror I caught glimpses of his

approval of the passing scene. He gazed at the flash of seaside
bungalows as if proud of having designed them. His way of
gloating over a racing row of shops suggested that they were
stocked with the spoils of the Orient. And he talked fast, needing that escape too, talking his system free of the shadows of
home.

'Many people misinterpret poor Edgar,' he said, as Hythe
zoomed into the past. 'They treat him as a normal male adult.
You and I know better. He's an underdeveloped area. When
I'm not looking, he toddles off to his room and builds castles
out of Meccano which he buys from a second-hand dealer in
Lichfield under a false name (age ten).'

'It's not possible.'

'It's a fact! He bicycles to the railway station and hides in
the lavatories on a platform ticket until he thinks the staff
aren't noticing that he's collecting train numbers.'

'I can't believe it.'

'It's a fact! At night when he's put me to sleep with his
platitudes he sneaks out with a net and comes back in the small
hours with a lot of moths which he impales on pins with
tiny shrieks of glee and won't show anybody his collection in
case they steal it.'

'Really?'

'It's a fact! He sits in a shed with the door locked and
makes models in balsa-wood of enemy submarines. And that's
a fact too. And he's forty! One day a little boy will run out of
him and hide in the bushes and there'll be only a suit left.'

All this puzzled me no end, as we roared through Sandgate
well beyond the limit. How could a man of Aitken's sophistica-
tion tolerate a spoilt middle-aged lad whose pursuits were so
infantile? I had no time to work it out, for now our triumphal
progress had ended at the quay in Folkestone and, breathing
gusts of salty air, Aitken stepped out with an alacrity that
suggested a genuine fear of missing the boat. The boat train
was in – I involuntarily noticed its number – and disgorging

tourists. The vessel hung high over the sheds. And it was then that the bottom fell out of this brave new world of fast cars, snap decisions, international gastronomy. I had no passport.

At once I saw my father flapping at a wasp on a pre-war beach, to protect me, but knocking the ice-cream out of my hand. This moment crushed me with the same whack of disappointment. A good French lunch lay there melting into the pebbles.

'Ah,' said Aitken, ogling the challenge. 'Let us go and hoodwink the whole pack of them,' and waddling into the customs hall he took his place at the front of the line of back-packs and holdalls that snaked back to the train in a muddle of unkempt youth and elderly fret. 'Make way for an old fraud,' he cried, and the head of the queue actually backed away in the manner of an affronted cobra. 'Young man,' he hissed, presenting his passport, 'I am suffering from terminal senility, my brains hardly function, I ask only to eat my last meal abroad before they put the black bag over my head, and here's a man of charity to see me safely on to the steamer – may he pass?'

The fingers riffling the thick pages handed the passport back. 'What was that again, sir?'

Aitken sighed. 'I am suffering from . . .'

'Hurry along, gents. You're holding things up.'

I was stateless. But the hawsers were cast off. The ship edged away from the quay. We moved out of harbour. Nobody in uniform bore down on our seats to question my right to depart. My father had bought me another ice-cream; life was full of both continuity and surprise. With no difficulty Aitken took up enough room to deter the holdalls and back-packs from joining us. The white cliffs passed into the whiter mists behind. The old man sat at ease revolving saliva round his mouth as though wondering what it was for. England disappeared.

'Champagne,' said Aitken.

The steward came with it. It was like freedom bursting out. He also brought nuts. Tankers loomed out of the fog and fell away to the west. Gulls ripped gashes in the grey view beyond the portholes. I headily felt as if I hadn't eaten or drunk for days.

'The first time I crossed the Channel,' Aitken said, sipping the fizz, 'was on the *Titanic*.'

'It's not possible.'

'I hardly believe it myself – so long ago. Eighteen I was. April, 1912. Goodness, it was something to go abroad in those days. It sank,' he said.

'Presumably you didn't go down with it,' I said, humouring the fellow.

'Still nobody knows why.'

'I gather it hit an iceberg.'

'Come now,' Aitken said, gesturing for his glass to be re-filled. 'The fact that events happened is of minor interest, isn't it? History is finding out why they happened. Aren't you interested in knowing why the *Titanic* hit an iceberg?'

'Of course.'

'Well, you've a lot to learn before we get to that,' he said amiably. 'They threw me off at Cherbourg. After only one meal. Fillets of brill and mutton chops. And champagne.'

He emptied his glass. I racked my brains for some reliable detail of the *Titanic* disaster, if only to confound this unlikely tale. The trouble was that in modern scholarship there was so much to know that an historian's discipline was to shelve facts until he needed them. I could expect no reference library on the high seas. Confirmation had to wait. Meanwhile I latched on to the dim view of the waters where the gulls hovered for garbage.

'When I met him,' Aitken said pensively, 'I never realised what a small boy Edgar was. He was eighteen. I made the mistake of intoxicating him with Billy Bunter. I told him all the tales. And, do you know, he rather took to the ass. After that he utterly devoted himself to me, as no woman has ever done – not even Wallis Simpson.'

'Who?'

'The Duchess of Windsor,' said Aitken.

'Now look here . . .'

'Before her marriage, that is. Which reminds me, were you aware that her husband was the model for Lord Mauleverer in the stories?'

'Just a moment . . .'

'Old Richards had the nerve to pick up all the gossip about the young Prince of Wales going round the Fleet Street pubs – no question of royal assent – and then actually got a fan letter from David, *The Magnet* being required reading at Balmoral, saying what a jolly character Mauly was and how he intended to base his public career on the shining example of His Lazy Lordship. But that's by the way. I didn't myself meet David until 1920 at that luncheon I arranged in Boulogne.'

'Luncheon in Boulogne?' I expostulated. 'But we're just . . .'

'I know. Indulge an old man. I only possess a past. You'll be helping me bring it up to date. We'll try for the same table, though there were eight of us on that occasion.' With a gulp he again drained his glass. 'What a beano! I'm the only one left. Even Jack Priestley packed it in a while ago.'

Once again chasms of novelty yawned in front of me. There was no stemming this tide of headlong memory or time to insist on chapter and verse. As the champagne bit into my faculties, Aitken set up a cry for another bottle. There were more nuts. For no reason he was now going on about Field Marshal Montgomery, and then Pandit Nehru received an inscrutable mention. I almost gave up listening. It was evident that interruption only insulted his flow. In any case we were nearing land. The window framed a picture postcard of French beaches, bathing-huts, breakwaters – all grey, as if photographed long ago. I tried to focus on Mrs Simpson. I saw her as young and slender and dressed in white and in a hat. A vast and courtly Aitken was breathing a compliment in her ear. Yes? No, quite unacceptable. It can have been no accident that

Bunter was portrayed in *The Magnet* as a phenomenal liar.
Richards had known his man.

'As for Mr Quelch, the Master of the Remove,' Aitken said,
as we bumped against the dock, 'Richards forged that mighty
figure out of a synthesis – creative chaps are so damn cunning,
as you know – of A. E. Housman and Jack the Ripper.'

Yes, yes, oh, yes. I chewed a nut and looked at him. I let
him finish his champagne and smack his lips. I willed him
to admit that he was pulling my leg. The back-packs were
already crowding at the gangway. We would soon be on foreign
soil. Tense with indignation, quivering too with a fear that this
trip could end only in disaster or dislike, I went on staring at
him. I felt my eyes bulging. He peered at me softly over his
glasses.

'Don't doubt so, my boy,' he whispered. 'Your charming
wife warned me you weren't the trusting sort. The loss is
yours. If you never credit the more unusual things people tell
you, you'll never grow up. Now look the facts in the face.
Frank Richards may not have known the identity of Jack the
Ripper – few did. But the fellow's exploits appealed to his
imagination. Perhaps he didn't meet Professor Housman either.
But that irreproachable scholar was also an ideal of his. Not
even the police had any means of ascertaining whether or not
they were one and the same man. So, to solve the problem,
he created Henry Samuel Quelch, M.A.(Oxon). Mr Quelch,
I assure you, tanned the hides off boys with just as much
savagery as Jack the Ripper dealt with the innards of ladies of
easy virtue. And Housman's small output of poems proves
him an author of no greater application than the schoolmaster
who set himself the holiday task of writing the History of
Greyfriars.' He paused. 'So now you have to write it,' he added
with satisfaction.

Aitken raised his body. I followed him out into the air,
which was laden with a breezy blend of cigarettes and coffee.
We were unmistakably abroad, and with how endearing an

intake of breath Aitken welcomed the spectacle of the continent. At the same time, one debated, what truth lurked beneath those airy efforts on his part to cast light on Greyfriars? Housman had ruined my youth with his sloppy verses set in a borderland of dreams; also the idea of Jack the Ripper had often frightened me into admiration, if only for his anonymous power. And, true, I had always sensed that dichotomy in Quelch. He would bear down on any boy for transgressing his iron standards; but next minute retire to his study and ponder poetics. If he were indeed an amalgam of two of the forces that had fashioned the twentieth century – perverted violence and a twisted sentimentality – I begged leave to wonder if Archibald Aitken was such a big liar after all.

At the sight of Aitken at the door the management was alarmed, then charmed. He offered a graceful apology for taking up so much room; his size was merely evidence, he claimed, of his respect for good food. His French was delightful. He recalled the *patron*'s grandfather who had so well served his party of eight in 1920. In turn the *patron* pretended to recollect from his boyhood how much that long-forgotten party of Englishmen had enjoyed itself. Was he therefore aware, asked Aitken, that as a lad he must have overheard a veritable top note in the grand duet which our two countries eternally sang on the stage of history? M. Lacoste, presenting us with menus as large as newspapers, digested this metaphor with a wary smile and expressed the hope that today history would again be made by his kitchens.

Duty done, comfort assured, Aitken sat back in a trance of anticipation over the bottle of Montrachet which a waiter whizzed to our table and gazed at the immensity of the bill of fare. I flatly wondered if they would take a credit card, whether Diner's would dishonour a debt that soared over the limit, and what means I could find of recouping the money on expenses. All this was deeply unworthy of the occasion, I felt very small, but could do nothing to allay my anxiety except drink the best dry white wine in the world.

The nectar worked. I soon put aside squalid calculation. As Aitken pored over the menu, savouring a dish only to reject it, balancing one delicious item against another, my mouth started to water, my mind to tingle. Never had I so relished someone else's open pleasure in an act of choice. No girl had enthralled me by such exquisite delay in deciding what to have; indeed Lesley's way of ordering her favourite things had only maddened me. But Aitken, as he dithered and discussed and swilled and stared, gave me the sense that, if life had any meaning, it was accurately contained in this shared, trivial, magnificent moment of selecting what he wanted from a variety of alternatives.

At last his mind was made up. He had only to raise a finger for Mme Lacoste to hasten to our table as though to throw herself into his arms, pad at the ready. I had no will left of my own; the Montrachet had seen to that. I would have what he had and be glad of it and pay with joy what we owed. Allowing for a few bits and pieces to taunt our appetite, Aitken began with *palourdes farcies*, he moved on to *sole dieppoise*, he settled for *canard aux petits pois*, he reached a conclusion with the *gigot d'agneau à la Bretonne*, then quickly added to that tasty climax a helping of *pommes dauphinoises* while popping in a sorbet after the duck. His voice fleshed out the words. Each syllable tingled on the tastebuds with more elegance than greed. Every dish sounded as rounded as an epigram. When he finished it seemed that he had at last expressed in spare prose the sum of human experience. No wonder he sat back with an air of fulfilment as though he had already consumed this huge meal.

By now I was fairly close to being drunk. He ordered further Montrachet to tide us over the fish, while thinking perhaps Volnay – no (he screwed up his eyes), Pommard – again no, far too heavy for the lamb; for a second he seemed to blunder after some distant perfection – and then it all came back to him. Yes, a bottle from that little vineyard up the hill behind Chambolle-Musigny. Mme Lacoste beamed and scribbled.

'Ah, how my memory frolics when Edgar's not there to bring on the amnesia,' Aitken said. 'In a matter of minutes we shall be eating the exact luncheon which I ordered for the Famous Five in 1920.'

Oh Lord, the old sybarite was trying it on again! My mind wavered after proof, precision of detail, perhaps a snapshot of the chaps tucking in, washing down the classy spuds with a splash of the little vineyard up the hill. 'Come on, Mr Aitken,' I said amiably. 'Out with the whole wretched thing. I've waited long enough. Are you trying to get me squiffy, so I'll believe anything you tell me? You must think I'm an absolute mutt.'

Aitken said nothing. He flipped a slice of sausage into his mouth. His silence sounded hurt – and shamed me. I began eating too, if only to clear the fumes from my head. He crunched a radish.

'The lads had come back from the war,' he said gently. 'The war wasn't like school. Your friends weren't swished, they were killed. The headmaster was God, and you didn't know what on earth He was talking about.' The stuffed clams reached the table in a cloud of steam, reeking to high heaven of garlic. 'Was the era of jolly japes over, we wondered? Had teas on the lawn gone for good? Was there no longer any order, propriety or class?

'But then,' Aitken said, slurping a clam out of the shell, 'I had such a great idea. *The Magnet* was still being published, for the delight of a new generation of schoolboys. There I still was, Billy Bunter, immutably on the cover, up to my usual tricks, asserting a normality that had vanished. All the other boys were dashing and flashing across the pages. I knew them. At least I knew by name one or two of them whom Frank Richards had used as models. So I wrote to those chaps, and they put me on to the others. I tried to make common cause with them. I suggested, as a start, that we form a luncheon club, and meet to have a whale of a time, and find ways of putting the ruined world to rights. I must admit, as now, that the food and drink came uppermost in my mind, which is why I proposed we all took a weekend off from our despair and met here secretly in France, yes, in this very restaurant. Does that suffice?' He quaffed the last clam. 'I really don't understand your doubt.' He swallowed juice. 'That occasion, after all, was very like this one.' He wiped his lips. 'It seems credible enough to me.'

My head was floundering. The sole arrived in a creamy sauce topped by a tumulus of mussels and prawns. Aitken wagged a hand at a long table set under the window where a bourgeois family munched without a word, jaws rotating in unison, bodies silhouetted against an exterior where mists swirled along the coastline. On the sands a dog leapt high to snap at a thrown pebble. On the quay a blowsy matron attended a shellfish stall. 'There in the window,' Aitken said. 'That's where we all sat.'

I capitulated. 'All right. Tell me who.'

'Ah, now then, the seating plan,' he said with renewed vigour, easing a fillet off the bone with skill. 'H.R.H. naturally took the head of the table, where that rapacious bank-clerk is gorging himself. He was Lord Mauleverer, if you recall. Next to him, where the little girl is, sat Harry Wharton. Or Anthony Eden, if you prefer it. Then, in place of that fat old termagant, begging her pardon, Bob Cherry. And passing round clockwise, we have Johnny Bull – that avuncular chap wiping his moustache – then Hurree Singh, that's where the ugly one's tossing bread into her mouth, then Harold Skinner and finally Fisher T. Fish, that's the nubile little miss minding her manners, and then me, of course, W. G. Bunter.'

'Who actually were the others?'

'I've just told you.'

'I mean in reality.'

'Reality?'

'Have you forgotten what it is?' I said with asperity. 'Who, for example, was Bob Cherry based on?'

'Oh, Bernard Montgomery, of course.'

'And Johnny Bull?'

'That was Jack Priestley.'

'And Hurree Singh?'

'Believe it or not, Jawaharlal Nehru.'

'And Fisher T. Fish?' I went on relentlessly.

'Some American poet fellow. What's his name? T. S. Eliot.'

'And Harold Skinner?'

'Poor old Oswald Mosley.'

'And where was Frank Nugent?' I asked, naming the only unmentioned member of the Famous Five.

'Well, that was Frank Richards himself, you know,' Aitken said. 'He couldn't manage it – or, to be truthful, I thought he might be an embarrassment, eating peas off his knife in front of all these well-bred fellows, so I didn't invite him. In any case he was probably too busy pounding out the next issue of *The Magnet* on his machine.'

I laid down my knife and fork, my mind in riot. I glared at the table, focusing hard against the luminous mist outside, and the figures he had mentioned did seem for a blinding second to materialise. At one time or another they had all vaguely qualified as heroes of mine, just as their counterparts in *The Magnet* had. Sir Oswald Mosley? Well, no, of course not a hero, but then Harold Skinner had rarely risen above his role as a rotter, a vicious little snob with knobs on. However, the whole notion was preposterous. Yet part of my mind, as inconvenient as a headache, wanted to believe that those men, still in the cocky prime of their youth, with great futures ahead of them, had sat there with Aitken one summer noon building a promised land out of the wreckage of the Great War, laying their plans – the plans to which a few terms at Greyfriars had inspired them – for the future of politics, art and me. Already, as the bones of the sole were borne away and the duck landed on the table, they were mulling over the standards by which I now lived, perhaps even setting them. My society was potentially in their power. They could form it as they would: stamp all over it or fashion a utopia.

'And then I looked at them,' Aitken said, with a glance at the tooth-picking party framed in the window. 'I saw that underneath they were still as eager as Richards had described them in his boisterous stories. But pomposity was creeping in. They were solidifying. Behaving as if they were famous. It dawned on me over the *canard* that there was little hope for our country if such men, whom Richards had put in the fore-front of every schoolboy's idealism, didn't stop being fourteen and really make an effort – but here they were, my guests, just tuning up their personalities at one another's expense. They had lost the fellow-feeling they had at school. They were hiding under a cloak of jokes the agony they had felt in the war. They were polishing their egos, flat out for themselves. Far more like the cardboard inventions of some novelist than they ever were in class.'

Aitken dispatched a mouthful of wine in several lingering swallows. 'And of course the buggers didn't take me seriously for an instant,' he said, giving his plate a push. 'I was as fat as ever. I hadn't fought in their bloody war. So they ignored my witticisms. They edged me out of their counsels. They treated me as a waiter. I kept saying that we all ought to get together at intervals, form a nucleus of good will and good sense, to stop our times going off the tracks, call a halt to the dottiness, fire people with the idea of a paradise that was surely within human grasp. But they just jested and drank and roared and reminisced. I remember the Prince of Wales, when I pressed him for a commitment, tittering consumedly over the prospect of occupying the throne. Pandit Nehru wasn't much better. He had but one thought – to cast his homeland into such con-fusion that he could sneak in and dominate it by the combined force of his personality and his police. How Oswald Mosley chuckled at this masterful sally! And that listless little gnome Montgomery, fingertips together, refusing to consume more than a few morsels of this munificent meal, frightening me to death with his strategy for the next war – even using the cruet to position his armies – which as a well-trained soldier he would do all in his power to bring about.'

Our plates were snatched away and I was being made to inspect a small leg of lamb on a salver. 'Aha!' said Aitken with appetite. Ramparts of pallid beans surrounded the crisp curve of the flesh. The waiter cut deeply and hot blood bubbled out. As with Aitken's revelations, I felt both repelled and ravenous. My appetite too was up, but so were my defences, despite the Burgundy which had crawled into the middle of my thoughts with the stealth of a terrorist. It was a superb vintage that sluggishly began to rock the saloon in front of my eyes and induce a vague impression that I was thinking with the utmost clarity. I then giggled.

'What is it, old lad?' he said, mouth full.

'The whole bloody thing,' I replied, still wanting to laugh.

'Understood!' Aitken said. 'Want some more?'

'I want everything.'

'You shall have it,' he said, raising his glass. 'They were all drunk, of course, except for Monty. That's why they ignored me. And I suppose I knew then that I had a subtler part to play in influencing events. At least I knew that dear old England couldn't, must not, fall into the hands of my school chums. I couldn't let it be dominated and distorted and dashed by these fellows, simply because they were old friends, sharing with me the weekly pages of a paper that was teaching far more in schools than the form-rooms were. All they wanted, for their own glory, was to repeat the horrors we had already suffered.'

Even if all this were true, flaws gaped: perhaps a sure sign of truth; but it needed contesting – and my brains felt slippery.

Aitken was now tackling his potatoes, crisp enough on top but sloppy with cream. I kept wondering where home was. England had slid from my grasp.

'Does Edgar know about that lunch?' I asked, feeling my way back.

'Edgar?'

'Your friend.'

'Friend?' he spluttered. 'Golly, yes, won't he be worrying now?' He looked guiltily thoughtful. 'Poor Edgar. Unfair of me. Not too good.' He winced over the moral dilemma. 'Damnation. He'll be going scatty wondering if I'm all right. Probably on to the local bobbies by this time.' He guzzled a last sliver of potato. 'Look, be a good chap, run and telephone him. Put him in the know. Tell him we'll be home to supper.'

I stood, slipped away, banged a thigh on someone's table, knowing all of a sudden that the thing I wanted was the lavatory. Occupied. Someone was straining inside it. I turned to the telephone on the wall. The slots for coinage attracted me strangely. How did it work? As an experiment I put in five of the francs I had cashed on the boat and dialled a number in Britain. Oddly it was Joanna's number. She picked up at once and the five francs vanished. I entered another coin behind the glass panel, stuttering a bit, and that too disappeared, and the line was suddenly clear as if I were in bed with her in the dark. The lavatory flushed. Was Joanna in the bathroom? Even the voice seemed to come from the man adjusting his dress with a rustle, snorting into a crackle of paper as he blew his nose. Or was it a woman?

'Darling,' I said.

'I think you must have the wrong number.'

'No, it's me, Patrick.'

'Is something wrong?'

'No, here I am, I've just had mussels and duck, and he's just coming out of the loo – ah, *bonjour, madame* – and believe it or not this phone works, and the old man's quite out of this world, we've run away together, escaped, and here we are having lunch.'

'So it would seem. Are you in Kent?'

'Kent? I'm not there. I'm here.' The coin dropped. 'I'm in –' The line went dead.

Where was I? I'd rung the wrong person, yes, I wanted to go to the lavatory, and just then a broad lady sailed into it. The lock clicked. I slammed down the receiver and for no reason a franc came back with a tinkle. As I picked it up my bladder leaked. My legs tightened. The phone was by Joanna's bed. It was only two o'clock in the afternoon. She had answered as if awaiting a call. A fart reverberated next door. Compressing my buttocks, I dialled New Romney – a long blah – then dialled New Romney again. I listened to the unbelievable relief of someone pissing close at hand.

'Yes?' answered Edgar.

'Edgar?'

'Yes,' said Edgar.

'It's A. J. P. Taylor. We're in France.'

'Yes,' he said.

'We're coming back. For supper. Got some of that oyster pie left?'

'Yes.'

'It needs eating.'

'Yes,' he said.

'I'm told to tell you all's well and stop being such a fusspot.'

'Yes,' he agreed.

The lock shot back. The lady who had sat where Field Marshal Montgomery had stood in for Bob Cherry emerged from the closet applying lipstick. Water gurgled behind her. By ringing off fast I just made it. Duty done, I voided my bladder with a luxury more delicious than any item in the lunch and gazed at the chain swinging back and forth at eye level. I felt a new man.

*

I dozed mostly on the boat home. During the intervals my
thoughts toyed with that group sitting through lap after lap of
indulgence in the restaurant so long ago, with the world at
their feet. Aitken snored. I didn't believe a word of his view of
things. More likely Aitken, in his longing to be Billy Bunter
and recognised as their head, had allowed envy to corrupt his
version of what happened. Surely the real fact was that all
these men – Nehru and Eden, Eliot for sure, Priestley perhaps,
even Mosley – were blind and boring idealists, and it was this
that had terrified our host.

I felt my logic tottering, but I realised with the wisdom of
wine that the effect of food and drink on Aitken was to reverse
the truth: not just to fail to tell it or at the very least to pay it
lip-service, but to stand it on end – where it swayed as danger-
ously as an alcoholic attempting a somersault. The sadness was
that the men at that lunch shared a vision of the future that
firmly excluded Archibald Aitken. Here was a fat man content,
then as now, to let things slide. If he made any effort at all – as
when we shot off in the motor-car leaving decent behaviour in
the lurch – it would be towards anarchy, folly, revolt. He
resented, as he had at school, their unity of diverse but well-
matched ego, which excluded him, if only for his interest in
food and drink, fun and games. By seeming inferior to them,
he had been made to feel a child. His gusto, the storm of life
that blew through him, his refusal to accept rules let alone obey
them, had quite properly dismayed those men on the make.

They were all aiming at power. So they had dismissed Aitken,
now as an ample reminder of the middle class questioning their
ambitions, now as a comedian who would laugh their plans
away. A balanced man simply couldn't fail, as he had failed, to
take seriously a Famous Five who had each prepared for and
met his historical moment, and it was absurd for Aitken to
minimise their presence in our annals just because his own
achievements weren't up to much. Little did I then know how
outrageously wrong I was in that assumption.

Still less did I know of the welcome that awaited me at Folkestone. But at this point, as the white cliffs came up on cue, Aitken briefly surfaced. 'One thing I never told you,' he said, as if he had otherwise told me everything, 'was how I once brought a noted murderer to book. The sea always calls it to mind, and it still hurts, he never merited the gallows, but I was only a boy at the time and didn't know any better. Just think of poor old Crippen looking with a wild surmise at the white cliffs of Canada, much as we are now, little suspecting that Inspector Dew, last seen in Hilldrop Crescent, was waiting on the quay to arrest him. How would you feel now if Folkestone over there contained the seeds of your exposure? To this day I wish I hadn't done it.'

I trod warily here. To judge by previous example, Aitken almost certainly believed that he was responsible for the execution of Dr Crippen. I believed he hadn't been. A gap yawned between us which, if not somehow bridged, would put at risk all the things he had told me which I really did want to credit. The safest step, therefore, was to enjoy the possibility that it might be true, while waiting until I had proof that it wasn't.

'Wasn't that in 1910?' I asked. 'You must have been about, what, sixteen?'

'Precisely so. I was still at school. I had just won a history prize. The guest of honour at speech day was Horatio Bottomley – of course he hadn't been exposed for fraud then, and I certainly had no hand in that.' It was amazing how Aitken could gain credence for his less probable stories by denying his part in others. 'You know what the Fleet Street pubs are like – well, doubtless from Frank Richards, old Bottomley had got wind of the fact that I was Bunter, which being on the fat side himself amused him no end, so he asked me over to tea at his place near Eastbourne, no great distance from the school. It seemed quite an honour at the time, though I've been careful to suppress it ever since. The Bottomley name, you know – bad to be associated with it.'

We drew nearer the coast. 'I then cracked a tooth on one of
his rock-cakes,' Aitken said. 'Terrible pain. I writhed all night.
So next morning he packed me into his motor-car and sent me
to London to consult his dentist, Hawley Crippen. The blessed
man yanked it out, but there were so many policemen around
his surgery that, being the usual adventurous sort of schoolboy,
I wondered what was up. In fact I followed them back to the
good dentist's house in Holloway, where it all turned out to be
a false alarm. But just after the police had left, giving him a
clean bill of innocence, the old rascal crept out with a suitcase,
met his receptionist slyly on the corner, and buzzed off at a
guilty trot as if going into exile.

'Well, what would you have done? Contrary to the picture
you have of me as Bunter – quite false, that, Richards really has
a lot to answer for – I was an almost priggish upholder of the
proprieties as a lad, and guessing something was morally wrong
here, I dropped a note in to Scotland Yard suggesting it might
be a worthwhile lark to chase after the eloping dentist. That's
all. As you know, they caught up with him, his nice receptionist
most perversely garbed as a boy, at the dockside in Canada.
Ah, we'll be coming in soon.' He yawned. 'I think I'll just go
and rest my venerable bones below for a few minutes.' And
Aitken slowly descended the stairway, as if the effort of memory
or invention had taken too great a toll.

I continued my effort to sober up among the seagulls. In
France, even on the boat at first, the drink had made sense of
Aitken's confidences while he was uttering them. But now,
bringing back all the facts he had unburdened to the rationality
of England, and bringing them back like contraband as mental
furniture of my own, I felt them turning sour under the weight
of wine I had consumed. The vessel bumped the quay.

An emergency vaguely developed as I went on trying to feel
my way to sobriety. Sailors shouted, the crowds were pressed
behind ropes, a wheelchair was hurried up the gangway. Unbelievably it was Soames who manoeuvred this contraption on

to the deck, where it vanished in a swarm of uniforms. There was a mood of controlled panic, or perhaps I woozily imagined it. Or perhaps the panic was only in me.

And then I saw Archibald Aitken. Bulging under a blanket, he was being bumped down the gangway with slow ceremony. His huge face lolled and gaped, a circle of blind pallor; under pressure he had beaten his customary retreat into the gaga. On the quay below stood the vehicle in which we had made our escape. Beside it a policeman was conferring with Edgar Smedley, whose eyes narrowly ranged the deck until they met mine. He raised a finger. I waved back. The blue helmet nodded.

Aitken was eased into the car, Edgar closed his door, Soames took the wheel, and the party moved at the pace of a hearse through the limbo of the customs hall and out into England. I shuffled forward in some perplexity. How was I supposed to get back to The Dunes? What had I done to be dropped like this?

At the gangway two young men awaited me in suits.

'I'm sorry to trouble you, sir.'

'You answer the description of a man we're looking for.'

'Would you mind stepping this way?'

'It won't take long, sir.'

I was led to a small room, my brain still numb with drink, and left to fume on my own. The policeman stood guard outside watching the vulgar herd crush into the boat train. Regulations were hooked to the wall in sheaves. On a filing cabinet stood a ship in a bottle. What the hell was going on? The harsh light throbbed in my eyes with the start of a headache. The London train drew out, then the two men entered. They considered me with a courteous severity that looked false.

'Now then, sir.'

'Your passport, if you please.'

My hand moved to my inside pocket before I remembered. It was a pity I was drunk; they noted this condition. It was also a pity I had no passport; they evidently hadn't known this fact.

'Not that you need one, sir, for a day-trip,' one said helpfully.
'We're just checking,' said the other with a shrug.

Both stared at me, oddly disconcerted, as though I were
indeed a wanted man who now had no identity, mistaken or
not. The only proof that I existed was my set of credit cards,
perhaps stolen. With an almost crestfallen air they begged me
to check my pockets again, which so convinced me that their
pretences were false that I fell into a woolly rage. 'You'll hear
more of this,' I think I stammered. 'I happen to work for H.M.
Government in a senior capacity and I'll see you answer for
your insolence. If you're so interested in who I am, telephone
my Secretary of State. He happens to be a personal friend of
mine.'

Having committed the tasteless error of mentioning the
Minister, I had no choice but to stand by my folly. Equally
the two young men, though out of their depth, had no alternative but to put my arrogance to the test. Ignoring my sodden
muttering, they began placing calls with an air of anxious
reserve. The Duty Officer at the Department of Trade naturally
had his tabs on Richard Rathbone, who turned out to be spending the night at Chequers.

I knew the form. I had once undergone a vetting there. They
would be in the thick of a dinner designed to tempt a Third-
World statesman into buying trucks from Britain. There would
be a token intellectual (probably Hugh Trevor-Roper) to add
lustre to the dull panoply of negotiation, and one or two lady
wives to spice the tedium in gowns as long as the speeches. A
phone call to guarantee the bona fides of a renegade junior
impounded at a Channel port could hardly improve the occasion. Give my Minister his due, however. Alerted to my
distress, Rathbone called back within minutes, and thereafter I
was treated by the young men with a degree of respect that
seemed even more scornful than their earlier patronage.

'You seem to be in the clear, sir.'
'We'll overlook the little matter of the passport.'

I was escorted to the railway, where exiguous apologies were exchanged, and stood stunned on the platform nursing my headache, wondering what damage I had done my career and why I wasn't closeted with Aitken sorting out the twentieth century, fact or fantasy. When the late train at last drew out I just had time to fall sound asleep in a first-class compartment before being awoken at Ashford to pay the excess. How savage an irony! Only yesterday this shadowy station had been the passport not only to Aitken and the Famous Five, but to the *Titanic*, Dr Crippen, *The Waste Land*, El Alamein, *The Good Companions*, Sir Oswald Mosley, the Suez crisis, the Duchess of Windsor, *et al*. I had travelled a long way in twenty-four hours and ended up nowhere.

Well, back in Victoria at least. Only when I stepped out of the train did I realise that my ridiculous arrest was just the kind of jape that might have been played on an adult in *The Magnet*, and I had risen to the bait, if not the occasion, by blustering and pulling rank in the time-honoured manner. It even struck me as possible that Bunter himself was at the back of the outrage. Had it been planned from the outset to show me how gullible I was? The episode certainly bore the stamp of Bunter. It was Aitken, after all, who had lured me out of my routine. He had got me squiffy. Humouring me with a lot of tall stories about the high and mighty, he had let me loose on a flying carpet of fantasy, only to pull it from under my feet. How Lesley would have relished seeing me stand on my dignity and regress into affront.

Safely home I brooded alone on my wrongs. If Aitken was the architect of my downfall, surely Edgar was the clerk of works. Less clear was his method. Somehow or other he had suborned servants of the Crown and persuaded the law of the land to make a fool of me. I recalled his eyes smouldering with triumph on that damp quay. He had risked my making a fuss in public. He must have guessed my power to make him jump, if I so chose. But he had gone through with the charade. And,

the unkindest cut, he had snatched Aitken away from me, by
means so underhand that I had no idea how to fight them, at
just the moment when I thought I was coming to grips with
him. Yet Smedley was a mere middle-aged schoolboy, not even
a grown-up one. I had to know how he had done it.

All next day I considered my strategy. After my call from
France I could hardly ring up Joanna. It would be to add a
confession of failure to my record as an alcoholic. In any case
I was determined to work out for myself what Bunter now
meant to me. I also felt ill. My body was no more accustomed
to the extremes of that luncheon than my mind to accommodat-
ing its surprises. It was a dispersed and nervous sort of Sunday.
The nadir was reached when the doorbell rang at about six in
the evening – the day's only punctuation, apart from pick-me-
ups – and there was nobody there. An old grey car was moving
off down the street, a figure in a peaked cap at the wheel. The
sight aroused what seemed like a race memory, but was only
from yesterday.

Starting down the steps in vague pursuit, I tripped over an
obstacle that slewed into the gutter. It was the suitcase I had
taken to The Dunes. It had a label addressed to 'A. J. P.
Taylor' – yes, in inverted commas. On the back, in large childish capitals, was inscribed a message: EFF OFF PROF. Though
fatuous, this touch of humour left my body chilled, my mind
hurt. It was plainly not Aitken's style but an obscene squeak
of triumph on Smedley's part. Perhaps to ask why, mainly to
enquire after Aitken's health, to thank him for a day which I
was now drugged enough by pills to judge unforgettable, to
request on any terms another meeting, I rang the New Romney
number several times in the course of the evening. But it was
always engaged. It was probably off the hook, which was more
than could be said of me.

4

A night's sleep convinced me that I had imagined the whole affair. Inquiries through the local exchange in Kent established that Aitken's number, though not out of order, was unobtainable. Worse, they knew no subscriber of that name. Joanna was so rarely late at the office that I thought she must have been spirited away, and luckily – but that didn't seem real either – there was no message from the Minister demanding explanations for my conduct at Folkestone. I appeared to have been forgotten.

I sat gazing at damp sunlight turning Green Park into a watercolour by a gifted amateur, then with an effort took out a couple of sheets of official paper. My idea was to appeal to the two experts on the past whom Smedley had mentioned as my rivals for the rewriting of history. At least Hugh Trevor-Roper existed; he had recently been elevated to the peerage by the authority for whom I worked. A. J. P. Taylor appeared often enough on television to be also regarded as a fact. Asking these men as equals whether or not they had been approached by 'Billy Bunter' jerked me back into the actual. I felt better. Historians never lied.

I had scarcely sealed the envelopes when Joanna bounced in

looking bonny and tediously full of herself. I felt a stab of jealousy. Instead of offering excuses or taking up pad and pencil, she dropped into a chair as if sitting for her portrait against a background of Green Park, then said, 'Shoot. All about Bunter. I can't wait.'

'Not in office hours.'

'Ask me to lunch then. I've got lots to tell you too.'

I frowned. 'I have an appointment at a comprehensive school this afternoon.'

'I only said lunch.'

Embarrassed by the suggestion that I had been suggestive, I looked into my diary. The school, where I was due to spotcheck adolescent grasp of literary culture, was just round the corner from my house. An early lunch could be accommodated. I had nothing in the refrigerator but stale eggs. However, we could shop. An erotic plot hatched sluggishly in my mind. An appointment at three o'clock seemed all at once as distant as the last trump.

I had forgotten what shopping with a young woman was like. It was as if the market were colluding with my desire. A music-hall vulgarity nudged us as we picked and chose our lunch. Repartee sprang to the lips of men selling fruit. The fish-monger delivered some rough-hewn innuendoes over the smoked mackerel. I kept not quite catching Joanna's eye. She had become gaily assertive after her weekend, as if she had already drunk the wine she was now buying us. There was a lot of sunshine about, as well as lip. I was desperate to know what had happened to her, and I felt years younger. Only then did it strike me that the stallholders probably thought she was my daughter.

We sat down to a simple feast, over which Joanna heard all about France. Eyes greedily following the story, she ogled Dr Crippen, stared aghast at Anthony Eden, raised an eyebrow over the Duchess of Windsor. She gasped at Aitken's audacity, while believing every word. Her appetite was up for every flavour of that lunch in Boulogne. She chewed Pandit Nehru with the lettuce, crunched up J. B. Priestley with the celery, digested the loss of the *Titanic* with the cheese. Squeezing a last drop of lemon on her fish, she saw it all.

I paused. Something was missing. Ah, yes, in the heat of the story I had neglected to open her wine. I splashed it into our glasses. How amazing the tale must be to have kept us so long from our pleasure!

'Cheers,' said Joanna.

'Your very good health.'

And then one sip, and out her secret poured. As she re-counted her version of the weekend, I could hardly believe my ears for either admiration or doubt. It was certainly a relief to discover no bedrooms in it. While I had been making a pig of myself abroad, she was sitting studiously at home, absorbing as much of the Bunter canon as the Hampstead Library could lend. While I had been bogging down in Aitken's variety of truth, she had gone back to the sources. Our contrary weekends were as glorious as a fugue. As I was swaying back on the boat, she had been scouring Foyle's for traces of the Famous Five. She had stripped the Charing Cross Road of every reference to Greyfriars, just when I was being arrested. Her free time had been lavished on my obsession as though it were her own. What did one say to that?

'You really are the tops,' I said, still faintly suspicious.

'Yes, but when you were living it up in France, didn't you think about the time Bunter sneaked the whole of that huge meal that was meant as an end-of-term treat for the staff?' she asked, giggling reminiscently.

'I don't recall coming across that story at The Dunes.'

'The Dunes? Surely you mean Bunter Court.'

'Ah, but there wasn't a Bunter Court. That was Billy doing his usual boast. He actually lived in some suburban villa in Reigate.'

'Exactly,' said Joanna. 'But don't you remember he took over

Combermere Lodge when the owners were away to prove to
his chums that Bunter Court really existed? What a gas!' She
tittered over the wine. 'And he nearly got away with it, didn't
he?'

'Not quite.'

A hint of boredom yawned in my mind. She was somehow
pushing fiction too far. I was moderately delighted by her
industry, but not by my lagging behind: at the textual level
Joanna now knew more than I did. But of course she had
missed the spirit of *The Magnet*.

'The point is,' Joanna said, picking at the strawberries, 'that
Bunter was always trying it on. And lots of the time it worked.
You're not like that, you're nice and cuddly, but all those real
people the Greyfriars lot were based on – Whatsit Nehru and
beastly Priestley and Co. – went on to get their own way with
life, twisted life round their little finger, and that's sexy,
Patrick, that's the key to not being unhappy for no reason, like
you are.'

'Am I?'

'Gosh,' said Joanna, 'I'll never forget the moment, it's really
great, when everyone absolutely knew Billy was lying when he
said he'd rescued the gipsy boy from sudden death on the
railway line – that was just after Bunter had ordered all that
food from Chunkley's (remember? yes? the department store?)
and then they had to eat their hats. Billy really had rescued the
child!'

'Had he?'

By now the boredom had settled in. I just wished she would
stop. Somehow she was dishonouring the age and experience
of Aitken with all this superior knowledge of his boyhood. She
had become a swot. I wanted to tell on her, or light a firework
under her chair, or rape her on the kitchen floor.

'What you don't seem to realise,' Joanna went on in relentless
tones, 'is that Bunter wasn't telling fibs just for the laughs. He
had a special gift. He used lies to finger the truth. It's like

philosophers do. Teasing us with the incredible, so we come
out taking a new look at things which we thought were facts.
And that's just what your Mr Aitken is doing. He's keeping
the truth up his sleeve until he can prove to the world it's not a
load of codswallop.'

She paused, but not long enough for interruption. 'And
don't you see, Patrick?' she said. 'That's what we're for.'

She sounded smug. Almost in panic I sought an escape.
Joanna had become too knowing for her own good. It didn't
seem proper for a girl to guess so accurately the secrets of
Greyfriars or treat Bunter as a buddy. I reached out for more
wine.

'That's why he's calling on us,' she continued. 'Knowing he
was Bunter, being too old for anyone to take him seriously –
not that anyone ever had, as if anyone would – Archibald simply
had to find somebody else to bridge the gap for him, the chasm
between the good old past and the horrible young present. Just
you think of that this afternoon when you're asking those kids
about Bunter.'

I jumped up. 'What's the time?'

'Three-fifteen – why?'

'Oh, goodness, I'll miss my date.'

'I thought your date was me.'

Casting one look back at her, I ran down the stairs and the
steps and the street, soon breathless, recalling with sorrow how
cheaply I had aimed to seduce her, if only she hadn't talked so
bloody much.

The corridors were suspiciously calm for a modern seat of
learning, but I knew the headmaster of old. Though forbidden
the cane, Cyril Venner was a stickler for the discipline we had
endured together at school in the forties. I regretted my friend
wasn't wearing a gown, and he seemed more depressed than
when last dining with Lesley and me at Haslemere in the years
when we all had high hopes of ourselves. 'Don't try to teach

them,' he said wanly at the classroom door. 'They'll think you're brainwashing. Make it a dialogue.'

Venner had put at my disposal a mixed form of fourteen-year-old low-achievers, who were draped over their desks in a limbo between scorn and indifference. They wore T-shirts that sported mottoes more catchy than the faces above them; their features advertised only junk food and inefficient cures for acne. They were nice enough youngsters beneath their inelegance and I saw at once that my approach must be to cajole. Verbal flourishes would miss their mark.

'I have a job to do,' I said, 'and need your help. The Government, which is paying for you to be here, wants to know what you read in your spare time. Now this isn't a test of your knowledge. It's having fun with facts. So don't feel threatened. There's absolutely nothing you can get wrong. Anything you say in answer to my questions will be what I want to hear.'

I spent the next half-hour pursuing my enquiry with rigorous patience. As a frame of reference, just to give them a narrative line to cling to, I told them of a splendid old buffer I had recently met, very much a fact, who when their age had become famous as a character in fiction. They would probably know him as Billy Bunter.

Pause. Well, did they? Or didn't they?

The class gazed slowly at windows and doors as though expecting the outside world to provide an answer.

In that case, I said, they were missing a treat. He was a story in himself, still full of spunk at pushing ninety, as eager for knowledge as ever, hacking his way through the jungles of modern history like an explorer, living his life as if he were the hero of an adventure. This man, I declared, was an example to us all. Even at his age he wasn't content with the world as it was. He wanted to shape it into something different, something his own, and he had stuck to this resolve by keeping his imagination alive, by recalling the stores of energy, ambition and initiative he had plundered as a schoolboy.

Pause. Nothing happened.

I hadn't meant to say so much about Aitken, especially after Venner's warning. But their reserve infuriated me. They were sullenly ensconced in their ignorance. At that point I knew that any question I asked would be blocked by a failure of interest, even in their futures. How many of them had heard of Rider Haggard? None, but who cared? Who had ventured on to a desert island with Robinson Crusoe or solved a case in the company of Sherlock Holmes? One, perhaps two, but did it matter? Could anyone tell me what Alice did in Wonderland? Not a soul. Or the disasters that befell Ulysses in *The Odyssey* or, for that matter, Dr Crippen on the high seas? Or how Eden gaffed at Suez? Or which enemy Montgomery had defeated at El Alamein? Or what anyone had done, in any place, at any time?

The answer wasn't just no, and no, and no again. From that class there wasn't an answer at all – no show of hands, not a smirk of recognition. They were lost in the void of adolescence. The riches of our culture, the twentieth century itself, were not so much a blank as a blackout.

'Told you so,' mouthed Venner from the rear of the form.

So I stopped asking questions. I had nothing on my notepad – also a blank that would barely provide a parenthesis in my report. I looked at them with concern – patronising? No, real concern. They had equal rights with me to breathe air, look forward to food, waste time. Their hearts beat too. All they lacked was the knowledge even to detect a lack in their lives, let alone identify it. I knew what it was: the absence of a story that took a line and made a pattern.

So again I told them a story, as if they were infants. Gilding the lily of invention, I told them how this fat fellow called Archibald Aitken – the name at least raised an unwilling laugh – had set out, years before they were born, to make an England not only fit for schoolchildren to live in, but jolly and jokey too. It was a country, possibly a paradise, where you could do just what you liked, provided the rules were strict and worth obeying. Then you could break them. If you were found out, of course, the penalties were terrible. Your bottom would be blistered, your spirit humiliated. You might be twisted for life. But this paragon of our times, Archibald Aitken, who had matured his cunning in the schoolrooms of long ago, had discovered a simple truth: that to grow up you needed an enemy. And for him that enemy was fact. Fact was always false. It lured you into ambushes. It jumped on you from the branches of trees. It hit you in the back of the neck. But you still needed the facts, even if you lost your battle against them.

'Isn't it ridiculous to be children in a world of peace?' I cried in peroration. 'A world in which you're so free to do what you want that you don't know what it is. Take no notice of the guff your biology chaps teach you. Each of you is not an individual but a species, which has to fight for survival. That's what I learnt from Bunter last weekend, so you'd better start reading him soon.'

Were they stunned? There was certainly no response. Had I gone too far? Yes, but no matter. Cyril was staring at me with a venomous satisfaction, hoping I had stopped but longing for further excess. I knew his urges as a boy. They were huge, he had hoped for everything. But he had gone flat. In the nick of time I remembered some words of Aitken: one said what one had to say, then left it to others to make sense of it.

I rose to my feet, gave the class full marks for concentration, congratulated them on their courtesy. Wishing I had a gown, I swept out. I heard Cyril's voice dismiss the form, which they managed with only a modicum of clatter. Perhaps they were starting to think.

A few minutes later we were sitting over cups of weak tea in a study hazed with pipe smoke.

'I made a fool of myself,' I said, fishing for a compliment.

'You took the stick to them,' Venner said. 'It's hardly their fault if they got hold of the wrong end of it. Billy Bunter? Come now, Patrick. You're way out of date.'

'Was it that bad?'

'I see my job as to contain the worst that can happen to these kiddoes,' Venner mused, settling back behind his milk returns and heaps of small-print admin. 'Preach to them about crime, and they're into it. One ill-advised exhortation on drugs, and they're all sniffing glue in the loos. To educate no longer means to lead out. They've hit on a new definition. It's drifting back to infancy on your own two feet. Oh, in the end they'll gravitate to the good things of life, but only on their terms.'

'When?'

'When they find that hard facts are too limiting.'

'Don't they know any history?'

'You're joking.'

'Art?'

'Never heard of it,' he said smugly.

In the fug that confused the outlines of Venner's den, I tried to consider these points. If true, they amounted to horrifying evidence of lack. I could scarcely blame the children for their despair. The teachers? Why should they nowadays be any worse than the cruel Quelch flashing his cane over an unlettered essay or the beaks who had flourished threat to squash my brains between the columns of irregular verbs? Yet there was a difference between then and now. As a boy I had escaped from the stress of the classroom into the ease of a story. I had crouched reading under a hedge until the sun dipped.

'Look, Cyril. Your children didn't respond.'

'They don't respond, Patrick. They reject.'

'They made me think the events I mentioned never happened at all.'

'Yes, you rather behaved as if you were inventing them,' he said, without fellow-feeling.

'Of course you've given them a smattering of historical fact. Ten sixty-six and not quite all that. But they know nothing of their own century.'

'Except that it's let them down,' he said chummily.

'Does that satisfy you?'

'Life goes on,' Venner said, relaxing into convenient platitude.

We looked at each other, friends brought up the same way,
middling chaps doing their best with middle age. A sensation
next door to sentiment tingled down my throat. I recognised
on his old face the smile he had had as a boy. It aroused self-
pity in me. Neither of us had any youth left. But he was in
charge of quantities of the young and my task was to report on
their doom. Smoke puffed out of his mouth as we considered
our lot in a more or less companionable silence. I looked for
gaps that divided us. We were too old to have many. Both of us,
in our heart of hearts, had given up. Yet had I? I thought of
my relatively young mistress screeching in the darkness of
orgasm. Cyril had been hitched to Berta ever since we joined
the Army and still lived near some stop on the District Line.

'Life doesn't go on,' I said to my surprise. 'Not unless we
force it to do so.'

'Well, Patrick . . .'

'You know what the trouble is?'

'I wouldn't be here if I did.'

'They don't read school stories any more,' I said. 'So they
have no mirror. We had. Look, we guzzled stories that were
simple enough to turn into myth. You know we did. We looked
into those mirrors and saw more than ourselves. Identifying
with Bunter or whoever it was gave a ring to our own lives, a
sense that an exciting event was round the corner, a feeling
that convention was there to be challenged as well as respected.
That was our drug, our crime, our escape from barbarity.
Wasn't it?'

'Patrick, I have to go now,' Venner said, with a last bitter
puff of smoke. He riffled through some test papers, gathered
them up, reset a picture of his family on the desk, took out his
car keys.

'Can I give you a lift?' he asked.

We walked in silence down the stone steps, crossed the tarmac of the playground, entered his car and fixed our seatbelts. At this rate, I thought, I would not be meeting my old pal for at least another decade.

'Give my love to Berta.'

'Surely.'

'Dear Cyril,' I wrote late that night after long thought,

'I worry about your charges, as I'm sure you do. I only mentioned Bunter (sorry you think he's out of date) because I was looking for a way of making the past real for children who don't believe in it. I know it's no good, but think of it as a first effort. I did tell you how I found out that *The Magnet* was based on real people, didn't I? Well, it just occurred to me that, if your kids have no idea who Anthony Eden was or how his conduct once rocked the country which they're supposed to be inheriting, they could do worse than discover what Eden was like at their age by making the acquaintance of Harry Wharton. If J. B. Priestley has nothing to say to them, perhaps Johnny Bull could laugh them out of their ignorance. It just seems a good notion to take them back to the people – manipulators of great events, mainsprings of social change, masterminds of art – who have contributed by more error than trial to the kind of children they are. A child can't believe Montgomery was anything but a crusty old warrior throwing his men into the jaws of death unless they can meet him on equal terms in the person of Bob Cherry. Pandit Nehru might be just the chap to rally your coloured contingent, provided they encounter him in the earlier form of Hurree Singh . . .'

I stopped, in deep water. I knew what I must say, but even to an old friend I couldn't say it: that those children, as homes broke around them and teachers lost heart, needed to be inspired – not by calls to arms, not by the facts and figures of the contemporary mess in politics and morals, but by the sweet breath of fiction. They were expiring from shortage of story. With few resources of their own, identifying with no one, with little sense of the continuity that alone made sense of life as it did of narrative, with no outlet to adventure except misdeeds, they were dying in a prison of our time's making.

I sighed. For the first time I felt a wave of responsibility for those hopeless offspring, which – since it put at naught all the work I had so far done on my report about the state of culture now – was almost bound to prevent my finishing, let alone posting, this or any similar letter to either friend or foe. I could say it only to myself.

I was just preparing for bed at well after midnight when the telephone shattered my peace of mind. It could only be a wrong number or a tease. I picked it up with a muffled hello.

'Did you know that Billy Bunter was a ventriloquist?' Joanna said in highpitched tones.

'Of course I did.'

'Well, just a tiny thought, wouldn't it be an irony – you like ironies – if he was still throwing his voice, you know, sort of figuratively, and you and I and Mr Aitken were just his dummies?'

I eased myself into bed with a dim sigh. 'Frank Richards,' I said, 'chose to employ ventriloquism as a somewhat contrived device for getting Bunter out of scrapes. It made a fool of the authorities when they looked the other way.'

'Right,' said Joanna, as if I had proved her point. 'And that's what we have to do, isn't it? We're his mouthpiece.'

At this late hour her grasp of logic was too much for me, or rather too little, and after a cool endearment I rang off. But resentment lingered sleeplessly. What was happening to Joanna? Her efforts over lunch to upstage my knowledge of the text had been bad enough. But this ardour in the small hours went far beyond the call of duty. I thought at first, as the void of the night loomed ahead, that I had fallen victim to a childish unwillingness to share so masculine a force as Bunter with the creature whose femininity now and then shared my pillow. But then I began to suspect an alternative explanation. Her desire to impress me, even at the risk of going overboard, must obviously be concealing a development which she preferred me not to know. Her enthusiasm at lunch had sounded false – but how much hollower now? In boasting of being so hooked by Bunter she simply wasn't being herself. Another voice was talking through hers. A secret was being brandished in my face.

This secret, whatever form it might prove to take, exercised my anxieties for much of the night. Twisting and turning, I argued thus. When I had first informed Joanna of my interest in Greyfriars she had taken the news calmly enough, indeed gazed at me with the indifferent scorn of someone mesmerised by bad television. There was no suggestion that her desire for me was so all-embracing that she would stop at nothing to share my concerns to the full. I had expected her hourly to dissuade me from my folly or at least to hint by a well-timed silence that I had gone round the bend.

Instead, over today's lunch, she claimed to have spent the entire weekend researching into Bunter's past. Jolly though she was, Joanna was not a girl whose free time anyone would associate with a concentrated study of prime sources. That wasn't where the action was. It seemed almost as if someone else, with far more eloquence than I could command, had inspired this outburst of loyalty, this gallop to the archives. I felt threatened, not only by the eagerness of her academic assault on Greyfriars which more than matched my own passion for the place, but by – well, what? Someone else. A figure in the background. A murky influence.

Gradually, as serpentine as suspicion, that black night of mine at The Dunes, when she had failed to answer the telephone, crawled back into my mind, only to begin preying on it. Where had Joanna been when I needed her, in whose bathroom, giving ear to what rhetorical excess? It now became evident in this darker night that, as soon as my back was turned, she had bumped into some young blade whose approach to Bunter and all he stood for was on a higher level of conviction than mine. That encounter had captivated, then captured her. She had fallen for Bunter. We had become rivals.

Absurd? I was certainly exhausted by speculation. Only as I fried bacon and eggs at sunrise did the light of reality dawn. It was all too clear. She had met another man. Yet rather like Aitken, if less believably, Joanna would divulge her secret if and when it suited her, and no sooner.

For days there was still no reply from Aitken's number or word from the exchange, which even refused to confirm that anyone of that name was on the telephone. But with interesting promptitude the two historians had replied by return of post. And somehow, by denying almost all knowledge, their letters suggested that a conspiracy was afoot.

Hugh Trevor-Roper arrived in the morning, A. J. P. Taylor after lunch. One thanked me for my inquiry and claimed that, while his mind was open to any further evidence that cast light on the smallest aspect of his discipline, he was unaware that he had been approached by Mr Archibald Aitken, but would be grateful to be kept in touch. The other asserted that he well knew that much of this century's history was still in the safe keeping of archives as yet undisclosed and though he suspected that posterity would view the whole matter very differently, he wasn't prepared to believe that Mr Archibald Aitken, from whom he thought he might have heard, would have anything of substantial importance to add for the time being. In other words, neither historian felt in a position to commit his reputation wholeheartedly to the facts as we thought we knew them. There were still lacunae.

I was disposed to regard these letters as a triumph for Aitken's view, if indeed the fellow still existed. For one thing they stopped me thinking that Joanna might be in two minds about the truth of the story I had unfolded to her. She simply assumed I had offended Aitken, perhaps by eating peas off my knife in France. So it was she who proposed that I should contact my ex-wife for further instruction. We were in the office pondering the letters.

'If you can't find him, what's wrong with Lesley?' she said suddenly.

'There's a lot wrong with Lesley.'

'But she put you on to him. She must know where he is.'

'Don't you understand about ex-wives?'

'I happen not to have one.'

With patience I said, 'They wait for you to make a bloomer, then invade the scene with cries of virtuous pity, and berate you for missing them so much that you misunderstood their point by being besotted with someone not in their class.'

'Heavens,' said Joanna. 'I can't think that someone you married would be like that.'

'We all make mistakes.'

'Do you think I do?'

'Only when you try to persuade me that Lesley is the answer to a maiden's prayer.'

'Well, I'm no maiden,' she said. 'You see to that. And I don't pray. It's unrealistic.'

'Not as unrealistic as asking Lesley for help.'

'Why not? The whole caboodle isn't really real, is it? You might just as well bring in a woman who doesn't exist for you in order to locate some boyhood hero you thought you had lunch with in a foreign country last week.'

Yes, it sounded improbable. But so would Lesley's way of life if I told Joanna what little I guessed of it. So I told Joanna. As far as I knew, Lesley fanned out with nationwide ambition from her nerve-centre near Haslemere to induce couples with bank accounts as big as their gardens to let her loose on their lawns, tearing up sods and putting down crazy paving, in an attempt to give Lesley not only a heavenly income but a touch of the divine afflatus. She razed coppices. She pulled out banks of rhododendrons planted in a more spacious age in favour of dinky displays suited to the suburbs. Lesley's burden, as she saw it, was generally to alter the appearance of things so that the past vanished. Her efforts wiped out history. Her sole impulse was to start from scratch, as if nothing that had happened before were of any worth. The same applied to her men. She wanted to rip up their roots too. Here was I, still suffering.

'She's only trying to impress you with her creative powers,' said Joanna.

'Balls, she's manipulating people into reluctantly changing their way of life.'

'Same thing.'

'Not at all. She imposes. She insists to these benighted people, who know no better, that her interference in their lives can only do them good.'

'Sounds a bit like Bunter,' Joanna said.

'What does that mean, for pity's sake?'

'That's all Archibald is doing, isn't it? Trying to rejig the garden a bit. Cut down this, plant that. Intrigue you with something new when you look out of your window. He seems to have rather a lot in common with your ex, in fact. And you're the one who talks about revolutionising! I think you ought to ring her right now.'

'I haven't the least idea where she is,' I said.

It would have been too much to hope that Lesley was at home in Haslemere hunched over her drawing-board. She never had been when I wanted her. I would drive at insane speed back from Oxford at dead of night to find the house as empty as the fridge. To prove my point, that the phone at home would ring on and on, I picked up the receiver and, with the nerve of a lover courting pain, dialled the long-remembered number. And of course Lesley answered at once.

'Well, well,' she said. 'About time too. I've just been thinking about you and all your many interests. I do terribly hope you're on to the right thing with that report.'

'How are you?'

'Oh, oh, oh,' said Lesley, as though climaxing. 'I can't tell you how exciting it all is. I've got a vast estate to get into some kind of order, but more of that when we meet. What's new with you, darling? You did call Archibald, I hope?'

'Well, actually, that was it. Do you happen by any chance to know where he is?'

'Of course I do,' Lesley said. 'I've just come back from a most wonderful lunch with him in fact. We went to France. You know, day-tripping. France is only worth it for the food these days, they've gone off culture. So in one way you're right with what you're up to – the trend is altogether here, darling, in merry England. Very good luck with your efforts. We really are on the same wavelength, and I somehow knew it would turn out like that. We had to part in order to be together. Isn't that an irony?'

There was much information here that needed sorting. With the phone pinned to my ear, I stared balefully at Joanna, who had a remote smile. On the face of it Lesley had lunched in France with Aitken recently, but hadn't known that I had done the same. In view of his relentless conviction that we were still married and happy, why hadn't Aitken told her? Or was she lying?

Lesley's habit was not to lie in any direct way; that didn't appeal to the fundamental honesty she flaunted as part of her character. Her untruths were of a subtler cast. They were designed to make one recoil a step and question one's own mendacity. Had I indeed lied to her? One never quite knew. She was capable of thinking that Joanna's presence in the room while I spoke truthfully to her was itself a species of deception.

'Are you in bed with someone, darling?'

'No.'

'I seem to hear a sort of slight susurration.'

'Not at all.'

'You don't desire me any more then,' Lesley said with spritely logic. 'Never mind. It's just good to talk to you. What is it you want exactly from your life, Patrick? Your friends seem not to know. I only wish I could help. It might bring us closer again, and you know how much we'd like that.'

In one form or another Lesley had been saying all she had so far said so many times that I could neither count nor discount them. Joanna sat prim on her chair, as though hurt that by saying so little I must be listening too much. It was time to secure some solid information.

'Lesley – where is Archibald?'

'At home, darling, where we all are. At least I hope you are, you naughty man. We rushed back from France yesterday – lots to tell you about that, he was quite wonderful about his war.'

'His war?'

'The First World one, poppet. And the dear fellow stuffed himself so much over lunch that he's probably too weak to answer his phone. Just try again if you're serious about it, and do be. Edgar was in smashing form, by the way – have you met him? Went all weepy over the battlefields.'

'What battlefields?'

'The First World War ones, darling. Anyway it's lovely to hear all your news. Incidentally Archie's commissioned me to design his tomb – that's so positive, don't you think? Monumental even in death. Talk soon . . .'

So the elusive Aitken was finally back at The Dunes after yet another debilitating jaunt. Not wishing to become enmeshed in the toils of Edgar's conversation, I asked Joanna to ensure that I spoke directly to the man himself. There was a slight wait; doubtless Soames had answered. Then Joanna, addressing at last her newly discovered hero, said, 'Mr Aitken? I have Mr Weymouth for you', and handed me the instrument with an air of suppressed triumph.

'Is that you, Archie?'

'No,' said Edgar, not even suppressing his triumph. 'It's Edgar.'

'Look here, I wanted . . .'

'Well, you can't. You're not the only one who can lure him to France, you know,' he crowed. 'Archie came with me this time.'

'Did anyone arrest you when you returned?'

'Why should they have done? I had a valid passport. You know-alls don't know everything, you know. Your wife is designing a free gravestone for Archie, and he wanted her to see the sacred places where the lost generation is buried. She was getting ideas.'

'Not for the first time,' I said; then, less sharply, 'Come on, Edgar, let me speak to His Nibs.'

'How many times must people be reminded that they don't own Archie? It's becoming quite a menace. It's like Caesar, you'd all rather bury than praise him, because you want to get your clutches on his fortune.'

'I thought he hadn't got any. Isn't he still waiting for a postal order?'

'His fortune is his story,' Smedley said. 'Why should you have it? I just may happen to want it for myself. I won't put up with anyone fiddling about with it. They'll introduce inaccuracies. It's preferable that it should die with me.'

'Is Lesley designing a gravestone for you too?'

There was a shocked pause. 'Bad taste is the last resort of the vanquished,' said Smedley.

'All right, you win. But just let me have a last word with Mr Aitken.'

'A famous last word?' he smirked.

'Edgar, I just want to make sure that he really doesn't want to speak to me.'

Smedley was gone some time. I looked at Joanna in faint surprise; I had forgotten she was in the room or even in my life. She was tense and glazed as though listening to bad news on the wireless. As the receiver hissed at my ear, ordinary life swam vaguely back. Green Park was misty, the traffic a murmur. A dim image occurred to me of the vacant corridors of The Dunes, as dusty as a school in the holidays. It was immensely sad. This search of mine made no sense. Nor did being in love with Joanna. In love? I hadn't meant to think that. Then Smedley came back. He sounded nervous.

'Archie can't recall how much or little he has told you,' he said. 'He requires to know what you intend to do with the confidences you extorted from him.'

'I intend to keep his voluntary confessions to myself until I have heard the whole story.'

'In that case, he asks, did he acquaint you with the details of how he sank the *Titanic*?'

'Not in full.'

'He doesn't wish you to have a false impression. Lest, I presume, you hear the truth from another source. A little learning isn't just dangerous, he says, it's an affront to veracity. Don't forget he was only eighteen at the time. Boys do pick up unconsidered trifles. You must be forgiving.'

'I seem to have forgiven you for playing the fool with me at Folkestone.'

'It was the pair of binoculars, you see,' Smedley said in a persuasive whine. 'He just found them. There they were on a lifeboat cover. Nobody seemed to want them . . .'

The immensity of a petty theft now stepped on to the stage of history. Aitken was on his way to America to rid his parents of a burden and to make his fortune. His Uncle George had paid his passage on the *Titanic*. Wanting to take a last magnified look at the old country as the Isle of Wight sank into the seas, the boyish Archibald had snatched up the said binoculars and was about to focus them on the chalky nostalgia of the cliffs when authority, in the person of a couple of officers looking for something lost, marched along the deck towards him. They passed him by. But by then, with a stab of fear, he had tossed the glasses overboard. Only later, when the mixed emotions of longing for home and a seasick premonition that he would drown caused him to disembark in adolescent panic at Cherbourg, did it strike Archie that those binoculars had been somehow essential to the survival of the ship. As he tottered below to lunch, they were now lying fathoms deep somewhere off the Needles. Four days later, paying dearly for their absence, the great vessel would follow them.

'Is that all?'

'All?' he echoed.

'Yes, well, it doesn't strike me as sufficient evidence.'

'It's not evidence,' Edgar spluttered, 'it's fact,' and rang off in a bate.

I was fairly cross myself. To tolerate Smedley's trifling insults was bad enough, but to be forced to deduce an effect as tragic as a shipwreck from a cause so piffling was to add injury to verisimilitude in a fashion so crass that it almost unhinged the mind. This was almost as perverse as Aitken's account of his role as *deus ex machina* in the downfall of Dr Crippen. Yet a doubt nagged. I had readily believed the Crippen story when it was Aitken who related it. Perhaps the manifest absurdity of this tale of the *Titanic* was proof only of Edgar's lesser gifts as a storyteller.

'That's that,' I said briskly. 'You and I will now pay a visit to the source of all truth.'

'Who might that be?' said Joanna.

'Who? It's not a who. It's a who's who. We're going to the London Library.'

As soon as we entered the relative privacy of the stacks (Science & Miscellaneous), our bodies brushed and Joanna leapt away with a hiss as if burnt, her heels clanging on the cast-iron gangway. It appeared our excitement was to be only academic.

'You take Crippen under Crime & Criminals,' I whispered, 'and I'll deal with the *Titanic* down at the rear under Maritime.'

We parted eagerly.

There were several versions of the loss of the *Titanic*. They differed in detail according to date of publication, for ever since the patent unreliability of the first eyewitness accounts scholars of the sea had been delving ever deeper into this most hypnotic of ocean disasters. The fact that a person unnamed, victim of a premonition, had been at his own insistence put off at Cherbourg grew in my mind as I read several references to it. Alas, there was no passenger list. But only in recent years had it emerged that, shortly after the ship left Southampton, narrowly avoiding collision with a docked liner, a rumpus had broken out on the bridge over the disappearance of a pair of binoculars earmarked for the crow's-nest, but this had died down in the fever of departure. Binoculars? My spine tingled. In an uprush of elation I became aware that, far from telling lies, Aitken was actually trying to digest a fact he had feared for years, not boasting at all but attempting to quieten his conscience by means of confession: that by the unwitting theft of those binoculars (how else could they have just 'disappeared'?) he had prevented the look-outs from glimpsing the iceberg in time and thus, through nothing more serious than a schoolboy prank, sent the flagship of the twentieth century to her doom. On the circumstantial evidence all this seemed highly probable. On the other hand Aitken might just have read the book. But, if so, why bother? What kind of a human being would really want to claim to have sunk the unsinkable as the result of reading a book?

At this point I heard a faint screech from Crime & Criminals. Once again I had forgotten Joanna, magnetised as I was by the tragic loss of so many lives counterpointed by Aitken's lifelong tragedy of feeling responsible for that loss, but only now daring to admit it. I hurried along to the forward stack, where she squatted on her heels, her fall of hair darkening the pages of an open volume of court proceedings. Her intensity of posture almost suggested that she was making love to the book.

'I've got it,' she hissed. 'It's all here.'

She staggered up, fingers caressing the vital paragraph, and I caught her in my arms.

'Whoops, I love it,' she said, as a waft of scent hit me in the throat. 'I think the old boy did it.'

'Who, Crippen? Of course he did it.'

'No, Aitken, silly. Archibald. Where can we talk? I'm stifled. It's too thrilling for words.'

I escorted her at a trot to the more generous spaces of the reading-room. Several researchers were snoozing in chairs as palatial as beds. A fusty silence encouraged conspiracy, and we huddled close to a shelf of encyclopedias exchanging the evidence in hoarse whispers.

'The Inspector had given Crippen up as a suspect,' said Joanna. 'He was closing the case. No clues. Just another missing person. But overnight something happened to change his mind.'

'What?'

'We can only guess. But I think he got a tip-off from Archie. Isn't that the sort of sneaky thing boys always do when adults give them a break? Don't forget – he saw Crippen going off with a girl. Anyway the fact is that next morning, for no possible reason unless you believe Archie, the Inspector got suspicious again. Went round to the surgery. No doctor.' Our mouths only inches apart, Joanna looked deeply into my eyes. 'He was on his way to happiness across the ocean.'

I took a deep breath. 'I think that Aitken sank the *Titanic* too,' I said.

'Ssssh,' scolded a female scholar starting out of a doze.

Even whispers, it seemed, interfered with the flow of inquiry. Yet the lady's protest solemnised the moment. We stared mischievously at each other in silence, I smelt breath. We were almost embracing in a place devoted to accuracy. In this very room discoveries of moment had been made; life had been proved to be other than people supposed; minds, when not dozing, had been changed, opinions routed, areas of history illumined by yet one more interpretation. It seemed just the spot for Joanna and I to consecrate our own particular contribution to novelty: our joint find that quite possibly Aitken was telling the truth.

We drifted out into the square, where the streetlamps were flickering on.

'Are we lying to each other?' I asked.

'We can't quite be sure of anything,' she replied.

'Perhaps all we need is an act of faith.'

'Or love.'

'Isn't it the same?'

'Let's go and do it,' said Joanna.

At last the call came. The Minister summoned me to a colloquy, his word. I guessed the upshot. I had known him at Oxford, where he disarmingly assumed that I was no less ambitious than he; he had always shared with me the secrets of his strategic cunning, his ache for power. Now my boss, still something of a friend, he was far too inquisitive to let my lapse at Folkestone pass without inquiry. We met in his office, not at lunch. That meant he was displeased. Equals never let you down, especially when they had become disciples.

'You play down your importance in and to high places, Patrick,' he said. 'The work you're doing for us – little short of gauging the impact of old-style culture on the current scene – is of vital importance. Culture? The term is very much out of favour. We'd like you to come up with a better, something with more appeal to the younger generation. You see, the children simply aren't going to get jobs, as you very well know. You are also aware that the Government isn't just trying to invent a commodity called leisure to take the place of an old-fashioned word like unemployment. It isn't as simple as that. Now I know that our predecessors in office should have started all this off years ago. But what do you personally think about it, as things stand? You're at the coal-face. I'm just an innocent bystander, as it were, with a mandate.'

These statements, though blunt, if confused, were moderately heartening. I hadn't seen the issue quite like that. I had certainly not been party to the idea that Government already had a concept which my report, whatever it might say, was designed to serve. This made me indirectly feel that Aitken's contribution, by drawing children back to the exploratory mischief of childhood, thus supplying their adult imagination with an inexhaustible food, might turn out to be greater than I had suspected. I wondered how to present this view to Rathbone without appearing to have gone off my head.

Then, tilting back in his chair, denying me time to think, Rathbone said, 'Are you sure you're the right man for the job, Patrick?'

'It's not for me to say. If you're in doubt, I'll go.'

'Now let's not be hasty.'

'But not, of course, without a public fight.'

'Come, come . . .'

'I must be allowed to conduct this enquiry exactly as I see fit.'

'That goes without saying,' said Rathbone soothingly. 'It's just that when a stateless drunk rings up Chequers to be baled out of immigration at an unsocial hour on a Saturday night, the odd eyebrow finds itself being raised.'

'It wasn't quite like that.'

'It never is.'

'I had been lunching abroad . . .'

'Perfectly acceptable. Ministers often do that on official visits.'

'I'd had a glass or two of wine . . .'

'Why not? We ourselves were well into the claret when your captors rang through to ask who you were.'

'I was researching in my free time into a matter germane to our purpose.'

'Look, Patrick,' said Rathbone, tiring of the narrative, 'come off your high horse. This isn't a security vet and there aren't any thumbscrews. Excuses bore me. We all boob. Just tell me what the hell you were doing.'

I looked at his vain face. It had become so proud and casual. I doubted how far I could trust an old friend who was also a self-seeker. At Oxford, with iron relish, with an application to the lure of power that was far beyond me, he had treated us all as voters in the making. The butteries resounded to his rounds of sherry. On committees his floods of manic rhetoric were precisely calculated to drown out the subtler voices. He had the gift of appearing eminent in his own eyes before anyone had heard of him.

But Rathbone was also a mischief-maker. He stayed out late at drunken functions not only to have the kick of climbing into college, but also to blame someone else for it by giving a false name when caught. He interrupted lecturers of high repute with populist points. He was always slipping off to London without permission, giving a speech which he hoped would make the papers, and brazening it out on his return.

Was the small boy still there? And why did I care a curse if he was or wasn't? I might want my job, but I certainly didn't need it. There were alternative ways of saying what had to be said and better modes of publishing it than in a paper which would end in tatters on the floor of the House of Commons. In other words, I had nothing to lose. I was vaguely conscious of a ravishing surge of independence, then my mind at once felt better. It felt like a mind.

'Do you remember Bunter?' I said.

His brow creased. 'Was he at Oxford with us?'

'Come on, Dick. Not everyone's had the advantage of a university education, or you wouldn't be in power. Billy Bunter. Remember?'

Rathbone looked cautious, his brain already leap-frogging

towards other matters of moment. 'Yes?' he queried, as if dredging his wits for a race memory. 'Why Bunter?'

'A fictional fatty, or so we all thought,' I said. 'But he's real. I've run him to earth.'

'Have you, by George?' He leaned forward rather like a doctor. Was he humouring my symptoms? 'I'm most interested. Tell me more. Not too much more. I have a meeting.'

In for a penny, I brought him up to date. I told him that at least one of Aitken's assertions – about his melancholy part in the sinking of the *Titanic*, not to mention Dr Crippen's arrest – was open to proof. I posited the idea that Bunter was no mere fiction; he had made history. I linked this daring statement with my contention, formed even as I uttered it, that Greyfriars might somehow be made the context for a brand-new and highly original launch of English culture, if at least a fraction of what Aitken had told me about the dramatis personae – Eden, Montgomery, Nehru – could be established as true, or as a working truth. My mouth was salivating as I spoke. This was great stuff.

'I'm offering you a ready-made metaphor,' I said. 'The facts of this century simply aren't good enough as they stand. We have to find some base to go back to – that's what you're asking my report to come up with, isn't it? Greyfriars is as good as any, particularly as the main character not only is still alive, but has a most unusual attitude to the events of our times. He has played no minor part in them, only a secretive one. He's a public figure who has lived his life in private. Let's get Bunter out of the woodwork, Dick!'

'Hmm,' said the Minister, frowning at his watch.

I chose to dash on. 'We must go about this carefully, of course. It can't be hurried. I'm only just on to it. But think how inspiring it would be if we could induce new generations to go back to *The Magnet*, start from scratch, relive through the microcosm of a school the utterly frightful experiences which this century has manufactured for itself. There's no better way of making the kids understand it, Dick. For us, it's beyond comprehension, we're too old. But they won't have any culture at all, unless we present them with something simple enough to enjoy.'

'Is this the central message of your report?' said Rathbone with leaden calm.

'No. We can't say it. It would look ridiculous. The kids know nothing – a fact which politically we can't reveal. The report will merely lead with unerring logic to just some such revival of the golden past as I have suggested.'

'Good,' said Rathbone. 'I think you're mad. Public money is being wasted on you. You ought to go. I shan't ask for your resignation. You're too old a friend. We've had good times. But I believe you should think twice about all this.'

Again he stared at his watch. 'I'm late, why has nobody buzzed me?' he said. 'I like an exciting idea, mind you, crazy though it is. Billy Bunter! Government's off its rocker too, of course. How splendid to be reminded of Greyfriars. It makes the House of Commons seem almost sensible – all that ritual, all those rules, popular chaps suddenly taking a nosedive on the strength or weakness of one remark, how we all jockey for position and end up where we started – well, just so, Greyfriars, isn't it? Or Oxford. Or anywhere. Do you know, Patrick, if only culture were a public school, how easy your job would be. You could just tell us all to read about Bunter, what?'

Clicking the lock on his briefcase, Rathbone stared at me hard. 'Let's dine one night. Don't do anything rash till my secretary rings you. I'll ponder some advice. You look as though you need a decent dinner. The club, shall it be? How's Lesley, by the way?' He moved to the door. 'Come along with me now. Let's get you past all these infernal policemen.'

5

It was the first time Joanna had used my bathroom for well over a week, and I was beginning to fear that research was eating into our privacy. Far from relishing the aftermath of our recent activity, we lay apart in bed, exercised by the problem of our next step. Only our lowered voices carried any hint of the amorous.

'Go and see the old man,' whispered Joanna. 'Just turn up. I know you don't do that sort of thing, Patrick, but these days it's not considered ill-bred. Nothing is.'

'We're not talking about today's manners. The Dunes is living in the past.'

'I thought you said Archie was more up-to-date than all those school-kids you interviewed.'

'In a manner of speaking he is, but then . . .'

'Then just swagger down there and charm your way in,' Joanna said. 'Take a bedroll. Treat it as a squat if necessary. The issues are too jolly big for pussyfooting. And what about time running out? If he keeps trundling over to France every time he fancies a snack . . .'

'I'm not even sure he's at home any more. Where's the proof? I only ever talk to Edgar.'

'The tiger in the woodpile.'

'Tiger?'

'I've been sifting through modern editions of the children's books you're supposed to be analysing in your report.'

Joanna was lying on her front, her voice muffled by pillow. A faint desire stirred in my belly.

'In any case what I want now, just to clinch things, is information from another source.'

'Lesley?'

The desire faded. 'A source I can trust. Lesley's no road to Damascus, and I want to see it all in a blinding flash. Otherwise Aitken will just go on running rings round us. Yes, I believe him, but I need more than that. It's my type of bloody mind – it's trained in doubt, it's lost the gift of enthusiasm, faith petered out with my first lot of brain cells that died at whatever age it was.'

'Oh, darling!' she said. Again desire murmured. Then: 'I'm sure Lesley knows more than she makes out. After all, she's designing his tomb. She's fending off his advances, so she says. To manage all that she must be regularly consulting her client. Please try her.'

With lazy irritation I abandoned any idea of love. Joanna, head still buried in the pillow, simply couldn't foresee the difficulties. To telephone Lesley was to ask for an escalation in her already dangerous stockpiling of concern for me. Divorce had changed nothing. Indeed she was far more interested in my welfare now than she had pretended to be when married. The best solution, if any, seemed to take the form of a surprise visit to Haslemere – except that Lesley wouldn't be surprised; any lunge of mine into a renewal of our relations would merely confirm her view of my endearing weakness of character. On the other hand, I stood a chance of discovering more about Aitken – from an acute angle, so to speak, but at least I had enough experience of the allowances to make. Perhaps it was worth the risk.

'All right,' I said. 'If that's what you want.'

'No, Patrick. I only want you.'

In a blur her head swung up from the pillow. We engaged in a fluttery kiss that for a moment confused me with old images of Lesley, then took on a force of its own. Time passed. Eventually I had a curt dream that I had left things too late, and awoke with a bumping heart.

'By the way,' said Joanna.

'Yes?'

'Just don't tell me when.'

'Why ever not?'

'Haven't you any imagination?'

'If I hadn't, I wouldn't be going to see her.'

'Well, just think.'

I thought, if a bit muddily. I decided in a doze that I had no notion what Joanna was on about, but sense enough not to disturb her further by giving away my ignorance. She was gazing at me in the gloom with an expression too warm for comfort.

'Very well,' I said. 'I respect that view.'

'Damn you,' said Joanna wryly.

From day to day I put my trip off, hoping for some event that would make it seem natural. One evening, when I offered her in our casual way a drink after work, implying thereby the usual dénouement in the dark, Joanna primly said that her library had run to earth an out-of-print biography of Frank Richards, and she felt she owed it to our venture to go home by tube and snuggle up and read it. This, though to some extent treacherous, was in other ways loyal. I saw her to the underground, then took a taxi to Waterloo.

The journey, including the gin and tonic in the jammed buffet, was like rushing at sixty miles an hour into my past. I was commuting back to marriage. A porter at Haslemere half recognised me, as if from a police Identikit. I dithered into the

station yard, almost expecting to be met, if only by a couple of
men who wanted me to help in their inquiries. Then I walked it,
uphill all the way.

Our house, now Lesley's, stood handsomely in a wood over-
looking a vale of bungalows. Lights were on. I resisted the
temptation of creeping up unseen to peer through windows into
rooms where our passion had run its course, as often as not on
floors or against painful pieces of furniture; a glimpse of the
carpet, I feared, might reveal A. N. Other entangled in his
trousers. Instead I rang the doorbell.

'Haven't you got your key?' said Lesley.

'I didn't know I was coming.'

'How odd. I was expecting you.'

'How so?'

'I always am.'

She flounced merrily into the living-room. 'Do let the eternal
optimist serve you a drink,' she said. 'It'll have to be a gin and
tonic after the one you had on the train, won't it? Or do you
mix things now?'

It was somehow outrageous to be in my living-room. I almost
expected a figure resembling myself to rise graciously and shake
my hand and ask me where I hung out and what I did for a
living. Instead Lesley reached up with a smirk and kissed me,
so that the drink slopped on to a rug notoriously hard to clean,
and said, 'Who you've really come to see is Archie, isn't it?
And you don't have to feel as guilty as you look, because I
don't mind one bit.'

'Is he here?'

'As good as.'

Without another word, presumably to fetch Aitken or recent
evidence of him, she left the room, her skirt swirling against
thinnish legs, and I looked around to see what had changed. Not
much. The room was as staid as a memorial to a shared life that
had never needed to end. The same glazed ammonite was on
the mantelshelf, lit by a nineteenth-century lamp bought cheap

in Woking, which cast a circlet of light on a coal-scuttle used as a wastepaper basket. Each occasional table was a shrine dedicated to the trinkets and *trouvailles* of a marriage entirely happy until we both started looking into it for faults. The one intrusive note was struck by a framed photograph, on a piano belonging to me, of a dashing chap called Sholto Pritchard, who had once persuaded Lesley that two marriages were better than one, and who was now, to judge by his cynical presence in that frame, reinstated like me, poignantly forgiven for having been left by her. Lesley now returned holding, oddly enough, a photograph.

'Here he is,' she said, handing it to me with a curtsey.

Though not in sepia, the picture had browned with age, and the crackling edges crumbled even as I held it. The image was slightly out of focus, but not so dim that I couldn't recognise at once the ramrod person of Sir Douglas Haig, attired in the breeches and boots suitable to commanding an army from well behind the front line. He was not alone. Indeed he was gazing with mulish severity at a fat young man who, had he not been dressed in the tweedy plus-fours suitable to a shoot, could hardly have been anyone but Billy Bunter, as immemorially drawn to illustrate a story in *The Magnet*. A château stood four-square in the background like ill-painted scenery.

It was not quite Bunter, though. This chap, for one thing, was in his twenties. His expression, as he peered through his glasses at the C.-in-C., contained little of the quaking fear or abject self-pity which Bunter would have brought to the occasion. In fact he appeared to be staring at the noted soldier almost with patronage, certainly as man to man. As far as one could divine the scenario, it seemed that two stubborn idiots had agreed after a long wrangle to differ about some such matter as which of them stood a better chance of winning the war. Both, in their outfits, looked like grown-up schoolboys. There was no doubt in my mind that Sir Douglas, whom I had rarely admired, was here pictured face to face with Archibald Aitken, whom I now admired more than ever – if only for his effrontery.

I was also oddly moved by this snapshot. The two men had the air of enemies engaged in silent attrition.

'Don't say it,' said Lesley. 'You think it's a fake.'

'When will you learn not to put words into my mouth?'

'When you stop putting the wrong ideas into my head. It's terrible to be burdened with intuition.'

'Well, it certainly could have been tampered with – faked, as you put it.'

'So could you,' said Lesley. 'How real are you, Patrick, I often wonder?'

'At least I don't go about producing false evidence.'

'You did at the divorce. You said under oath that I was sexually insatiable. What you meant was that I loved you too much.'

I sighed. 'Let's get back to this photograph. What's the provenance?'

'If you mean where did I get it, the answer's all too obvious. It can't have been from the Field Marshal because he died in 1928, the year I was born.'

'I thought that was 1933.'

'Since you left me,' she said, 'my age is a fact I have learnt to live with.'

At a certain point in any dialogue with Lesley, the knees ached, the toes tensed, one had to sit down. I sat down by the piano under the other snap. I took a swig of gin. I waited, as my muscles warily relaxed. In any dialogue with Lesley one also knew that it was hopeless to ask, with hope of answer, any further questions. She must proceed in her own way.

Her way on this occasion was to lodge the photograph against an ammonite above the fireplace and, hands clasped at her belt, stand back as though to worship it. Her voice deepened into a tone of throaty respect. The truth, as Lesley was inclined to view it, was no mere matter of fact. I was in for a story as long as a sermon.

Summarised, the story was as follows. To appease Edgar

Smedley, who had taken so badly to our jaunt to France that he had decided as a sour joke to punish me by mobilising for my embarrassment those immigration chappies who happened to be former members of a youth club Edgar ran in Folkestone, Archibald had promised to repeat the treat for Edgar's benefit, provided he was allowed to include Lesley in his party. Behind this hospitality an ulterior motive lurked. Aitken wished to take his last look, not only at the battlefields of the Somme where so many of his generation – much of Greyfriars, so to say – had perished, but at the cemeteries that bore such a resemblance to English gardens that Lesley might be inspired by their kempt lawns and cottage shrubberies to an even better idea for Aitken's tomb than she had so far sketched. He wasn't quite sure what he wanted, but his vision was hovering between something as simple as a plain white cross and an erection as grand as a cenotaph.

'You don't know what challenges are any longer, Patrick,' Lesley said. 'I was almost in tears – you know, fighting it all back for his sake, but longing to let it go for mine.'

Rather like tears, honesty now shone in her eyes, even if she didn't quite realise what she had said between her lines: that all emotion, as I believed, as she didn't, was self-indulgent. Never mind, I had my gin. And all of a sudden the story became very simple indeed. Even Lesley lacked the intellect to wreck it.

It all started in 1914 when Archie volunteered with the rest of the lads. He was, of course, rejected amid much regimental laughter, a fact he attributed to Frank Richards having made such a fool of him in print. Resentful but resilient, he holed up in a couple of rooms at Folkestone to be as near to the battle-front as was consistent with not fighting. He hoped his school-fellows would pause for any good cheer he could provide on their way to the trenches. He wanted to be well placed to hear the gunfire, so that he would feel involved.

Archie had little money. The one point to which Richards had been faithful in the stories was that Archie's career at school

had been dogged by the paternal failure to send him postal
orders at moments of need, but his Uncle George – also slipped
into *The Magnet* without permission – happened to live rather
handsomely in this residential hotel at Folkestone, so squared
matters with the landlady and gave young Archie a pathetic
reward for being non-combatant in the form of weekly pay. It
wasn't enough. Food was short, yes, but appetite spoke louder.
Archie soon found that his income was smaller than his intake.

Vaguely getting wind of the funds which his mentor Horatio
Bottomley – 'who introduced him to Dr Crippen, you know,'
said Lesley with due pomp – was raising for the war effort,
wanting to take some slight revenge on Frank Richards, Archie
determined, on the strength of his fictional name, to launch in
the Folkestone area a scheme for comforting the troops. It was
a big idea that seemed to need big money. He kept wondering
how to launch a scheme unobtrusively but to large effect. And
it was then that fate threw up a catalyst.

He was loitering by the dock one day, envying the soldiers in
their eagerness to get to grips with the enemy, when a group of
snooty officers started chortling in his direction, having identified him as Bunter. They were *Magnet* readers to a man. One
of them, taking pity, came up to Aitken and whispered, 'Don't
worry, old chap, I'm in the same boat, you're not alone. They
call me Harry Wharton, but the name's actually Eden, and I
can't describe to you what a bother it's been. Too boring. But
this Big Push'll be the death of me, I don't doubt.'

'Big Push?'

'That's the ticket,' Eden said with a rabbity grin. 'Dead
secret, don't tell a soul, etc., but Haig's going to attack on the
Somme on 1st June next. We Greyfriars boys' – he laughed
hollowly – 'must stick together. See you after the war.'

Lesley was no bad mimic; our dinner parties had been famed
for their malice. In her account of that scene I heard Eden's
thin strangled tones that for me had always smacked of sixth
forms and sport. But the effect of those words on Aitken had

been instantaneous. At a hint from a fellow-sufferer at the hands of Richards, a fellow just off to suffer even more at the front, his whole scheme clicked into place.

Bunter Bonds! That was the ticket!

A week later small advertisements announced Bunter Bonds in the local papers, an offer aimed at involving the workers in the war. Dig into your mattresses, the small print said, bring out your savings, send in your postal orders – and the great Bunter will ensure that every soldier waiting for the Big Push on the Somme on 1st June won't be short of either food parcels or more glamorous fare, to inspire him with home comforts, to give a touch of reality to the ideals for which we were all fighting.

For a week nobody, except perhaps the Germans, noticed this modest betrayal of an official secret in the environs of a port in Kent. From labourers in the wheaten vales behind Canterbury, from wives of slaving miners up Ramsgate way, from hinterland rectories touched by any effort to blunt the edge of war, the postal orders flocked in so fast that Archie, whizzing up to London on unexpected expenses, began ordering hampers from Fortnum & Mason to be despatched to the front c/o H.Q. in Amiens and photographs of scantily clad vedettes in plain envelopes to be hung up in dug-outs on the otherwise monastic night before the assault. He had no thought of personal gain. This was his war work: to ensure victory by donating a last-minute happiness to the troops or at least, if funds ran out, to the officers who led them over the top in the dawn.

But official ears at length pricked up. The moment when that photograph propped against the ammonite would be taken was fast approaching. Aitken was briskly interviewed, but not arrested. How had he come by his information about the Big Push? Thoughts of Greyfriars guaranteed that at this dread moment not a word escaped him. Across the very seas on which he had eaten well on the *Titanic* four years earlier, he was taken under escort to a château behind the lines and brought before Sir Douglas Haig.

Snap. Here was the picture to prove it. Lesley stared. So did
I. The evidence stood on the mantelshelf as contentiously as the
shot of Sholto Pritchard on the piano.

'What was said?' I asked.

'How should I know?' said Lesley with impatience. 'They
didn't have tape-recorders in those days. And I wasn't there.'

'But presumably you believe your prize witness, or you
wouldn't be telling me all this.'

'How dare you suggest that Archie is lying?'

'I just don't want you to be hoodwinked by him, that's all.'

'You're being selfish again,' Lesley said, sniffing.

Slowly the story got under way once more, Lesley making it
plain by more sniffs that I wasn't worthy of it. Haig, it seemed,
was writhing in rage about Aitken's give-away of the date of
his attack, but dared not act against him for fear the enemy
might learn that he had now changed that date. He had perforce
put it back to 1st July. But his yet more cogent reason for failing
to lock Aitken up or have him shot was the rumour that the
character of Bunter, hero of his junior officers, was based on
him. The will to fight might plummet if the lads heard that
Bunter had been treated as a traitor.

Aitken then made his next mistake. He told the C.-in-C.
about the luxurious gifts that even now were on their way to
his troops. Haig at once stated that he considered them both a
risk to the morale required and an affront to the rations provided. If they arrived they would be impounded. It was time
civilians ceased to interfere in a war that was none of their
business.

Harsh though all this sounded, Archie was let off. So who,
Lesley wondered, in her belief that all life was a mafia that
excluded only her, had interceded on his behalf?

'Harry Wharton, I expect,' I said without thinking.

'Darling, don't you mean Anthony Eden?'

'Someone like that. It might have been old Mauly, I mean
the Prince of Wales – he was in the front line too.'

She frowned; this was obviously news to her. Then she said, at her quietest, 'You do realise what then happened?'

'No. I'm waiting to be told.'

'Well, of course, Archie was dispatched home with a flea in his ear and ordered to keep a very low profile, and the attack on the Somme went forward a month late.' She paused for effect. 'It was the biggest disaster in the history of warfare, and that includes you touching up other women when we were still married.'

I sat back and gazed at the ceiling that had once been mine. There were all sorts of problems to be tackled here, and I longed to be elsewhere to tackle them. They were matters of such moment – the whole of the Great War, what had happened as a result of it, the future it shaped – that to put them in order a man needed the privacy of his own pad and, ironically enough, though I felt absurdly at home, this wasn't it. Yet my mind couldn't cope on its own. I needed to spell out the obvious. This affair was too big for the confines of thought.

'Do you honestly mean to say,' I asked, 'that if Eden hadn't leaked the Big Push to our friend, it would have been launched a month earlier and achieved the proper degree of surprise, with the result that the war would have ended two years earlier and millions wouldn't have died?'

'You said it,' replied Lesley.

'And are you actually implying that if – what did you call them? – Bunter Bonds had provided the whole of the front line on the eve of the attack with whatever you find in a Fortnum's hamper, game pie, port, duck, a slice of smoked salmon, plus a few pin-ups in frilly knickers showing a bit of leg to put heart into the men, the whole pack would have rushed over the top, sated with good living and cheered by a naughty glimpse of what they were fighting for, and hounded the Germans all the way to Berlin?'

'You said it,' said Lesley.

In the long pause we stared at the snapshot on the mantelshelf. It was probably faked; you could almost make out the dark-room division between the two men. I suspected that if I looked at Lesley I might begin laughing. A great ache to laugh seized me in the stomach. I had no idea how else to react. We were sitting at odds in a room that had once belonged to both of us. We were discussing, as if we believed it, a moment of history that must never have happened, or happened not quite like that, just one version of events that might or might not have taken place, and that moment was somehow too serious to be taken solemnly, yet so funny as to be almost tragic. I had a staggering glimpse of our limitations, of the fact that we were human constituting a prime obstacle to any understanding at all.

I looked at Lesley. Ever so gradually we began to start to smile. From proper gloom her mouth turned into a hesitant half-moon of not quite assertive amusement. The lips trembled on the cusp of a joke. I couldn't bear to encourage this collusion, yet I too was close to breaking up. There was honestly no alternative. In a few seconds I had passed from a cool examination of the evidence proffered at one remove by someone I loved – yes, now I realised it, I loved the old fool – to a session of hysterics rolling all over the upholstery with a woman whom I tried to forget I had once been in love with and now considered a threat. I saw her denture. Her hair literally came down. Screams pumped out of her diaphragm. There had been nothing like this in our marriage, nothing so wild, nothing so short of breath, not even the act of love.

When it was almost all over Lesley said, 'Would you like something to eat?'

'All they had before the attack was baked beans,' I replied, not knowing what to say.

'What about after it?'

'They were dead' – and Lesley just as abruptly as her laughter started crying and threw her body into my arms.

I refused to stay the night. On the other hand I missed the last train. I essayed the steep hill back, but her lights were out.

The pubs were shut. In the main street the hotel showed a glimmer. When I knocked gently at the door, it disgorged a gang of hilarious young men in evening dress. A trail of maids in a trance of fatigue were bearing trays of smudged glasses through a swing door. If the Great War had been cut by half, their forebears would have sired different daughters and other men would have been wearing the black ties. The ironies of history were not ironic. They were merely a fact. The middle-aged duffer who took my credit card might never have been born.

As a last test of the evening I sidled into the phone box, which choked me with stale tobacco, and dialled the number in New Romney without caring a jot if I woke anyone up. It was as if I needed more laughter or a hand to hold. There was no reply. I giggled. Here was a nadir that seemed like a zenith. I hardly existed myself. I went up and slept in a bed that would otherwise have been empty.

'I tried to call you late last night,' said Joanna quietly in the office, 'to find out how you got on.'

'Oh, really?' I started guiltily. 'How did you know where I went?'

'Because you didn't tell me.'

'But that was our agreement.'

'You don't have to be so literal, Patrick. I can take bad news. I couldn't sleep, reading that Frank Richards book – remember? he wrote the Bunter stories? – so I rang you again at four. No reply. You're getting as elusive as Archie.'

'Oh, well, yes, I missed the train. Ah, any messages?'

'So you had to stay the night, I suppose.'

'Yes, that's right, the hotel, I found a hotel.'

For once Joanna seemed tired, not her usual self, her eyes listless, as if she had spent the small hours in kip with someone.

'I imagine Lesley hasn't any spare bedrooms.'

'Five, in fact.'

'You counted them.'

'It used to be my house too, you know. Any messages, did you say?'

'And they were all occupied. I didn't realise it was to be a party. Was Archie there?'

'In a sense. Well, no. We were alone. But I'll put you in the picture when we've dealt with all this wretched correspondence. Very exciting it was.'

'I'm sure it was.'

These asides were best ignored. 'I think Archie may have been responsible for our nearly losing the Great War, certainly for prolonging it.'

'Oh,' said Joanna without interest.

'Why don't you come out with it?' I snapped. 'You think I've been unfaithful.' Anger! I hadn't known anger of such deep relish since Lesley threw me out of the very house we were discussing.

'It doesn't concern me if you are. I'm not married to you. I never have been.'

'I mean unfaithful to the cause. You think I had a peach of an evening and got sloshed and tumbled the old girl with retroactive lust and Bunter never got so much as a mention. Is that it?'

'If you say so.'

'No, it's you who say so. And you who advised me to visit Lesley. And you who are now behaving with a total lack of decorum, not to mention efficiency. Are you my assistant, Miss Feathers, or a harridan paid by the Government to extort from your boss a craven confession of what you can't quite call adultery, even if it had taken place? What the hell are you doing to me? I ask you a simple question – are there any messages? – and your answer is to accuse me of raping my ex-wife. Now let's try again or you're for the high jump. Are there any bloody messages?'

'Yes,' she said in a small voice.

'Divulge.'

'The Minister would like you to dine with him.'

'When?'

'Tomorrow night.'

'I can't.'

'I'm afraid I'm not privy to the details of your personal diary, sir,' said Miss Feathers.

'I've put tomorrow night aside to punish you, Joanna,' I said with attempted affection. Her bitter calm didn't flinch. 'Ring back and tell him any other night. Who else?'

'Mr Smedley.'

'Not Edgar!'

'Alas, I'm not on such familiar terms with the gentleman.'

Still stilted, still silly, not giving an inch.

'This really is exciting,' I said. 'What on earth did he want?'

'He said he would ring back when he arrived in London.'

Oh, dear: in the office one couldn't, but I didn't even want to, take her in my arms and say sorry or cheer up; or indeed 'I love you', if this were love. One could only try jokes.

'London!' I cried. 'You can't let Edgar loose in London. Someone will mistake him for a second-hand suit and throw him away.' Not a flicker. 'But this might be the break we're looking for. Oh, God, must we sit all morning waiting for a call that might never come? He probably doesn't know how to fit a coin in a coin-box.' I glanced at her for an answering humour. 'Anything could happen.'

'Everything has,' Joanna said miserably, dowsing me once more in needless guilt.

She stood up, uncertain, verging on emotion, perhaps to muddy the waters still more by stamping out, to blub in the tube, to lurch into her flat, to turn on the gas. I never knew what, for now the phone rang and discipline took over with a snap. She picked up. I overheard a lot of bleeps. Joanna sighed, biting her lip. A silence, then a voice. It was Edgar.

Contrary to likelihood, that call resembled a return to sanity. I gathered that Edgar had come up to London to make arrangements, at Aitken's former club, for a discreet celebration of his ninetieth birthday in the coming month. He begged to see me on business. For economy's sake he was putting up at a boarding-house behind Victoria station. His manner was suitably humble. Generous in victory, I asked him to dine with me at home just round the corner. He said he preferred to meet, if at all, on more neutral ground. As I racked my brains for a no-man's-land that would satisfy his obvious desire for anonymity, he specified the Golden Arrow platform on the station concourse. The fact that the Golden Arrow had gone out of service years ago seemed not to perturb him.

We were to meet at six-thirty. I thought I might tempt him across to Overton's for a few return oysters, as it were, but the sight of him standing there, hunched in yet another handed-down suit that surely must have once belonged to Aitken, suddenly overburdened me with the wish not to entertain him at all, indeed not to be seen with him. For a few moments I circled him at a distance. He was peering across the misty platforms of the rush hour as if shiftily collecting train numbers. Or perhaps he was locked into other fantasy; the homeward girls seemed to be giving him as wide a berth as the crowds permitted.

'Edgar!' I said.

'Oh, it's you,' he replied with a wan humour. 'I was expecting A. J. P. Taylor.'

'No, no,' I cried gaily – why did the man always arouse falsity in me? 'He would have insisted on meeting you at his club.'

'It's that which I need to talk to you about.' Faces passed at a trot, eyeing the indicator, grey after a day's work. 'Do you belong to it?'

'To what?'

'The Athenaeum.'

'I have friends who do.'

'It needs big guns, I tell you, does Archie's birthday,' Smedley said. 'The little chumps won't listen to me. They say

Archie isn't a member, so can't have his dinner there. They've never heard of him. It's only thirty years since he resigned, but it's as if he never was. Wiped off the slate.' He stared at me with those canine eyes that looked huge and haunted in his narrow face. 'It upsets me. I've never failed him yet. And I'm not very used to these London things. I want help.'

I looked out over the barriers to the dim platforms, and it wasn't pity I felt for Smedley then. Partly it was shock – that a man of Aitken's stature should depend exclusively on the support of a hopeless adolescent – but also an access of cunning: as the trains muttered southward and the announcements of delay echoed in the roof, I felt power pass at last into my grip after days and nights of fruitless effort. I had Smedley at my mercy.

'Leave it to me, Edgar. My Minister is a member, and he's sympathetic to the cause. I'll have a word in his ear.'

'I have to protect Archie, don't I? No one else will.' He sniggered bleakly. 'They think he's a dead duck. Goodness, how blind can people be! It's like saying the twentieth century is a mistake.'

At this declaration my sense of power strengthened. I saw that a great opportunity had played into my hands. Smedley, if anyone, knew the truth. He had been immured for years in the monastery of Aitken's confidence. Bunter was his lord; the train numbers, the collection of moths, the castles he built from outfits, were no more than a substitute, the rituals he performed while waiting for a resurrection. The long delay in the world's acceptance of Aitken, for whatever achievement, for however little or much, had held Edgar back, stunted his growth. He was still a small enthusiast in short trousers patchily disguised as a middle-aged pedant in long ones. He was standing on this platform to say something that mattered to him because the spaces of a terminus felt as cosy as one of his hobbies. A second coming for Bunter? Well, Edgar should have it, but on my terms. I wanted the truth out of him, every last word.

All London was at our disposal. The bright lights? What

would he consider wickedly out of bounds? 'Come, Edgar,' I said softly, wincing at his reflex as I took his arm, 'let's cab to my club, shall we, and discuss it all? An opportunity to get to know each other which I hope I'm not alone in welcoming.'

'I'm not coming to any club after today's little experience,' said Edgar with a petulant shrug.

'But you're my guest, my dear fellow. I'm repaying you for your hospitality.'

He edged slyly sideways as though to escape, and then I was manoeuvring his shabby form, with some effort, rather as he assisted the reluctant Aitken, towards the taxi rank. I helped him in. He sat bolt upright as several districts of London sped past his scared eyes. Thus kidnapped, he would allow no word of confidence or betrayal to escape his lips. Meanwhile, searching for the strings that would animate the puppet, I talked easily about my career as an investigator of culture, my boyhood dedication to Bunter which had led in adult life to a decent adherence to the values which Greyfriars had taught me, my only mistake having been to believe that women – my wife, Lesley, alas, had thrown me over – were brought up similarly to respect a workable balance of mischief and convention. At this reference to the fair sex, Smedley's features formed a mask of distaste that lasted through most of Mayfair.

Luckily for me, if not for its future, the club was more or less untenanted. A bearded boozer swayed alone at the bar, his loud halloas diminishing crossly as we mounted to the dining-room. At a corner table some barristers were barracking one another with salty tales of the court-room. I steered Edgar to a corner darker than theirs and with resolve began to seek topics to put him at his ease. But as I opened the menu he stood up so suddenly that his chair tottered back with a crash. Across the room a lawyer barked reproof.

'I won't eat,' Smedley said.

'Would you prefer a drink?' I suggested, though dreading a return to the bar.

'Thank you indeed, but no. I don't know why I'm here.'

'Would you care for a game?'

'A game?'

'Cards? A bout of snooker? We needn't play for money. There's nobody about.'

'I'm good at snooker,' said Smedley, looking more pert. 'Shit-hot.'

'I beg your pardon?' But he was already halfway out of the dining-room. 'I'll lash you,' he said, descending the stairs at a trot.

We entered the billiard-room where an oblong umbrella of greenish light bedevilled the shadows. 'Ah,' said Edgar, taking out a small coin and slapping it on the mahogany. The fellow seemed instantly at home. I lost the toss. Picking a cue with care, he looked to make sure the scoreboard stood at zero. His mouth widened into a competitive grin which it was hard to regard as amiable. Yet if I wanted him to talk I had probably produced the master-stroke. I had given him a game to play!

'Did you say just now,' said Edgar, limbering up as if for a cross-country, 'that your lady wife had given you the chuck?'

'Well, yes.'

'Good riddance,' he said.

'Of course you've met her.'

'Yes, and I've watched her through a keyhole,' he said with pride. 'I know what kind of woman she is, yes, I do. I'll break. I like to see the balls go all over the place, sometimes I get one in.'

The reds parted company with a mighty crash. Two found pockets. For an easy black Edgar arranged the folds of his suit across half the table, as though climbing into bed. At the end of these manoeuvres I was still wondering if I had heard him aright. A keyhole?

'How did that incident come about?'

'She wasn't fully dressed either,' said Edgar, smugly completing his break. 'She was in her knickers.'

I went in-off an easy red just to keep him talking. My mouth was dry after his refusal of drinks. It was hard to frame the right question.

'Where was this keyhole?'

'Where do you think? You're the self-appointed expert on women. She comes down whenever she likes, and I knew from the first she was up to no good. Needed watching. She tried to make up to me – brought me a present. Chocolates! I never touch them.'

'I take it, then, that she was in her bedroom at the time.'

Smedley bridled over his perfect aim. 'If she had been, do you think I'd have been looking? A peeping Tom am I now? I have to look after Archie. It's my life. I don't want to be always pestering him with questions about whether he's dead or not, do I? So every hour or two I look through his keyhole. Your shot.'

He flicked up a break of seventeen for himself on the score-board, but it was too late to protest; I hadn't been watching.

'So you spied on my wife,' I said bluntly. 'I suppose you enjoyed every minute of it.'

'Oh, no, it made me go all funny inside,' Smedley said. 'I'm not used to it, you see. I felt ill. She took off her stockings. They were black and had holes in.'

My mind reeled back to our meeting weeks ago. Was Lesley still wearing the same laddered pair as when she had first accused me of being as fat as Billy Bunter? Perhaps even then she was on her way to the old boy's bedroom, there to sacrifice her dignity in those preposterous arms. But no, it wasn't possible. Even Lesley would scarcely go the whole hog merely to secure a commission for a tombstone.

'Archie said it hadn't happened to him since Mrs Simpson gave him the raspberry back in the late twenties.'

'What hadn't?'

'Taking a liking to a lady.'

'Falling in love, you mean?'

'Through a keyhole,' said Edgar sagely, 'you have such a small field of view.' It sounded like a proverb.

By spreading his body all over the table Edgar notched up another few points. I watched his toes vaguely to make sure he was sticking to the rules. For some seconds he panted over the pink, then missed.

'My eye isn't in,' he said.

'Perhaps you've been looking through too many keyholes.'

'That's witty,' he said. 'But I'm winning.'

'Try an arras next time. It improves the value of the evidence. You can hear as well as see.'

I botched a simple double, then my desire to compete shrank, matching my score, to zero. I had no wish to win against such opposition, though in normal circumstances I could have wiped the floor with him. Badgered by an unwilling image of Lesley approaching with alacrity that mountainous bed, I cleared my throat and asked Smedley where he practised his game.

'In my youth club,' he replied. 'I can beat anybody I like. There's no fun in losing. You ask my boys, if you ever come down again. They're a modern bunch of lads.' He paused to smirk. 'They know all about the other side of keyholes. You've met them. Some are in the Customs and the police. But they do what I tell them.'

We were now down to the colours and I foresaw that Smedley would pick them off one by one. All I wanted was a drink, but I couldn't help feeling that if I slipped off to the bar Smedley would tamper with the balls behind my back, as if it mattered. In any case there was the bearded boozer to negotiate. I put down my cue.

'What did happen, Edgar?' I said quietly.

'Oh, there were some groans. If you can't see through a key-hole, clever, you put your ear to it, don't you? I very nearly called the doctor in, but it all subsided after a few seconds.'

He took the yellow.

'A few seconds?'

'You can't expect a lot,' Smedley said. 'Archie hasn't had enough practice.'

He sank the green. In despair I looked at the meagre possibilities of score left on the table. I would need a dozen snookers to come anywhere near this demon of the baize.

'Had he practised on anyone at all?'

He potted the brown.

'You can't count Mrs Simpson, if that's what your dirty mind is thinking,' said Smedley. 'He was her knight errant, so horseplay didn't come into it. He was never selfish, Archie wasn't. In his better days he had a big house near Melton Mowbray where the meat pies come from. That's where he generously introduced the Prince of Wales to her, when she said she wanted a bit more class than even Archie could give her.'

'Do you really believe that, Edgar?'

He polished off the blue.

'You're not doing at all well,' said Smedley, nastily turning on me. 'You must have rigged this game just to worm out a confidence. And you tried to force me to have alcohol. Your wife's the worming sort too. That's why I can't stand her.'

He lay face down on the table as if to demolish the pink. For a few moments, long enough by his account to achieve satisfaction if you were an old man, he lay there motionless, setting up his shot, then his head dropped and, believe it or not, he was sobbing. 'I don't like her,' he cried in muffled hiccups. 'Go away. She's not good enough for him. You've spoilt it all, you and your family, I wish we'd never run into you.'

At that point the door staggered open and the bearded man from the bar tumbled in and fetched up at the rim of the table.

'Ah, a loser!' he bellowed, as Smedley with a crushed face righted himself and slithered back into shadow. 'Let me deal with this renegade!'

Handing me his drink with a slop and snatching a cue, he sent the pink angling at speed round the cushions, followed in mad pursuit by the black, so that for some seconds, in total silence, three balls were missing one another by several narrow squeaks.

'Gentlemen,' he cried, as the balls slowed down, 'what you need is a psychiatrist and here I bloody am – I'll take on the pack of you for not less than thirty guineas a frame.'

Moving over to me, sniffing, Edgar gazed damply into my eyes. It was as though we had reached, at this extreme of anti-climax, a new understanding: that we would never reach one at all. Never could I hope to break through to the truth about Aitken. He was too well defended by the vulnerable.

'Could I have a glass of water, please?' said Edgar.

Without thinking I handed him the intruder's gin fizzing flatly in my fist. Edgar slowly, in several swallows, tossed it back, while I debated how to get rid of him and sink my sorrows in the company of this loud lonely shrink who was setting up the balls again.

'I want to go home,' Edgar whispered.

'Give me my drink,' the champion shouted.

I was in for a difficult evening.

6

For some days Joanna remained unforgiving. Every morning in the office we exchanged notes on our progress, oral memos that did nothing to soften our relations. We had no talk worth talking about. Such intercourse as her resentment allowed us had the formality of an exchange of letters between parties engaged in litigation.

So I told Joanna about playing snooker with Smedley, pretending that he had won only by sharp practice, and failing to mention the rumour that Lesley had strayed beyond the bounds of propriety with Archibald.

So Joanna told me that she had finished reading the Frank Richards biography, noting as a sinister omission the fact that Aitken made no appearance in the index, despite a lot of references to Bunter. This she explained on the grounds that no artist, when creating his characters, liked to be exposed as a predator on normal life.

So I told Joanna about Lesley's account of Aitken's version of the mass of deceptions that had become notorious to historians as the First World War.

So Joanna informed me that she was now deep into George Orwell's lucubrations on schoolboy fiction, in which Bunter played a star part, though observing that the author of *Nineteen Eighty-Four* had neglected an essential element: the lower middle-class origins of Aitken himself, which might have cast a stronger light on the truth, had Orwell but known that fact.

Meanwhile her reading sprees went on unchecked. At this uneasy point they seemed designed principally to keep her away from me. In the office Joanna looked almost with awe at the books that weighted down her carrier-bag. With an urgent step she went off visiting libraries in the lunch hour as though every bay of shelves concealed an amour. My own position, if I still had one, was impossibly frustrating. To propose dinner would be taken as an act of disloyalty to Bunter. The very idea of inviting her home to my bathroom carried the seeds of a vulgarity that could produce only the blossom of guilt. It made the situation no more palatable that I had almost gone to bed with Lesley on the eve of Edgar's revelation that she had been to bed with Aitken.

This growing distance between her preoccupation and my desire made a mockery of office life. If she attended at all to business – I was now putting in order my notes on the ignorance of our own times in children about to go out and change them – it was to shorten the time before lunch, when she could shoot off to her illicit rendezvous with a library. For her our report had become an irrelevance. She had already as good as implied that many more of the origins of twentieth-century culture were to be found at Greyfriars than in the British Museum.

'If the things Mr Aitken says are true,' she hinted one morning, 'the children aren't ignorant. They're just misinformed. All the assumptions in the report will have to be changed.'

'Don't jump the gun, Miss Feathers. There's a long way to go yet.'

But her remark perturbed me. My mind span as I sat at my desk in the posture of Dornford Yates, who had also earned his keep by spinning yarns behind the scenes of the century. As an entertainer he must have been acquainted with Frank Richards.

Even Conan Doyle's collection of books, which honourably soundproofed my walls against the outer traffic, was full of downright lies, which the old magician happened to have had the skill to make convincing. I felt besieged by doubt, as well as by Joanna's evasion of my personal needs.

Nor had I been too successful at the Athenaeum. The secretary interviewed me loftily, as if I were begging for membership. This too was a bitter setback for credulity, for Aitken's name had never featured on the club's books, and the fact that he had been the original model for Billy Bunter, who must have been fondly known to most members, did little to unfreeze my icy reception. Yet I went away still believing that the ninetieth birthday of such a man, distinguished if only by the quality of his self-deception, demanded the kind of festivity which the Athenaeum ought to be generous and amused enough to give it, and I decided to have a word with the Minister when he came back to me with the promised dinner, perhaps in that very club. The date of this, according to Joanna, had not been fixed.

The problem of Miss Feathers was daily no nearer a solution. I had to talk to her; yet talking to her would crudely imply that talking to her was the last thing I wanted to do. I had left it too late for anything natural to happen, or happen with the discretion of our earlier rituals. But then suddenly, I knew not why, for I was still hunched over the same desk and regarding her without hope, I chose to reverse the usual procedure, which was to allow formality to ease unnoticed into its lewd opposite, and say, to her surprise, not to mention mine, 'I want to go to bed with you tonight, Joanna, and I don't give a bugger if you're up to your eyes in studying the minutiae of Greyfriars life or having dinner with a boyfriend or whatever falsehoods you've been palming off on me, nor do I want any nonsense about going to the bathroom, you can have it on the sofa if you like, but do let's get together on this thing because you're the only friend I've got.'

This last appeal sounded soppily like Smedley, I almost denied saying it, but it worked. On Joanna's face pleasure rapidly succeeded the bewilderment that at speed had followed shock. Indeed she seemed to be breaking down. Her eyes screwed up without her knowing how ugly she looked. Her mouth became briefly undesirable with emotion.

'I'll bring my notebook,' she said, making a last lunge towards sanity. 'What time will you be expecting me?'

Only later did I feel shamefaced about the use of force. There she was! It was like looking through a keyhole to see Joanna for the first time naked. Her body appeared far more vulnerable than in clothes. At least two table-lamps were on, for we were denuding ourselves in the relative publicity of my sitting-room. I was anxious not to appear unseemly in the act of removing a pair of trousers; it was what drunks did only with difficulty. It wasn't long since Lesley, so Edgar had said, had gone through the same motions, so I couldn't stem the thought of those knickers tossed aside, the stockings torn off, for the brief delight of a man who, if nearly dead, was still lovable for his sense of life.

Not wanting to see Joanna in the buff vied with a curiosity about how poignant she would look. It didn't help desire. Reality was sometimes too naked. I turned off one of the lamps, and with an unforgettable twist of her body Joanna reached up to extinguish the other. A faint glow came in from the street as we settled on the carpet into the hues of a Renaissance painting that needed a good clean. When we woke from a rough and tumble that seemed to last for ever, the champagne bottle was still there, the telephone hadn't rung, her face was drained of the scholarship that had stultified it for so many days, and I felt we were back at the beginning we had never really had.

'You're a different man,' Joanna said lazily.

'It wouldn't have happened without old you-know-who.'

'Yes, it would,' she said. 'The you-know-what would have taken longer to get better, that's all.'

In due course we crawled to bed. Joanna emphasised the
irony by spending well over ten minutes in the bathroom. But for
once I knew that I had behaved accurately in having her. Just
as there was now no choice about taking seriously the footnotes
Aitken was adding to the text of history, there was none over
pretty well raping Joanna on my carpet. It had to be; if things
had been otherwise, they wouldn't have been as good.

When Joanna tripped back from the bathroom at lights out,
I settled into the pillows in sheer wonder.

'You're a different woman,' I said.

'You know why.'

'I think I know how.'

Hours later, when my watch had stopped, her disembodied
voice said, 'I've been checking up on Mrs Simpson', sounding
deliciously familiar, as though we had been mulling over these
realities for ever. 'He just might have met her. You said he had
a house in Leicestershire in the late twenties. It's true – I flirted
with the county surveyor on the phone to find out. The Prince
met his future bride at about that time.' Her voice was soft and
speculative. 'And somewhere up there in the Midlands it was.
It's a bit obscure, because not too many people want to claim
credit for almost bringing down the monarchy.'

'Aitken wouldn't mind claiming that,' I said.

'But only if he had done.'

I eased my slack body up on an elbow. 'Joanna, this night of
all nights, tell me if you think he's telling the truth?'

'As much as anyone,' she said fondly. 'And, as I've now learnt
not to trust anything I hear, far more amusingly. Isn't that
enough?'

'I suppose we'll have to go along with it now,' I whispered.
As usual we had lowered our voices as if someone were eaves-
dropping in the bathroom.

'Of course. How could we possibly stop?'

'You really feel the same as I do?'

'I'm in it up to my neck,' she said with a giggle.

'It would alter our lives completely, wouldn't it? We'd have to think of everything we assumed in the past from an utterly different angle.'

'Haven't you always wanted to do that, Patrick?'

'Not much.'

'Oh.'

A faint disappointment stretched between us in my narrowish bed. I knew of course that the entire venture, the glory of the chase, the arousal, were far too interesting to give me a chance of turning back. Yet still I rummaged around in my mind for an authority to support this madness.

'Act, in spite of doubt,' I murmured. 'Wasn't it Bertrand Russell who said that?'

'One can't be sure.'

'What do you mean?'

'How do you know it wasn't Bunter?' said Joanna with quiet reason. 'It's just the sort of brilliant sally a philosopher like Russell might have stolen off Aitken without giving him any credit. People do that all the time at dinner parties. Like you muttering just now that my breasts were like lilies.'

'Did I really say that?'

'No, the Bible did. You nicked it.'

I thought back to our unforgettable excess an hour or so earlier; I had almost forgotten it. She had probably made the lies up.

'I wonder,' she mused, 'if Frank Richards thought of using Bertrand Russell at all.'

'He could have been Mr Prout.'

'Not Mr Paul Pontifex Prout, M.A.!' She giggled again. 'I can't believe it.' The bedsprings groaned.

'It's quite on the cards. Old Bertie was already teaching when Richards was out looking for material. He must have needed some brainy master to offset the effect of the boys.'

'I know, I know, and I know what proves it,' said Joanna with sudden elation. 'There was a boy called Russell in the school, in

Greyfriars. Wasn't the philosopher known for having lots of illegitimate kids? Richards probably put the boy in *The Magnet* for a laugh. Dick, his name was. An awful bully. Always going round with Bulstrode.'

Commendable though her knowledge of the text was, Joanna's reference to the results of Russell's darts hither and thither through decades of willing bedrooms gave me a moment's pause. Why my irritation? Then memory jogged me. Hadn't Bertrand Russell fathered a child when well into his eighties? Until that moment I had refused to credit, on grounds of age alone, the scene which Smedley had observed through the keyhole. Now, by some unwelcome alchemy, the combination of myself in bed with a secretary and the image of a public figure putting his senility at risk to bring yet another child into the world – allied to the mean fashion in which Edgar had scored off my ignorance by his alleged glimpse of my ex-wife's uncontrollable libido – filled my spirit in that darkened room with near panic. It was the hysteria one felt in the presence of the irrefutable.

Joanna lay beside me. Happiness, which had perhaps touched me earlier when I first saw her bare legs, had now slipped out into the rain beyond the window, while in its place a stab of the truth had crept into the black acreage of the bedroom: you cannot have truth and happiness, it said. Happiness was frivolous; so it vanished. It went as soon as you started following up a feeling that had the lineaments of truth, however ridiculous they looked. In a reflex of disillusion I got up sharply and bounded over to the bathroom and spoilt everything by switching on the wrong light. Joanna's eyes closed in pain at the flood of illumination and she uttered a cross grunt. I had probably ruined the evening.

I spent a while in the bathroom looking at my face. At first it looked honest enough, but as I unblinkingly confronted that hitherto well-known friend it began to take on the gauntly stubbled stare of a criminal in a prison mug-shot, a man adept at avoiding any brush with the truth, let alone telling it. In the clinical detail of the mirror I was hypnotised by the features, the unreliable quirks and bulges, somewhere behind which a brain was busy day and night risking my job in favour of folly and my sanity in the interests of sex. I poked out my tongue. It was furred.

When I slipped back to share all this self-knowledge, and run through our plans, and decide in concert how far we had progressed and what we should do next, and how much the evidence to date had shifted the way we need look at our life and times, Joanna was sitting upright in bed with an air of lascivious reproach.

'I think it's very unfair,' she whispered jauntily, 'that I haven't even met Archie yet. How do I know you're not inventing him?'

'Is that likely?'

'Very. From the start you've been keeping too many things up your sleeve.'

In bewilderment I gazed at her immaculate contours. How dared she accuse me of exactly the crime of secrecy she had herself committed? The old question reared in my mind: why, after first thinking me both nutty and infantile in my devotion to Bunter, had she suddenly become dead keen on the subject? What new force had entered her calculations during that earlier weekend which she claimed to have dedicated to private study? Who had been feeding her all those details of Greyfriars life that outshone my own recollections of the place? Yet, as I looked again at the pert bosom barely concealed by a froth of sheet, it seemed not the moment to start these hares. Our nakedness was too fresh in my memory. It struck me as a better idea to take further advantage of it, instead of ignoring her body in the interests of a confession that might embarrass me even more than making love to her yet again.

'Leave it to me,' I said masterfully, lunging back into bed.

*

I simply had to see Aitken. I had given up the telephone as an instrument of clarity; it produced either silence or muddle. So the next morning, without showing up at the office, I took the train down to Ashford with a view to bearding whoever was left in the den. On the opposite platform, as I alighted, stood a wheelchair. It had an abandoned look which somehow encouraged me. Then, to my amazement as I hurried out among the taxis, Soames was just climbing into the old Wolseley. My illogical notion that he had been sent to meet me was swiftly dispatched.

'Just put them both on the train, sir, safe and sound,' he said, as though reporting to a supervisor.

'Where've they gone?'

'It's the master's first trip to London for, what, couple of years at least,' said Soames. 'First class, thermos, all the trimmings.'

Behind me, just at the edge of perception, a fast train from the south crossed points, braked with a grind, slowed to a halt.

'Where?' I shouted, backing away.

'Gone to that club, fix it all up, pull a bit of rank.' Soames shouted back, joining in the fun.

An announcement boomed across the footbridge. I ran. My heart heaved up the stairs, then sank down the other side. I caught the train by a whisker, wrenching my shoulder on the door's recoil, and at a guess I was less than ten minutes behind not only Aitken's first trip in a train for an age, but a scene of heart-rending humiliation at the Athenaeum which would put paid to everyone's hopes for a ninetieth birthday to remember.

There was no sign of lonely wheelchairs at Charing Cross. The Athenaeum was a brisk walk westward under pigeons and Nelson and rain. I knew that my quarry had eluded me when the secretary appeared at my request looking unruffled but severe. 'Ah, Mr Weymouth, isn't it?' he said, as if I were about to be blackballed. Still panting, but with nothing to say since Aitken wasn't in view, I fumbled a question about whether the

Rt Hon. Richard Rathbone M.P. had spoken in my interest. His eyes grew wary. Not surprising. I had forgotten that I hadn't mentioned the matter to my chief and by this intrusion had seriously reduced even his chances of mentioning it with influential effect. 'Don't trouble yourself to pop in again, Mr Weymouth,' said the secretary, escorting me to the doors. 'Just pick up a telephone.'

A taxi returned me in a rage to the office. I swept past the switchboard girl who wanted to flap a message in my face. I entered my room, intending to throw myself on Joanna's mercy. My behaviour, last night, this morning, all along, had been absurd. In my chair, hands affably clasped over the dome of his belly, sat Archibald Aitken.

'Oh, good morning,' I said with a glance at Smedley who was gazing nervily out of the window as if frightened of Green Park.

'Ah, Patrick, we have been making friends with your charming assistant,' Aitken said. 'I was informing her of the little luncheon we enjoyed with your wife in France last year.'

'Last week, Archie,' said Smedley.

'I wasn't present,' I said rapidly for the record. 'You must be confusing two distinct occasions.'

'Did you not foot the bill? Did we slink out? Shall I have to avoid the place in future?'

'His brain's going,' explained Smedley. 'The journey took it out of him.'

'I was just telling your lady friend that Oswald Mosley – we called him Tom, of course – gave me this stick in exchange for an idea,' Aitken went on, thumping an ivory cane across the files on my desk. 'I had the best of the arrangement. The idea landed him up in prison, whereas the stick is supporting me to this day. Now to business. Take me to your club.'

'But the Athenaeum . . .'

'Not the Athenaeum. I never belonged to that stricken institution. Edgar has a bad memory. I wouldn't be seen dead in it, unlike the other members. I need instead to inspect your club – which Edgar tells me needs a leg up in the world – with a view to taking it over for my birthday party. Pity we can't include Tom among the guests. That idea of mine led him to an early grave.'

'He's rambling,' said Edgar. 'I'd better take him home.'

Picking up the cane, Aitken raised his voice to the edge of petulance. 'Mr Weymouth is kindly giving me luncheon again, Edgar, this time at his club. If my memory serves me, ladies will not be admitted, so you may offer refreshment to our delightful hostess here. Patrick, would the petty cash run to standing my friend some modest type of sandwich?'

'I'll look after him,' said Joanna, with an air of stunned pleasure. For her, of course, these characters had stepped straight out of fiction into her office. After all her reading she must almost feel she had created them herself.

As for me, only now did I realise the extent to which being out of touch with Aitken had rattled my faith. His absence had left me without a future. The story of my life had been cut off in mid-chapter without hope of a dénouement. But now we could push on. New energy throbbed in my mind, a revived purpose. A taxi was waiting. We drove off. Aitken gazed out at London, mumbling a street name or two, as if touring the ruins of a city he had known in its heyday.

I had failed to allow for Aitken's effect on the clutch of members I half knew swopping gossip at the bar.

'Who's your Bunterish friend?' muttered a critic as I drily ordered the obligatory champagne.

'It's Billy Bunter,' I said.

'Got an exeat, has he?'

A lawyer looked askance at my bottle. 'That's going to cost you a postal order or two,' he said, swallowing beer.

We retired to the panelled corner most likely to give Aitken half a chance of looking unobtrusive. To my surprise he eased his body into the upholstery with a grimace and an expulsion of breath, playing his age much as he did in Edgar's presence, and after a sniff took no further interest in his champagne. His spectacles glinted in the glow of a distant table-lamp.

'I'd forgotten how these places depress me,' he said glumly. 'They're so deafened by their own voices that they can't hear the facts. An awkward reminder of the number of times I haven't contrived to alter the course of history.'

'I'm afraid we won't be able to put you up much of a lunch either.'

'I'm not hungry,' Aitken announced. 'That's even more depressing. The truth is, through no fault of my own, that I've been overdoing it. Not a whisper to Edgar, by the way. He'd wheel in those damned undertakers who call themselves a medical practice. You should never have tempted me across the Channel, I fear. I know you meant well, but that luncheon turned out to be a frontal attack on my liver.'

'How very sorry I am.' I was too. This moment of suffering aroused in me the filial tenderness that had struck me once before: how little I could bear to lose him, how much I wanted to know him better. 'I'm so sorry.'

'I might manage a grilled chop if the kitchens are up to it,' Aitken said, rallying slightly. 'With a dish of soup and a glance at the cheese-board. What a fall from grace! I have to keep this body of mine going somehow. The spirit's healthy enough whenever I can catch a glimpse of it, but it's under siege, surrounded by this huge mutinous army of cells that's used to marching on its stomach. And clubs reek of yesterday's vegetables, my boy, and I don't wish to become one.'

Members were drifting loudly down to the dining-room. Glad to have my back to them, if only to protect Aitken, I detected in their voices the ringing tones of another age. None of their concerns was mine. They had gossiped their lives beyond history into a limbo where they clung on for some inkling of hope, the divination of a brighter future than getting drunk at lunch.

'But you believe me?' said Aitken suddenly.

'Of course.'

'You're a fine young fellow, Weymouth, I observe in you a moral rigour which I suppose I lacked, but I shall be much pained if you humour me.'

'Isn't that Edgar's function?'

'How you misjudge him,' Aitken said. 'Edgar is there for me to trick and bully and cheat, so that he can at once feel virtuous and take his revenge behind my back. He'll be the death of me, I don't doubt. But I cannot abide the thought of his being my only convert. He lacks the presence for it. When I drop out of the reckoning, he won't have the backbone to go forth and tell everyone else how wrong they were. That's why I stuck out for you, old chum.'

'Many thanks.'

'Over there in France I may have waffled a bit,' he went on, 'but I was looking out for your affection as well as your integrity. If I haven't been keeping in touch it's because nature made me a joker in the pack, a fool, a cap-and-bells man, and I brooded long over deciding how I must present myself to you, if you were to view me as I am. Do you believe me?'

'Wholeheartedly.'

'Good,' said Aitken. 'You've given me the vigour to die a happy man.' He picked up his glass and drank it down with a shudder, then half stood, sat down again with a thump, cursed, then found his feet. 'Lunch, I take it,' he said bravely, as though about to be led to the gallows.

We occupied a guest table under the long windows which from urban backyards strained acid light into the dining-room. Aitken took on a pasty look and soon began mopping sweat off his face. Various members stared at us in a silence as obvious as a buzz of rumour. His shape was so vastly outlined against the light from outdoors that no one else could see the deathly white of his features, as he made every effort to rise to my hospitality. In the end, after asking me to recite the menu, he settled for corned-beef hash, by far the least expensive item, and with a sad smirk said he would prefer water to wine. A fat finger reached with difficulty inside his collar to ease the pressure.

'Are you sure you're feeling up to it?'

'I don't know,' said Aitken. 'My sensations are all so far away from my brains. It takes time for bad news to reach me. My guess is that I'm in good trim, but I'm not quite easy in your company, you know.'

'Oh, surely.'

'I'm taking so much from you and giving little in return.'

'Heavens, what's a lunch here or there, a few favours?'

'Favours, you say? Yes, old chum, that's the euphemism we used to use for it, and in that regard my sorrow is unfathomable. I haven't behaved impeccably. I fear' – he paused, sweat tracing parentheses down the amplitude of his cheeks – 'I fear that I have taken your wife away from you.'

'Not at all . . .'

'Yes, yes, I knew you'd say that. What a thing to confess to a man in his own club, while drinking his champagne – or water, is it? Many might judge it not to be the mark of a gentleman. But the cad never comes clean, he awaits the additional thrill of being found out. And my private ethics cannot permit that to happen, Patrick. I want you to know the worst. Otherwise how can I expect you to trust any word I utter on other themes?'

I said, 'Did Lesley not explain to you that we parted ten years ago?'

'Parted?' His eyes bulged. 'Because of me? I say, we can't have that. I'm too old to be dragged through the courts.'

'It's ten years, Archie.'

'Don't upset me with threats, Patrick. In your own club too! I just want us to agree to a friendly arrangement. Your side of the bargain is easy enough.'

'But we're not married, Archie.'

'I never said we were,' blustered Aitken. 'And I'm not making things difficult for you. All you do is to grant me various facilities, such as inscribing your name in hotel registers when the need arises. Or passing myself off as your wife's consort when we're invited as a couple. In return I offer you my memoirs – a generous proposal in view of the mess Frank Richards made of my life when given similar rights – and make you the exclusive arbiter of the way posterity will reckon me. I am putting myself in your hands, Patrick. Don't let me down. There's been all too little love in my life. My mother perhaps, bless her, Edgar of course, dammit, Wallis Simpson . . .'

'Mrs Simpson?'

'Is this the hash?'

A waiter had bent over him. Aitken stared at the food as if uncertain of its purpose. A grey steam curled vaguely off the plate like the smoke signals of an illiterate. Aitken put a hand to his forehead.

'Have it removed, old boy,' he said. 'It's love. Love plays the devil with the appetite.'

My chop was served. I glanced at Aitken's pallor. Were his symptoms truly signs of a stricken heart? Forking up some potato, I thought back with care to my adolescence: gripping hands across a table, unable for the emotions that convulsed the belly to down so much as a bite, the brain ricocheting between shyness and gauche wit. Well, given the gap of years, either a condition poignantly similar was afflicting Aitken or he was on his last legs.

'Eat on, eat on,' he said. 'Don't give me a thought.'

I cut into the pork. Aitken eyed the juices that seeped among the peas.

'What can I tell you of all people about love?' he said. 'If anyone informs you that the twenties were a riot of romance, a decade of decadence, and we young ones floated on a tide of jazz and bubbly, don't you believe them, old fruit. It was much worse than that. I tried my best, mind you. I kept up with all the old Greyfriars boys, hoping they'd see sense and help me to scramble together a time worth living in. But they would have none of it.'

'Oh, really?' I said vacantly. This cutlet was good. For once the club was excelling itself.

'Look,' said Aitken, 'can you imagine Pandit Nehru in a Mayfair nightclub at midnight foxtrotting my little Wallis into independence? Or think of that old wet-blanket Eliot writing a slim and graceful poem about her figure on the tablecloth, as you or I would have done? Or Bernard Montgomery in full-dress uniform holding her hand while sicking up the Bollinger in Berkeley Square at dawn? Doesn't fit, does it? These men had changed. They weren't the stuff of Greyfriars any more.'

'So you were disappointed?' I said, chewing the last of the fat.

'No, no, no, I was winning,' said Aitken. 'It was a triumph for Bunter, don't you see? I alone was true to myself. Anthony Eden was busy at Westminster denying the Harry Wharton in him by deceiving the electorate into supposing he was the cat's whiskers. Instead of being old Bob Cherry distributing high life to the populace, Montgomery was plunging his bayonet into the premonitory sandbag of the next war. Even Johnny Bull turned his back on Wallis and all she stood for – for I soon saw that Johnny was dead and buried in the ample figure of Priestley, writing stories to gull people into an artificial escape from their doom, while amassing a fortune. Why wasn't he writing tales to read Wallis in bed as she recovered from the perpetual headache of not meeting the right man?'

'I don't know,' I said, putting down the last of my wine.

'I wasn't that man, alas,' said Aitken after a pause. 'There was only one Greyfriars boy worthy of her.'

I wiped my mouth. 'The Rt Hon the Earl Herbert Plantagenet Mauleverer,' I suggested.

'How did you know?'

'You told me.'

'Did I? Must have slipped out. I thought it was a deadly secret about H.R.H. being Mauly. Never mind. According to our bargain I'm telling you now. So having begged Wallis to drop a smart date or two to motor up to my place in the back of beyond – separate bedrooms, of course, though her door was jammed for some reason – I discovered old Mauly was staying next door about ten miles away. I lay awake all night, with only the sound of striking miners for company as they poached rabbits on my land, wondering what to do about Wallis. I wanted to give her a future, you see. That, as now with your excellent wife, was the nature of my love for her. In those far-away days, if courting, you had to trick hotels with a false name, and never could I descend to a lifetime of that squalid stratagem with a girl as womanly as Wallis – so I thought to myself: give her a party, let an old school chum have a chance, keep it in the family, get Lord Mauleverer over to try his hand. I couldn't have known that his hand, bejewelled as it was, turned out to be the one Wallis wanted in marriage.'

'Are you implying,' I said ponderously, 'that you introduced Mrs Simpson to the Prince of Wales?'

Aitken looked huffy in the now emptying dining-room. 'I didn't just introduce them, I did better than that. I vacated my own bedroom and left the door wide open. I recommended His Royal Highness to sign a false name – well, Mauleverer, not that false – in my visitors' book, so that history would never know. I left the couple alone in my study with some new effusion by D. H. Lawrence, not a Greyfriars boy but a local lad, lying in manuscript on the table – since I inspired it, he'd given me a first peep.'

'D. H. Lawrence?' I said.

'Also I spread the word among the other guests – a bishop, I think there was, a statesman or two, if I'm not in error – to behave as if the two of them didn't matter or even exist, which of course hotted up the gossip no end.' Aitken paused, then shrugged. 'That night I did all in my power to ensure that the 1930s was to provide one of the greatest royal progresses, not to say retreats, of all time. I wasn't to know that Herr Hitler would outclass me with his rather less intimate war.'

Aitken offered up a faint smile and sipped some water

abstemiously. To recover from the weight of fresh information
I now had to digest, I looked round the dining-room. The few
faces left, mostly of servants, were swivelled our way with ill-
disguised impatience, as though they had overheard Aitken's
attempt to subvert the monarchy but only wanted the bill paid.
The waiters indeed looked more rebellious than usual. I had a
strong feeling that the revolution which I now knew to be at
hand – if only in my inner view of things – had crept as subtly
as a laxative into the very bowels of the club. The atmosphere
was distinctly uneasy. Soon the staff, catching my mood, would
all be rushing out to block the streets.

'Can I go to your lavatory?' said Aitken.

Touched by this echo of Joanna's habitual request, I led him
through the morning-room, where one or two members shifted
off their bottoms to not quite greet my companion, and left him
in sight of a row of tiled cubicles that smelt a good deal better
than school.

'I'll be some little while,' he said, squeezing between the
jambs. 'These matters take time when you're my age, as does
the more amorous side of things.'

'How long exactly? I thought I'd just nip up and have a word
with the secretary about your birthday.'

'Give it a quarter of an hour,' Aitken said, banging down a seat.

Clipped and nervous, Hugo Wheeler slid a batch of set menus
out of his drawer, then slammed it.

'Your friend has been recognised,' he said. 'But nobody can
think who the hell he is.'

'You mean, they can't believe who he is.'

'Well, who is he?' said Wheeler sourly.

'Does Billy Bunter mean anything to you?'

'Don't patronise me. Of course he does.' His hand shook in
shuffling three-course dinners across the desk as if dealing me
a bad hand. 'A frightful example to children. Do you know why
I'm under the doctor? Because I thought I could get away with

anything. For years now I've been insulting my entire system. And now it's fighting back. I feel ghastly.'

'That's not good news.'

Wheeler blinked through his glasses at a wine-list. 'You know what being young is, Patrick? It's learning the lying lesson that life goes on for ever. You're always as well as you feel at fourteen. But look at me now. I'm paying the accumulated bills of a life-time of believing that middle age was only an up-market version of youth. It's not. It's a killer. That's what I blame your friend Bunter for. Creating illusions. Going on as if youth were for real.'

'Surely it's as real as anything else, Hugo.'

His heavy head brooded over a price-list. 'No – it's a brief romantic spasm. I rowed for my college. I ran. I bowled leg-breaks. I ate and drank in moderation with the boys. I didn't even smoke. And all the time I was storing up trouble. Building up my health just in time for it to fail me.'

'Is there any alternative?'

A steely eye stared at my nose. I wondered if he had noticed his assumption that Bunter, if nothing else, was real. 'Oh, there has to be,' he said. 'Life must be better than this. This is just not on. However, brass tacks. We think we can accommodate you this time. How many guests? Do you want to discuss the refreshments? They'll need to eat, I imagine. And drink. Only drink will make the speeches seem witty enough. I'd suggest – we like a deposit – the usual sort of deal. That works out at a glass and a half of the white, then two glasses max of red, a shot of port, and of course for the real men the bar's open at normal prices.'

'I'll pay for it,' I said.

'All of it? You'll need to dig into your savings.'

'Don't patronise me, Hugo. I'll look after it.'

A white fingernail trembled over a column of sums. 'We're looking at twenty-five pounds a head or so,' said Wheeler. 'Say thirty to be on the safe side.'

'Look, sorry, I must go and rescue him from the loo.'

'Who?'

'Bunter,' I said. 'By the way, what's actually the matter with you, Hugo?'

'Cancer,' he said.

Aitken was not in the lavatory when I descended. There was only a biggish button on the tiled floor with a shred of blue cotton attached to it. As if following a trail, I hurried with a quaking heart upstairs. There were no buttons in the morning-room, but a group of men bent like mourners were gathered over a sofa in the bar. Their murmur sounded like an hilarious litany.

Between their dark suits it was just possible to glimpse Aitken. He was lying back, flies agape, gasping slightly, as if indulging his senility for Edgar's benefit, while a helpful member was stuffing cushions behind his head to inhibit his breathing. Aitken's fat hand kept pulling them away, seemingly in jest. It was evident that all these hardened drinkers thought that he was drunk. Admittedly he looked quite comic.

'Who does he belong to?' said the critic, his eyes alight with drama.

'Mr Aitken happens to be my guest,' I said, stepping into the controversy.

They all turned so lightly to me that his plight became secondary to the fun. 'Your chap seems to need a helping hand,' whispered an elderly banker in my ear.

'He was just allaying our fears,' boomed a lawyer I almost knew, 'when he fell back.'

'What fears?'

'That he wasn't Billy Bunter. He is, isn't he? He must be.'

'Is there a doctor in the club?' said an advertising man with a snigger.

'He told me,' confided the banker, 'that T. S. Eliot only made a bosh of *The Waste Land* because he didn't listen to your fellow's advice. It's as well to know, I dare say . . .'

'He might be lapsing into coma.'

'Aren't we all? It's that sort of club.'

'Witherby's the man for him.'

'Witherby's probably working off his lunch in the billiard-room.'

'Who's Witherby?' I asked, by now at a complete loss.

'The noted shrink,' said the lawyer.

'Pills in every pocket,' chuckled the man in advertising.

'Weymouth, why is your guest tossing our cushions all over the carpet? Doesn't he know the rules?'

I looked with care at Aitken's face, a sweaty mask, then down to his body, which was palpitating as though the heart were pumping too hard, then at his legs, which were writhing in their trousers. And a fraction of a second later I looked again. He simply couldn't be putting it on. At that moment his feet rucked up the rug. Soon there would be further protests about maltreatment of club property. Panic seized me.

'Fetch Witherby!' I shouted. 'For God's sake get him here at once. This man's dying.'

'What's this?' said Aitken, when we had sped in a taxi from the club to the consulting-room. 'Not a deathbed, I trust.'

'It's the usual couch.'

'May I recline on it?'

'Make yourself comfortable, Mr Aitken,' said Witherby, whom I now recognised as the champion who had ruined Edgar's snooker. 'And just say whatever comes into your head, that's the idea.'

'Have you any brandy? It often helps.'

Witherby wagged his beard at me in query. I nodded. Opening a drawer of his desk, he withdrew a duty-free half-bottle with an apologetic shrug, fetched a pair of tooth-mugs from his washbasin and poured out a couple of generous measures.

'Sometimes,' he said, grinning, 'it loosens the tongue.'

'Oh, I don't believe I need my tongue loosening,' said Aitken. 'Can't keep it still, in fact.' He uttered a gruff snigger. 'I know you doctors are supposed to have seen it all, but do you want to know how Lady Chatterley met her lover?'

'If you want to tell me,' said Witherby professionally, taking an enormous swig.

I sat watching Aitken's equally huge face. As before, when his thought moved into the past, his features set into more babyish lines, as if being reborn into calm. 'I don't have to reveal myself, do I? Or take any clothes off? You could well be taken aback. Ladies usually are.'

'Just be yourself,' said Witherby, settling down behind his brandy.

'I'm so many people,' Aitken began pensively.

'Good.'

'But rather than talk about me,' said Aitken, who by a miracle appeared to have recovered his health in the limelight, 'here's a merry tale of yesteryear for you to analyse. Lorenzo! We called him by that nickname to tease the bugger for always slipping off abroad at the first hint of trouble, with a foreign woman who was trouble personified. But actually when I met him he was – rather like you, Patrick, or you, doctor – trying to collect material. His aim was to dig one last great novel out of a return trip to the Midlands where his pater, a collier by trade, had given him a bad start in life – and, golly, how well I understood that after my few terms at public school.'

'So you identified with this Lorenzo?' said Witherby.

'Thin little cock-sparrow with a beard like you, as I recall,' said Aitken. 'Anyway he couldn't get into the local hostelry or persuade his seamy relatives to give him a bed – he liked to think people were dead set against him, as I expect you do yourself – so his foreign Frau knocked at the door of my mansion one night and explained all to my butler. No room at the inn! As it happened, another person of foreign birth was staying the weekend, and I thought they'd all rub along rather well together at breakfast, so my answer, conveyed through servants, was a reluctant affirmative.'

'Why reluctant?' said Witherby eagerly.

'You never know how clean people are,' said Aitken.

'And who was this other person?'

'Or dirty, for that matter,' Aitken went on. 'Next morning over the kidneys poor old Lawrence took one lingering look at Mrs Simpson, and that was it. It put paid to his appetite, not that he had much. He kept peering at her through the shrubbery when she took a stroll as if she were the opening chapter of a masterpiece. Then, when I came out to sun myself in my wheel-chair – I'd taken a bit of a knock while trying to bring the General Strike to a satisfactory conclusion – something snapped in Lawrence's brain. He rushed to Mrs Simpson in a distinctly threatening manner, like a character in one of his own novels. Naked passion!'

'What did you do?' whispered Witherby.

'I had no choice. I loved her. I had to protect her. But I was out of commission,' said Aitken, stretching back comfortably on the couch. 'So I summoned my gamekeeper, an old boy called Mullins. One glimpse of his twelve-bore, and Lawrence whizzed off back into the bushes and left Mrs Simpson to her own devices.'

'What happened then?'

'Oh,' Aitken said, as though abruptly tired of questions, 'he went off abroad and wrote *Lady Chatterley's Lover*, all about Wallis and me in my wheelchair and dear old Mullins who wouldn't have hurt a fly. Luckily all this bohemian stuff happened before I introduced her to the Prince of Wales – though he may well have read excerpts from the manuscript I put out for him on the fatal night.'

'If you cared for her,' said Witherby relentlessly, fingering the half-bottle, 'why did you bring in a royal personage?'

'*Faute de mieux*, alas,' said Aitken with what seemed a genuine melancholy. 'A chap in a wheelchair is in no position to make demands on beautiful women, even if he loves them to distraction.'

'Did you love her? This is important. You might still be suppressing it.'

'Oh, I am, I am, I'm certainly suppressing it,' said Aitken with verve. 'A thing of beauty is a joy for ever, even if one dies before being old enough to fully appreciate it – eh, Patrick?'

Lesley? Could the man possibly mean Lesley? I had never viewed her as a joy for ever. Even as a thing of beauty she left much to be desired. Perhaps I was still confused by his story of D. H. Lawrence's furtive libido. If so, poor old Witherby was very much in the same boat. At the first mention of Mrs Simpson he had begun to look progressively more manic, though the brandy can't have helped.

'Could we have a private word?' he whispered behind his hand, as Archie lay on the couch mulling over those scenes in the primordial forest not far from Melton Mowbray. We withdrew to the window, which overlooked a tangle of fire-escapes.

'Is anything wrong with him?' I said.

'Everything is wrong with him,' Witherby said with hushed professionalism. 'A physical examination would merely prove that he ought to be dead. In any case he won't benefit from my kind of help, which is intended to stop a patient's mind running off course. He's beyond it. He's enjoying himself too much to profit from treatment.'

'One thing I don't need,' shouted Aitken from the couch, 'is a hearing-aid.'

'I was just telling Mr Weymouth that there's nothing wrong with you that time won't cure,' gabbled Witherby with an air of guilt. 'Just keep an eye on him, Patrick. Let him do what he likes – that's the key to his problem.' And with a slam he shut the brandy in the drawer as if closing the case.

'I feel wonderful,' said Aitken, waddling on to the pavement in Harley Street, where a young cripple was being helped painfully out of a limousine. 'That quack said I could do whatever I liked. I really should have asked him for a prescription to show Edgar.

We'll have tea at the Ritz. It'll build up our strength to stroll along to Quaglino's in time for their five-course special.'

'Archie, I don't think the Ritz does that sort of tea any more. And Quaglino's went out of business, oh, years ago.'

'Sorry I didn't put up a better show over your lunch,' he went on. 'Nothing wrong with me, of course. It was having to confess my peccadillo that drove refreshment out of my mind. I was afraid you'd send me packing. That member who recognised me as Bunter seemed jolly interested in Fisher T. Fish's poetry. I was just telling him that the waste land was a patch of ground behind the house where I was intending to grow peaches, when I keeled over – probably from lack of nourishment. Or because for once I wasn't telling the truth.'

'Shouldn't you go home and rest?'

'Rest? If I rest at all it will be in the luxurious arms of a suite at Claridge's. You probably have special rates there, your club being just round the corner. But we have oceans of time before us. I'd like to look up some of the old places. Where's Harry Wharton – what's his name? Eden – interred, do you happen to know? I'd relish a glance at his tomb, if only to avoid the same mistakes with my own.'

'He may well be in the Abbey.'

'That's where Priestley's memorial service took place – Johnny Bull was the last of us, apart from me.' Aitken paused to survey his memories congregating in Hanover Square, then blundered off between the hooting taxis. 'Or I'll introduce you to my tailor,' he said over his shoulder. 'Old Cowie in Cork Street, the only craftsman with the taste never to ask me which side I dressed. Or my shirt-maker in Jermyn Street. Or Fortnum's for the fun of it. I must be the only customer in the history of the firm who once popped in to order twenty thousand of their hampers to be sent to the western front with my compliments. Let's potter in and see if old Mason remembers.'

'I doubt if Mason will be there any longer.'

'His grandson will be,' Aitken said. 'A fine family of tradesmen. The Mason in my time scored 226 not out in the Old Boys' Match in 1880 – according to Frank Richards in one of his stories, though he didn't always get his facts quite right. Is there any cricket on anywhere? Edgar never lets me watch it in case I get too excited. By golly, I've so much to tuck into before I go.'

'You're not at death's door yet, Archie.'

'Who said I was? Before I go home, I meant. I trust I can recall which station the trains run from. I'll instruct the man at Claridge's to put me in a cab in the morning. Meanwhile let the flower of cities all open her honeyed doors to us!'

As it turned out, these plans were reduced by shortage of time to a brief foray on the ground floor at Fortnum & Mason, where Aitken bought a small pot of caviare by borrowing a less small fortune from me, a glance at the erstwhile tea-room of the Ritz which in Aitken's view had lowered its standards since he had once eaten pastries there with Sir Oswald Mosley, an embarrassing moment outside Boodle's where Aitken succeeded at last in unscrewing his pot and started thumbing caviare into his mouth, a vain search in Cork Street for his former tailor who he then claimed must have gone bust as a combined result of lavishing too much material on his suits and failing to be paid for them, an interlude with a tobacconist in the Burlington Arcade whose memory wasn't up to reminding Aitken of the brand of cigarette which Pandit Nehru used to smoke, and finally – I was dying on my feet by now – a visit to his shirt-maker.

'Ah, Mr Aitken, isn't it?' said the middle-aged manager with threatening courtesy. 'It's been quite some time, hasn't it, sir?'

'What? Well, I've been abroad. No post forwarded. Now, as to shirts. My friend requires a shirt.'

'There's a little matter of . . .'

'Bless the fellow!' said Aitken. 'When Oswald Mosley asked me where I bought those black shirts you used to run up for me, where did I tell him to go? His order must have reached the same heights as the hampers debited to my account at your grasping neighbours over the street. My business has kept London afloat. The stock market has perceptibly responded to whether or not I persuaded my many friends to buy things in your shops. I wish to present Mr Weymouth with a shirt. Bring some out, while he writes a cheque for whatever you say I owe you.' As the manager bustled towards the shelves, Aitken favoured me with a huge wink. 'Out,' he mouthed briskly, and the next moment we were hurrying down the pavement, cannoning into people who paid their accounts on the nail. 'Saved you a fortune there, old chum,' he said in a breathless gust of generosity, and without warning swivelled into Paxton & Whitfield with a cry of 'Cheese!'

If only to recover in comfort, I took Archie to tea at the Piccadilly Hotel. 'Nobody knows where I am,' he said, wolfing a sandwich. 'That's how I get away with it. I've been dead for close on thirty years. It all goes back to the time when I stopped interfering with history just to sit back and see what the results would be. But enough of philosophy. The point is that in 1957 I drew in my horns, let the whole dilemma look after itself, retired to an unknown address and an unlisted number, put an announcement in the deaths column of *The Times*, ignored such correspondence as filtered through to me, let my property fall into rack and ruin, spent several years waiting in vain for the inner call that would drag me back into action – and then suddenly realised that I was free! Free to observe the self-generating mess that consumed the nation, free to gloat over the outcome of all the mistakes I had initiated, free to relish the effects that had sprung from my causes.'

Aitken finished the sandwiches with a flourish, flipping the last of the egg and cress into his mouth. 'Mind you,' he continued, 'I have suffered much from this chosen anonymity. I really wanted to be hoicked back into life by the ear and made to pay up and apologise to one and all and serve six months – or whatever the society I had tricked required of me. But the trouble was that those who knew I was Bunter – all the ex-

Greyfriars fellows on their way up in the world – wouldn't have dreamt for their own sake of revealing the fact. They too were living on pretences as grand as they were false. Drugged by power, ambition, greed, their achievements depended on persuading others that greed, ambition and power bore no resemblance to a public school, though of course they do. But for Eden power had to look democratic, for Nehru ambition had to seem altruistic, for Mosley greed had to resemble a normal human desire to better everyone else's lot. So, having set out to produce a century in my own image, I have been alternately chortling and blubbing for thirty years over the results, in an isolation which alone has enabled me to assemble the whole picture. You should look at my notes. You must cast an eye over the treasury of material I have collected, a culture in itself, a civilisation packed into boxes.' He paused, eyeing the cake trolley. 'You see before you a man who has become the next best thing to a god, but a god in whom nobody believes. Except perhaps you. Not forgetting Edgar, of course – he'd believe anything.'

'My secretary Joanna believes in you.'

'Ah, how sound of her. I've always thought a female admirer must be the choicest of all.'

'There's always Lesley.'

'Your wife is not merely a woman,' said Aitken, snapping his fingers at a waiter. 'She is the best human being I have met since I brought Winnie out of the wilderness. She's designing my catafalque, you realise?'

'Winnie?'

'Winston Spencer Churchill,' said Aitken, fingerprinting a chocolate éclair. 'I got him to take over a war which I for one felt we needed.'

'That's an outrageous statement.'

'I dare say it is,' Aitken said, his mouth full. 'But have I never told you that Frank Richards once saw his son Randolph Spencer Churchill in the cradle and, with a brilliant flash of prescience, turned the infant into Sidney James Snoop, that ghastly boy who was always hanging around Skinner – or Mosley, if you prefer it?'

'No.'

'I don't seem to have told you much.'

'No.'

'There's more to come.'

'I can't wait.'

'Read some history, Patrick.'

'I will.'

'Trust me.'

'I do.'

'Even about Winston?'

'I think so.'

'You must be off your head,' said Aitken. 'True though it may be, I wouldn't believe you if you paid me a thousand pounds.'

'I'll do better than that.'

'You'll pay for this sumptuous tea?'

'With pleasure,' I said, and Aitken cackled in delight as a waiter alerted by the noise hastened forward with the bill.

7

Tea over, Archibald Aitken sheepishly asked to be conveyed in a taxi to whatever terminus served Ashford, Kent. It seemed no accident that when I took him to Charing Cross a girl not unlike Joanna was vanishing into the crowds and Edgar Smedley was waiting at the gate to escort his master home. Obviously Aitken, let off the hook for the afternoon, had been keeping an eye on the clock. Talk of Claridge's for the night or five-course meals in long-dead brasseries had been so much window-dressing for an escapade designed to taunt me with further scraps of questionable truth, which would later be narrowly confirmed by printed facts in the London Library. This encounter at the station was all part of the plan. But what plan? I felt thoroughly manipulated.

Amid promises to meet soon, I waved them off down the platform. My last sight of Aitken was of Edgar heaving his bulk into a compartment as if overloading a luggage van. As the whistle blew relief flooded me. To be honest, I was a little exhausted by being compelled to look in a novel way at supposedly well-known facts; it wrenched me out of true. I had an impulse to buy the evening paper to put myself straight.

Walking home, crying out for solitude to absorb the reckless

fatuity of an afternoon when Aitken had nearly died, then walked
me off my feet, then risked arrest, then consumed a starchy tea,
then claimed acquaintance with Churchill, I decided to delay
telephoning Joanna with the details of this sob-story, so slipped
into my quiet house and sat back with an unusually large whisky.
Whereupon the telephone rang.

I let it ring, then caught it just in time.

'We must meet,' Joanna said eagerly.

'Can't it wait till tomorrow?'

'You won't be there tomorrow,' she said. 'People have plans
for you. And I've got some information you should have before
you leave.'

'I can't take much more mystery, Joanna. Where am I supposed to be going?'

'The Minister is giving away the prizes at your old school's
speech-day,' she said. 'He particularly wants you to accompany
him. He has some facts to put at your disposal.'

'More facts!' I cried. 'Why is everyone belabouring me with
facts? They've stopped making sense.'

'You'd better listen to mine,' she said with a hint of threat.

'Where are you now?'

'In the phone-box across the street.'

'That sounds just as fictional as everything else.'

'Wait till you hear what Edgar told me.'

'I'll be at the door.'

Perhaps still charged with memories of last night's excess,
Joanna blew into my house with an air of ownership, tossed her
scarf on to my favourite chair, threw off her shoes as if marking
out territory, dropped to the carpet and sat up on her haunches
like a guru. Her eyes were aglow with not desire but foreboding –
yet another Joanna. Each of our meetings these days cast a
different woman into my presence; her features were now so lit
by emotion that they looked borrowed. My own day seemed
dramatic enough in retrospect. Hers had evidently been melo-
dramatic.

She had taken Edgar Smedley to the wine-bar round the corner for a snack and, tossing aside a lifetime's resistance to alcohol, he had imbibed a whole bottle of Valpolicella in tiny doses, like swallowing a patent medicine for his nerves. Almost too quickly he got a lot better.

'Does Mussolini mean anything to you?' asked Joanna with an air of anticipating ignorance.

'He made the trains run on time,' I said drily,

'Just what Edgar told me,' she said, snapping her fingers. 'Which is why Archie caught one to Rome in the twenties. He was a train buff, you see. Like Edgar is now, the copycat. He wanted to see the railway system for himself. At least that was the cover.'

'For what?'

'Well, this Mussolini was fat too and only a bit older than Archie, and everyone must have teased him at school for being so big and boastful and puffed up, but now nobody was laughing at him, because he had power. And Archie thought if only he could meet Mussolini he might learn how he did it – not just the trains, but gaining all that respect from his fellow-citizens. It's pretty obvious, really. Since leaving school Archie hadn't found many people he could identify with, poor boy.'

'This is a ridiculous conversation, Joanna.'

'It's only what Edgar told me after his third fix of the house red. I didn't say it. I didn't strap him to the stool and pour the stuff down his throat. I'm not inventing, I'm reporting. I just listened – for your sake, Patrick.'

'Did he meet Mussolini?'

'I'm not too sure,' Joanna said. 'Edgar got a little muddled...'

The likeliest version of the tale which Joanna now recounted was that the Duce, through his roughs, had got wind of the presence in Rome of one of the original heroes of British school-boy fiction. Some sycophant had advised him that our system of government had a weakness for the type of well-born bully who dominated the dormitories when voters of the future were at their most sensitive to the arguments of cosh or cane. By all accounts this Englishman had the right qualities. As Billy Bunter he had already achieved the notoriety required to win friends in his homeland for the cause of sound politics. All he lacked, since aristocrats as a class were wilting under the punitive blows of democracy, was cash.

Thus the young Aitken, according to Edgar's fast disintegrating evidence, had waited only a few days, not only for his hotel bill to be covertly paid, but for a secret proposal to be whispered in his ear by the unsavoury satraps of the Duce. Bunter, closet fascist of *The Magnet*, was to return to his fatherland and with due cunning pave the way for a similar regime to dawn naturally upon the English scene, in exchange for a regular supply of the postal orders for which he had been waiting in vain since boyhood.

With a grimace Edgar had taken another dose of Valpolicella. Like a public school, he then said, the Rome of those days was a whirlpool of licensed crime, and Archie, whose own country had thrown him in at the deep end, had no moral raft to cling to. Young gangs roamed the piazzas like fourth-formers on an outing. From alleys hung with washing authority suddenly pounced on the feeble in shirts as black as gowns. In its noisy chaos the whole picture was as Latin as a lesson at Greyfriars. Archie felt at home. He had no choice but to take on his first job.

At Rome his train left on time, however late it was destined to arrive at Victoria. Edgar thereupon finished the bottle and, sitting back well-satisfied, nearly fell off his stool.

'Why do you suppose Smedley told you all this nonsense?'

'A bit to get his own back,' Joanna said. 'Edgar's very touchy about you taking Archie over, you know. But also showing off. He seemed really proud of Archie for accepting the challenge of clearing up the mess in England, while letting me in on a secret that would get Archie into trouble with you.'

'So it would, if I believed it.' I paused. 'But this is calumny of the lowest order. Edgar's off his rocker. You let him have too much medicine. Do you honestly think that Archie would have taken financial reward from a foreign power for subverting the social order in his own country?'

'He also got money from Hitler,' Joanna said casually.

'Oh, for heaven's sake . . .'

'But that was later. Perhaps Mussolini tipped him off about Bunter at one of those meetings they were always having on the trains that ran on time.'

With some difficulty I forced a grin and beamed it towards Joanna. She gazed up at me straight-faced. So I deliberately broadened the grin. It was meant only as an invitation to disbelief. She went on looking solemn.

'You weren't there,' she said.

'Thank God.'

'You can't know how serious he was.'

Fixing the grin on my face, I let all the humour drain out. I felt lonely and small and young. 'I think you're ganging up on the truth with Smedley,' I said pettily. 'I think you're herding the facts into the gas ovens. I think your cosy lunch was a cellar for torturing the life out of common sense. Hitler almost destroyed our world, I remind you. We're lucky to be sitting here – or lying here in your case, yes, lying – joking about it. I could just about credit the Mussolini part – Italians are so stupidly boisterous – but it's not possible that Aitken received funds from the Nazis to extend their foul work to these shores. My father fought them, Joanna. He killed Germans. Oh, Christ!'

'Archie's still living on it, Edgar says.'

In some pain I kept up the rictus of scorn that seemed to have paralysed my face. 'It is evident,' I said with tight logic, 'that Smedley will stop at nothing to traduce his employer.'

'Ah, so your hero has to be whiter than white, is that it? You can't accept that Archie is as human as you or me.'

'Don't argue with me, Joanna . . .'

'Do watch it, Patrick – if all your geese have to be swans, they'll end up as albatrosses.'

The grin still in position, I bent down and swished the flat
of my hand across Joanna's brainless face as she sat upright in
her peculiarly smug version of the lotus. She toppled sideways
on my white carpet, looking suddenly as small as a child, her
feet splayed out, ankles touching. I dropped to my knees, hung
over her, with no desire to comfort, with only an urge to make
my point clearer by damaging her more. Her hip was uppermost, clothed in blue denim, a contemptible material. Her
behind curved amply away from it, a normally inviting target
for a slap of fondness or lust, but at this moment a cynosure of
hatred. I belted it hard, hurting the ball of my thumb, then
again and then once more. Joanna merely moaned in a passive
fashion that further enraged me.

I stood up unsteadily; then, hovering above her, transferred
my loathing by an act of will to my own property: dashing to
the carpet, where it failed to break, a cache-pot empty of
flowers which Lesley had given me one Christmas, kicking off
a low table a pile of books which I had thought I needed for my
work, fetching my fist up short against a bottle of the very *vino*
which had prompted Edgar's dubious *veritas* over the sandwiches. All these impotent gestures of destruction were no more
than a hideously difficult effort to refrain from kicking Joanna
to a pulp.

And then all at once it changed, the shame and sentiment
swam in, and I rolled her over as though to inspect the wounds,
and her dry eyes gazed at me from the floor without reproach,
and her mouth at last grinned, then broadened its grin, and
humour crept into it, and in a minute we were making love in
most of our clothes amid the not very serious wreckage of the
room.

'You can't take it either,' she hissed during a transport.

'What?' I gasped. 'This? This? I can take any amount of it.'

'Don't be crude. I mean, the fact that facts about people you
love sometimes have to be horrible. You can't bear it.'

'Yes, yes,' I whispered, and there was a moment of collusion, brief and total, before we subsided in the aftermath of love on to the floor where all that earlier hate had run its course.

'Ah,' she said drowsily, planting a kiss on my mouth. 'Wait till you know more about me. I've got guilty secrets too, you know.'

My belly jumped.

'What are they?'

By chance I had hit upon the opportunity I had missed time and again: getting Joanna to come clean. Perhaps only violence brought the truth blurting out. Perhaps coitus fingered dishonesty.

'Dare I say?' she asked coyly.

'I demand it.'

'Don't dither, Patrick,' she said, stretching a foot that dangled a pair of tights. 'Tell me what you want to know.'

I breathed in. 'What were you really doing that weekend when I rang you up late at night from The Dunes and you weren't there and you pretended, with an enthusiasm more suspect than persuasive, to have spent the entire weekend reading up the Bunter canon?'

'I see,' she said. She was lying with her knickers half off, eyeing me warily. 'What you're asking is, why did I get so buzzed up about Billy Bunter all of a sudden.'

'Put it any way you like.'

'Fair's fair. You went down to visit Archie in Kent. So I popped up to see my dad in Beds.'

'Beds? The county? Your father? Who's that? Why don't I know about him?'

'You never asked. You never do ask. It's a flaw in your make-up.'

'Don't tell me he attended Greyfriars.'

'Too right,' Joanna said. 'Well – almost. He coaches cricket at some dump near Luton and keeps a pub.'

'Keeps a pub?'

'I mean, he runs a country-house hotel,' said Joanna, cycling her legs to disentangle the underwear. 'In fact his fancy piece does all the work, Debbie, an air hostess he met coming back from a tour of India. She's about my age.'

'How old's your father?'

'He's about your age.'

'What a lot of coincidences,' I said weakly, feeling sapped by an ambush of jealousy, pulling up my trousers with hands that had gone awkward. A sense that here was the most crucial exchange, though trivial, which our joint excursion into Bunter's world had thus far thrown up filled me, not with the joy of at last finding out, but with a rage that I hadn't been told before.

'He played for his county in the fifties,' Joanna said on a chatty note of pride.

'What was his name?'

She clucked crossly. 'Feathers, of course.' Squatting on her nude calves, she peered into the laddered heel of her hose against the underside of a table-lamp.

'Not G. H. G. Feathers?'

'Don't say Gerry was a hero of yours?'

The homely chaos of the room faded to Lord's, years ago, a damp afternoon, the ball turning, a squat chap coming in fifth when the Gentlemen needed 17 to win against the Players, losing all his partners, then out to a dolly catch two runs from victory or rain stopping play. How could I forget? The suspense had nearly killed me. It was like a school story, if less cheery than most.

'You'd get on with him,' said Joanna generously.

'I doubt it after that terrible afternoon.' I watched her re-clothing her lower limbs, legs swanning in the air. 'He let down the side.'

'Is that a serious remark?'

'I was only nineteen.'

'So was he,' she smirked.

The secret gradually emerged as Joanna continued to adjust

her dress on my carpet. At my first mention of Bunter she had thought I was mad. Yet because she so wanted me to exhibit a passion, any passion, that might liberate her too, she had at once telephoned her father to ask if he had ever heard of Grey-friars. He nearly exploded with wrath at the thought that anyone might suppose he hadn't. So, to coincide with my first visit to The Dunes, Joanna had risked a night of Debbie's cuisine and Gerry's reminiscences to find out more: to nail the Bunter myth, as she put it.

As I listened, half my mind was still on the cricket. The thought that that burly figure glued to the crease had sired this woman – I saw him even now hunched over his bat, bottom stuck mulishly out, eyes following the line of every devilish ball until the last that skied his team to defeat – and that he and I were of an age, and had grown up miles apart, and had pored over *The Magnet* in our own little worlds, and then leapt off with the ambitious bounce of youth into careers so different, suddenly made Joanna, as she lay there with her skirt up, as vulnerable as a child, lost somewhere between us, still aching for the love which her father's generation, stuck in ruts, hadn't had the heart to give her. And that included me. I had failed her too.

'But you didn't nail the myth?'

'No,' she said, reaching back to the catch on her bra. 'I fell for it.'

Her life, she went on, sitting upright primly, had got off to a shaky start. With averages like his, G. H. G. Feathers had never had the cash to extend her education beyond a year's shorthand, so she had picked up her pretensions from night school, any old cultural course she could fit into a secretary's leisure. Her late teens were dogged by boys who were only allowed to take her home if they first took her to the theatre, by books read at top speed on buses, by poems tightly memor-ised between typing memoranda, by the hit and miss of self-improvement. She had no idea how to penetrate a club as exclusive as great art. There was no discipline to her efforts and in the end no point. Joanna had emerged into the muddle of her mid-twenties with a ragbag of too much South Bank: her shoulders rounded and her brain warped by silent films and loud acting, abstracts and readings and rock. She had longed for culture to seduce her; it had led only to loneliness. It was when she saw the advertisement I had put in *The Times*, and looked pretty at the interview and won the job on her speeds, that she knew how badly she needed a tutor to make sense of it all. She found me.

Her first few months of my higher culture, she now confessed, had dismayed her. The names I dropped trod on the toes of her ignorance. She felt as small as the kids whose inadequacies were the subject of my daily dictation. And then brusquely, just as she was giving up, whizz-bang, out of nowhere, out of character, I mentioned Bunter, and she recalled that once her father, in some bate about the slack manners of boys in the nets, had invoked the ancient ethic of Greyfriars and then raved on about standards going to pieces, and that was the moment when, slipping out of my ken for a night, she had taken the train home to the family hostelry near Luton and asked her old man – not that old, in fact – just what Bunter & Co. honestly meant to him or, for that matter, to anyone else. And she got the works, the full treatment. Not only bags of detail – all those school incidents which she pretended to have culled from her reading – but a staggering late-night slightly sloshed spiel about how much better this country and culture not to mention its women would be if only we had all stuck by the inalterable tablets brought down from the mountain, not in the poems or movies or jazz or dramas that were knocking his daughter's mind for six, but in the pages of *The Magnet*.

Pause. Her legs were crossed. She looked impregnable. 'Why did you believe your father and not me?' I asked quietly. The jealousy still stuck in my gullet.

'Even little girls have heroes, you know,' Joanna said. 'Only child. Famous dad. Worship the ground he walks on. Never find a man half as good. Where's your Freud?'

'Why didn't you tell me before?'

'No more questions.' She grinned. 'Just give me an answer or two.'

'Why have you put your clothes back on?'

'For someone to take off.'

I grinned. My hands moved up her thighs as she sat on my favourite chair. The elastic round her waist expanded over her hips, then slackened towards her knees. I pulled downwards. If not much mistaken, I had never wanted anyone more or at least more often.

'Oh dear,' said Joanna with a sigh. 'Oh, dear Patrick.'

The Minister picked me up in his limousine at ten-thirty the next morning. As we drove between pavements that kept their distance, the upholstery made it hard to feel resentful over this summons to a wasted day. Besides, it was amusing to revisit in style the school we had attended together. At the traffic lights our stately vehicle drew glances from the cut-out ranks of extras glued to the windows of buses. They glared pastily at our self-importance. As Westminster receded at speed, it took Rickie Rathbone several hundred yards of the Embankment, a bridge across the river and half an underprivileged borough to tell me how honoured he felt to be returning as a giant to the establishment where he had once been treated as a pygmy. By any standard it was one of his better speeches, style outweighing content with a suave assumption that his audience felt the same. And so I did.

Then he said quietly, 'What I'm about to say must go no further.'

Staring at the back of the driver's head, I nodded.

'I've had occasion to look into the files. Your man went to our school, were you aware?'

'My man?'

'Aitken. And he's a bad'un. Unbelievable, what? But that's what the files imply.'

'How quite amazing,' I said incredulously, with the day's first flutter of excitement.

'That he wasn't expelled?' said Rickie. 'Well, yes. But he certainly came to grief later. Aitken, Archibald Trent. Age at the time, thirty. Fat young rogue, no fixed address, no known employment, nothing on his record until 1926 when he was questioned at Dover after a trip to Italy – by then a power already needing to be watched from a security point of view – and then, quite a while on, he made contact with a worthy but restless Labour man, ex-war hero, practical joker, unreliable loyalist to any party or cause that took his fancy, called Mosley.'

'How did they meet?'

'God knows, but a tea at the Ritz was where our boys picked up the trail. Yes, Patrick – Oswald Mosley. The man who tried to let Hitler in through the back door, the misguided patriot whom no true Englishman can ever be forgiven for lifting a finger to help. Now correct me if I'm wrong, but wasn't it your proposal to base a fresh approach to English culture on the very chap who the evidence suggests played an undercover part in setting Mosley on course to turn our great country into a suburb of the Third Reich?'

'What actual evidence are you putting forward?'

'Would that I could tell you, Patrick. You will simply have to believe me. The papers in question, though long due for release under the thirty-year rule, have been held back, I know not on whose authority, and they may in fact never see the light of day.'

'I suppose they blacken the reputation of individuals still alive?'

'No, they embarrass the entire century,' said Rathbone with unusual candour. 'They make history itself look ridiculous.'

'Doesn't all human behaviour have that effect?'

'I see your point, but this absurdity is on a different scale,'

Rathbone said. 'Enquiries at the time, you see, revealed that your friend was indeed the model for Billy Bunter, and this discovery, as you may imagine, was suppressed with some rigour. Think how public knowledge of it would have added to the glamour of Mosley's movement! Consider how cosily English, how steeped in tradition, Mosley could have claimed his vile leadership to be! Not a threat, not an alien regime forcing its values on the nation, but a jolly political jaunt based on a school story that everyone knew by heart. Just think of it – the common man feeling at home in the common-room, democratic procedure turned into a rag. Why, millions might have been converted by the sheer fun of the thing. And then, before you could say knife, the Nazis would march in with fixed bayonets.'

We were now turning into the forecourt of our old school. The limousine swished over the gravel to draw up in front of a squad of boys in cadet uniform who sprang limply to attention as the handbrake was applied. Governors shuffled forward in a group of loose suits. While regretting the lack of discipline, my heart vaguely quailed; school still exerted that old power to unsteady the bowels. Rathbone, however, surged up the steps with a practised wave that combined arrogance and informality, and within a minute we were closeted in the headmaster's study with a dour ration of sherry between our fingers.

As soon as Rathbone was securely giving ear to the governors, I sidled up to the headmaster. 'I gather,' I said in an almost guilty whisper, 'that Billy Bunter is an old boy.'

Dr Trench raised his eyebrows in evident shock, then stared at me eagerly. 'Oh, goodness me, yes, years ago, before the First War, but sssh, yes, true, the eminently unsatisfactory character of Billy Bunter was, according to legend, it's little enough to be proud of though of course it has its funny side, based on a boy who attended this institution.' He lowered his voice. 'It does seem – it may only be literary gossip, of course – that the author of the Bunter stories, of whom our geography master, Mr Pocock, has made quite a study, ferreting away as

he does in the byways of the school's history, was invited by the
then headmaster to select a boy (it's quite a feather in our cap,
you may or may not agree) to become one of the most memorable
figures in that vast gallery of eccentrics who have peopled the
pages of the English novel.'

There was little news here and still less syntax. But the fact
that Aitken had never named in our talk the minor public
school we had both attended on the fringe of London somehow
imparted a higher degree of probability to everything else he
had told me. Nobody would boast by choice of this particular
school; yet he had never for effect claimed association with one
more famous in the annals of privileged education. Apart from
that welcome hint of the man's trustworthiness, it gave me a
frisson of pleasure to think that not only Archie in his boyhood,
but Frank Richards in quest of Bunter, had bent over a chair
or sipped a little sherry in this very den.

'Of course,' said Dr Trench, spoiling my thrill of rapport
with the past, 'the school premises were in the Strand in those
days, nearer the centre of things.' I might have guessed that an
indolent hack like Richards wouldn't have strayed far from
Fleet Street in his search for material. 'Most of the records
were, alas, lost in the move, but the good Pocock did manage
to discover that Aitken carried off the History Prize in 1910, so
he must have had a brain or two in his head, unlike his counter-
part in fiction. Such a pity he departed this life so relatively
young.'

'Departed? That's the last word I'd use of him.'

'Yes, our subject died in 1957,' said Dr Trench, as if taking
a class in elementary history.

'Are you sure?'

'Whatever his faults,' said the headmaster, plainly wondering
what mine were, 'Pocock never slips up on detail. As I recall,
Aitken's executors wrote cancelling his subscription to the
annual newsletter, so of course we announced his death in it.
Being a bit of a Bunter man myself, I only wish Pocock had

unearthed some nuggets of information about the use to which Aitken put his life after leaving school in such a blaze of glory. His memorial, if anywhere, should be here.'

'Perhaps I can help,' I said wickedly. The thought of Aitken's papers (soon to be mine) combined in a spasm of hilarity with the idea of a home (at last) for Lesley's tombstone or tablet. 'I happen to have access to the archive. Rather a privilege.'

For this or any remark I could hardly have wished more dramatic a response. The headmaster gobbled at me, his hands quivered and clenched in inarticulate elation, he swallowed hard, his eyes opened wide, blinked, then shut incredulously. His road to Damascus was at hand, but it was at once darkened by the loud entry of a tubby figure with a cropped black beard, who cast a look of overall hostility into the study and, in an officious bellow born on the sports field, cried, 'Time to go in, head. Face the music like a man, eh?'

'Good of you to remind us, Pocock,' muttered the head-master, adding in a whisper to me, 'Good work – you've handed me the key to my speech.'

Rathbone, after bestowing a spurious smile on the author of this crude interruption, moved towards the next challenge, followed by a trail of governors. 'Get the show on the road, fellows,' Pocock was saying as they filed out. 'No backsliding now.' About the man and his manner floated a pathetic suggestion of saloon-bar camaraderie. As a slouching cadet opened baize doors ahead of us, the half-broken voices of an assembly of restive boys pierced the dusty air. 'Ah, you'll be the Minister,' Pocock said in tones of crass familiarity. 'How's politics these days?' Rathbone sailed on with an unchanging smile.

We took our positions on the platform as the school showed its respect by replacing a maximum of noise with a minimum of silence. The Minister's bonhomie gazed down on the disorder of his younger self. As master of ceremonies Pocock fussed over the seating, then accorded the piano the rough treatment he had offered the guests. The school song rent the air; the rafters rang; tears jerked at the rims of my eyes. It felt solemnly right to be back in the atmosphere which my month's experience of Aitken had revived in my life. I had an urge to giggle.

We settled back into the speeches. Dr Trench was pleased to welcome the Minister for the Arts. He was an alumnus who had made good. He now belonged to those responsible for ensuring us a better life. He was an example to us all. The headmaster did not know what the Minister would choose to say, but he knew full well that we would be the better for hearing it. It was no accident that he and his party were in power. The parents of many a boy here present had elected them to office to preside over their best interests. The Minister was, however, not the only remarkable student to have left this school, gone on to higher things, or borne a name that resounded throughout the land.

I had been nodding. It was probably that thimbleful of Amontillado. I now woke sharply to witness hundreds of earlier selves gazing up at me in bored hope. With an abrupt lowering of his voice, Dr Trench changed tone from eulogy to obsequy.

'Boys,' he said. 'Many of you will mourn with me the twenty-seventh anniversary, which falls this month, of the death of Billy Bunter.'

'Hear, hear,' cried Pocock at the piano. The entire school stirred and stared. Rathbone frowned very slightly.

'Some of you will have read the stories about him. All of you must be aware of his existence as the fattest boy since records began. Well, Mr Terence Pocock has discovered that the original Owl of the Remove attended this school, I won't trouble you with dates, which you are adept at failing to remember, but it was long, long ago, in the days when pedagogy was an art and science virtually unknown. I am therefore making an appeal to our distinguished guest, who I am sure was boy enough when young to have enjoyed the antics of this classic of the classroom, who with all the mischief at his command has kept boys and masters alike on their toes for longer than I care to remember, to request of his colleagues in the Government some form of help, I cannot say what, to set up in the school a species of museum or monument to celebrate in perpetuity the age-old battle fought in schools up and down the country between us, the cruel authorities, and you, the downtrodden underdogs. Greyfriars, boys, was, I hazard an informed guess, this very establishment, so it is only proper that we should accommodate a museum to Billy Bunter and his well-loved friends, as a means of keeping the past in focus while concentrating our energies on the present . . .'

Throughout this statement of an eccentric case I was busy trying to keep my head. Clearly none of it qualified as the smooth introduction which a politician as used to banality as Rathbone wanted to hear on ground he considered safe, if not sacred. That didn't matter. But for some reason the idea, however admirable or at least amusing, struck me as a bad one, as well as badly expressed. I wished I hadn't spoken to the headmaster. I positively didn't care for even a mite of the secrets Aitken had told me to be exposed to official criticism as yet or perhaps ever.

The other problem was that I had taken against Terence Pocock. His tiny feral mouth worried me, as did the beard that embedded it in a surround of soft fur. The button eyes were predatory, but he was too soft, all bluff, an animal designed by nature to confirm the survival of the fittest by not surviving. One wanted to stroke him, while knowing he would try to bite. To place in this man's claws even a hint of the surprises Aitken had confided in me would be to invite their exposure as ridiculous. And I didn't want this. I really didn't.

To anyone who knew him – almost as though Bunter were playing a prank on him at a remove – Rathbone was severely embarrassed. He hid it well. Also, of course, he would blame me. Any evasion on my part, or even the truth, would be judged not only a lie but a stab in the back of our friendship. Slightly reddened by annoyance, he stood up to the school with an icy

affability that none the less gave every sign of pleasure to
Dr Trench.

'Boys,' said Rathbone, 'your headmaster has presented us
today with a wonderful idea, which amazes me as much as it
probably does you. Perhaps indeed we should all feel proud
that Billy Bunter, the world's most noted ignoramus, was educated in this venerable institution which we all respect. Your
headmaster is tolerant enough to suggest there is some virtue in
being a dunce, some special glory we should celebrate in being
fat – and a fathead.'

Dr Trench beamed evenly. At that moment I began to understand just as much why Rickie had entered politics as why
Aitken would never be heard. There was a riveting duplicity –
people called it charisma – in each of the syllables that moved
on suavely through Rathbone's slight smile.

'But this school today is a different place from the school as
it was when the likes of Bunter were being fed dead languages
and nourished on battles. The school now is a modern school,
thanks partly to the enlightened theories practised by your
headmaster's worthy staff, but also to the advanced equipment
placed at their disposal by a Government that is determined to
give young people every chance in life. The notion of a museum
for that old style of teaching, when boys were beaten black and
blue for the slightest error, a museum that would display to
every parent the horrors of a system that allowed boys as thick
as Bunter to hoodwink it, that notion, boys, is a wonderful one.'

Rathbone paused. 'For this reason,' he said, finger in the air.
'Museums are places where the dark ages are fossilised and
forgotten. Places we visit for the purpose of learning from,
perhaps laughing at, other people's mistakes. Places that inspire
us by the presence of death to regard the future as our only
reality. I can only say that if this school, by founding that very
splendid museum in its midst, though I shall give it all the
support I can, were to identify with Greyfriars by perpetuating
it, I don't think I would be quite so happy to be an old boy as

I am now, and as you will be, when you carry off into your individual futures the prizes, so well-deserved, which I shall now be even happier to award you.'

The speech, if not witty, was certainly brief. It ended with nobody quite knowing what the Minister had really said, least of all the headmaster, who led the applause. Once again Rickie's naïvety, an enthusiasm that rated as rhetoric, had won the day. He had the knack of sounding valiantly positive even when he sought to destroy. If challenged by colleague or columnist, he could either defend his corner by reference to his words as spoken or assert beyond contradiction that he had meant the opposite. It was one of his better political efforts. The only oddity was that he had thought it worth putting his brains at the service of cracking so small a nut.

The bigger nut, as luck would have it, sat next to me at lunch. For a while Pocock ignored me in favour of his food. My plate was awash with thin stew and my thoughts were equally unappetising. I couldn't help feeling that my old school badly needed a dose of just that discipline in which Aitken had tried to interest Sir Oswald Mosley. Down the hall a hungry chaos ruled. Lads slopped water on tables and pigged their rations with shouts that deafened talk. I thought warmly of the kind of punishment I had meted out to Joanna only last night.

Sucking meat out his teeth, Pocock eyed me sideways. 'What did you say your name was?'

'I didn't. It's Weymouth.'

His bearded jaw dropped an inch. 'Hey, you're not the Weymouth I know of?'

'I'm not a Channel port, if that's what you mean.'

'No, no, Pat Weymouth, great scholar and all that, spouse of the more famous Lesley spelt with a Y?'

'You could put it like that.'

'God dammit, man,' exploded Pocock, 'I just heard from Arch. Call that a coincidence. It's got to be meant. I've spent ten years trying to pinpoint the Bunter grave, it being an old school tale that this dump started off in life as Greyfriars, and then out of the blue comes this letter from one Aitken, saying he was here, not dead like we all thought, and just the chap rumour had it was the Bunter look-alike.'

'And what did he say about me?'

'He said just check with you. If I was looking for proof, you were the boy.'

'One can never be sure.'

'Come on now, Pat, this means a lot to me,' Pocock said. 'And a lot of other people. You know what – if Bunter turns out to be real, then all the Jeremiahs have got another think coming to them. The one and only thing *The Magnet* suffered from was not being fact. But this is a real turn-around. Opens up a lost world. Start me in at the beginning now, tell me all. Let's be partners.'

'Possibly some other time – Terry, is it?' I stood up. By a happy chance the celebrations were drawing to a close. At the front of the stage the Minister was pressing the hands of governors as if tipping them. The headmaster, who had been ogling with avuncular pride my special relationship with Pocock, now snapped his fingers at the geography master. 'Oh, it's that man again,' said Pocock rattily and heaved his bulk towards the piano. After a final chorus of the school song, the boys raised three ragged cheers. We passed down the platform at the pace if without the majesty of a state funeral, then hurried out to the waiting car.

'Very clever of you,' said Rathbone, sinking back.

'What was?'

'Putting him up to that trick about Bunter. I suppose you realise you could have made me look fatuous.'

'Only you can do that, Rickie. And you didn't.'

'I did my best to honour the occasion. And you didn't.'

'I thought you eluded his blandishments typically well.'

Suburbs passed. The chimney tops of detached mansions peered conservatively over walls. A few voters were airing their dogs in the gutters. It looked like Bunterland, but bored stiff, awaiting a surprise, a laugh, a challenge.

'I also thought the museum rather a good idea,' I said. 'It certainly wasn't mine. Until you told me I had no idea Aitken was an old boy or our Alma Mater gave birth to Bunter. Aren't you fond of the place that reared you? Why, Bunter is its only claim to fame – apart from you, of course. You could at least have given the scheme your blessing, instead of pretending that the school, which you know quite well hasn't changed an iota, is now so modern that it's leading the country into a golden age.'

'I don't have to discuss it,' Rathbone said petulantly. 'I'll drive you home and then I think we'd better part company for a while.'

'Are you giving me the sack?'

'Not officially. I don't want any martyrs peppering the news-papers with empty controversy about the work of my depart-ment. I want you to rethink your position and then come back to me privately having changed it. I never wish to hear the name of Bunter mentioned again. Alive or dead, Bunter is a trouble-maker. He's also making a fool of you, Patrick. He's trying to get beneath the skin of society by the most underhand of means – just spreading rumours that things aren't what they seem.'

'That sounds perilously like a definition of art.'

'And he seems to have demoralised you,' said Rathbone. 'We can't run a country if our best men start believing that the whole process, including government, is a farce, a tissue of lies, a function of madness. Modern life is more serious than that, Patrick, and I expect you to keep well away from me until you've wiped the grin off your face. I'm surprised a sensible woman like Lesley lets you get away with it.'

'How many times must I tell people that Lesley and I are no longer married?'

'Oh, of course,' said Rathbone, recognising out of the window a landmark in inner London. 'That explains it. You're on the

loose. A dangerous time, middle age, Patrick. I've seen all too
many of our contemporaries go off the rails, chasing women all
over their offices, getting involved in fraud or spiritualism or the
like.'

'Have you been talking to your psychiatrist?'

'It is not I,' said Rickie, shaking his head at the Thames as we
crossed it, 'who needs treatment. Nor I who indulges in schoolboy humour at the expense of the country in which he's fortun-
ate enough to live. Nor I who has lost the love of an excellent
wife.' The Houses of Parliament were blotted out by glassy
verticals of high-rise offices. 'You never had a son, did you,
Patrick?'

'No.'

'Thank your lucky stars. With your example before him he
might have grown up into another Bunter.' He gazed at me
sidelong. 'Now where is it you live exactly?'

It was time, painfully enough, to take stock. Even if worse were
to follow, I had survived, albeit shaken to the roots, a couple
of days disastrous to my opinion of myself. Counting up the
shocks, I found that I had struck Joanna in the face as an
alternative to half killing her, I had been threatened with the
loss of my job if I pursued a subject that interested me far more,
I had been told that a man whose word I trusted had been
responsible for introducing fascism into this country, I had met
an uncouth teacher of geography who shared and even surpassed
my enthusiasm for Billy Bunter, I had gathered that an octo-
genarian for whom I had yesterday bought a big tea had been
dead for a quarter of a century, and I had faced the fact that
just when the whole story seemed to be fitting nicely into place
it had started disintegrating before my eyes.

I thought I could manage it all if only I were left alone.
Indeed, taking the next afternoon off from an office that now
chilled me, I had half formed a plan to remove my person to
Sussex for the weekend, perhaps visiting that evacuee village

where my father had first poured out the riches of *The Magnet* for my delight, and to sort out, by reading between the lines of suitable texts, the new version of history which all the revelations by and about Aitken were forcing me to shape. The volume of the Oxford History of England covering the years from 1914 to 1945 struck me as a solid foundation for my scheme. It was by A. J. P. Taylor.

Yes, a good air-clearing, heart-searching plan, which in the evening I outlined to Joanna. I would be going back to my roots in an abundantly English place, the green and pleasant land where Greyfriars was built into my boyhood, as well as to the sources of the events of my lifetime. It was then that darkness fell and Lesley struck. With her customary instinct she was to provide me with even better reasons for a swift and solitary retreat.

Joanna was in position on my carpet, toes tucked under her kneecaps, tights straining against her thighs, and by then we were not only discussing the question of whether Aitken had really been in love with Mrs Simpson and only by a sweet-natured act of altruism had passed her on via D. H. Lawrence to the Prince of Wales, whose dipping that night into the manuscript of *Lady Chatterley's Lover*, also inspired by Aitken, might well have fuelled the flames of passion in his blue blood, but we were also looking forward, in a more personal way, to a night of our own to remember. The amiable narrative of the evening lay before us – drinks, supper, talk – ending, if all went well, in the climax one expected of a good story. And then here in Pimlico, in the heart of our privacy, the bell rang downstairs.

It rang not once, not even twice, but continuously as if short-circuited, like a fire alarm. Joanna jumped away from me. As my hand slipped from hers I overbalanced, hissing out of habit, 'Just keep quiet, I'll go,' and ricking my back slightly when springing sideways to my feet, I hastened down with rage in my spirit, pain in my side, and a version of not-today-thank-you on my lips.

Whether by chance or calculation, Lesley's entrances on the
stage of my life always stole the show, though she had yet to
catch me in bed with someone. 'Patrick!' she cried in a throaty
whisper, 'I can't tell you what's happened.' It sounded tragic,
but more excitement than misery animated her tone. Breathing
fast but solemnly, she sidled past me at a run, and as I stared
at her back retreating down the passage, she suddenly turned
and fixed me in the eye as though she had just caught me in bed
with someone. 'I must talk to you, I don't care who's here, are
you giving one of your famous dinner parties?'

'Calm down. There's nobody here, well, not a lot of people.'

'Is there anyone? You were probably doing one of your
girls.'

'What, fully dressed?'

'You lonely men are capable of anything, don't I know it.
Take me upstairs and I'll tell you.'

'Tell me now if you don't want to be overheard.'

'I can't talk in a passage – it's too long. Or without a drink –
I need one. Or not sitting down – I'm tired. Oh, Patrick, I'm
so tired. Who would have thought it would come to this?'

'Who would have thought you'd resort to platitude?'

'Words, what are words, you only think of words. Come
along now, take me up and introduce me to her. You're going
to tell her anyway if she's worth her salt or even if she's a whore.
I've got nothing to hide.' She raised her voice perceptibly. 'We
were happy together once, weren't we, my darling?'

Lesley's gift of not just ignoring but actually not seeing a
person now came into play. And by then Joanna was seated
with such dainty anonymity in a chair that the introductions,
which I had long feared, passed off not only without incident
but almost without happening. No words were exchanged, but
with a faint nod Joanna suggested a how-do-you-do, while
Lesley coolly implied how-pretty-you-are. Then she said, as I
poured her a whisky, as her eyes darted over my curtains, my
wallpaper, my pictures, my books, but positively not my

mistress, as Joanna herself just sat and stared, 'Darling one, Archie, yes, Archie, has asked me to marry him.'

I sniggered. Joanna narrowed her gaze at the cracks in the ceiling. Lesley looked at me with an intense air of hostility as though willing me to come up with a counter-proposal. I raised the snigger into a laugh.

'There,' Lesley said, 'you can't take anything seriously.'

'Are you taking it seriously?'

'Would you care if I did?'

'It's so preposterous an idea that you'll have to give me a year or two to get used to it. Beyond that, I always approve when one friend of mine likes another sufficiently to want to go on having breakfast with her for the rest of his life.'

'Breakfast! Do you know what he has for breakfast?'

'In my limited experience it's a water biscuit and a cup of thin tea.'

'You're out of date as usual,' Lesley said, ably concealing her relief that she could now speak of this great proposal only in trivial terms. 'I don't think you realise how much he's kicked over the traces since meeting you. You should never have carried him off to France. He's taken up his old habits, all those strains he used to put on his system before Edgar, sweet man, started reforming him. I happened to be there the other day when Edgar brought him up his normal breakfast in bed. He dashed it to the floor. While Edgar was picking bits of sodden biscuit off the carpet, Archie plunged downstairs in his dressing-gown, raving mad, with Oswald Mosley's stick in his hand, and forced Soames under threat of dismissal to run him up a pair of kippers, followed by eggs, bacon, sausages, mushrooms and tomato, plus a pile of hot buttered toast and the kind of sweet tea strong enough to give a lorry-driver a heart-attack. If you think that's funny! The whole house reeked of fish and fat and Archie just bolted himself into the dining-room and worked his way through all that dreadful food like a bulldozer at a banquet, not even reading the paper.'

'How do you know?'

'We looked through the keyhole.'

'It seems a popular sport at The Dunes.'

'It was in case Edgar had to dash to the phone and call an ambulance,' Lesley said.

'So you think he might die at any moment?'

'I've always thought that.'

'Is that why you want to marry him?'

'Who said I wanted to?'

'You wouldn't come racing to your ex-husband in a state of panic if you hadn't said yes,' I suggested. 'It's not advice you want. It's relief from guilt. You require to be told that your motives are honourable. Well, I suppose it's not exactly cradle-snatching, unless you believe in second childhood. Perhaps,' I continued, warming to the theme, well aware that Joanna's presence had sharpened my audacity, 'you prefer fond memories of a man to the bother of actually living with him. It's not un-common for wives to enjoy life only as widows. It makes them the talk of the tea-parties. Or do you long to bring such womanly comforts as infidelity, neglect and absence of mind to the last hours of a great man?'

Bitter it sounded, bitterer than I meant, but uncontrollably the news had released a gush of bile and I couldn't hold my tongue, despite a warning glance from Joanna, whose eyes were otherwise fixed on Lesley with a pity that verged almost on affection, and that hurt me too.

'One of your endearing qualities, Lesley, is not knowing a thing about yourself,' I said, 'and then never listening when someone tells you what you're like. Your only policy, therefore, is to behave just as your fancy dictates without questioning it. You've decided to marry Archie – not for his money surely, it derives by all accounts from such a disgraceful source – and now you're attempting to palm off your guilt on the only man who would have been more than content to stay married to you, if you had stuck to the rules. I won't be deceived, deluded or disillusioned by you any more. It makes me not like you, when in fact I'm only hating myself. And I want to like you, just for what you are. And for the record I also happen to love Joanna.'

Even in this extremity it struck me as bizarre to make an open statement of love for someone else to a former wife who was now all set to marry another. Joanna looked up acidly. In Lesley's eyes a pair of glassy tears bulged as if I had just proposed to her. Unaccustomed to declaration, Joanna now took refuge in looking faintly offended. Everyone was reacting the wrong way. How did one break this spell? All I knew, not without feeling, was that I was handling the situation as well as the situation itself enabled a flawed, muddled and good-natured chap to cope with it. Not much comfort there.

The situation went on imperceptibly developing of its own accord. Lesley's face was preoccupied with her own emotion, the inner stir caused by someone who normally caved in to her whims rushing without apparent motive to an extreme of opposition. I sensed both Joanna's regret at the pain I had occasioned Lesley and her smug pleasure that I had admitted my love for her in the presence of the one person who might least appreciate the news. All in all it was a devilish moment which Lesley, now freely sobbing, still upright on a long sofa with the ice rattling like the chatter of teeth in her fingers, had the cunning or honesty to make far worse.

'Will you give me away?' she said in a tiny whine.

'What, tell on you? How could I? Who'd be interested?'

With a screech of outrage Lesley then let her glass slip, roll over on the carpet, ice melting into the pile, and put her head in her hands, so that her dark hair fell into the curtain of despair I had witnessed in agony when she first announced she was leaving me for a landscape gardener called Sholto, and Joanna said, reaching across the sofa to touch her, 'You mean, don't you, will Patrick give you away in marriage?'

'I haven't got a father,' cried Lesley.

'You will have, if you marry Archie,' I said, still blundering into some revenge I had no wish to take.

'Patrick,' whispered Joanna, and I heard in that intonation the door slam when she left me, as Joanna would, I heard echoing in her use of my name all those years when the person I most wanted to be with didn't want to be with me, as Joanna wouldn't, and when I looked up again from that instant vision of loss, Joanna had Lesley in her arms. As in a seated waltz their heads were swaying together against the back of my sofa, and Lesley was fighting against crying in huge intakes of breath, and Joanna, just as bad as tears, was murmuring comfort into her ear, as a lover might.

'Come on now, the two of you,' I said.

Neither of them snapped out of it, and in a flash I realised the incredible: they were ganging up on me. Whatever Lesley's motives for getting hitched to an overweight oldie with a moral record that should have earned him a life sentence, they both thought it a great idea. Joanna was on her side. They were entering a conspiracy of sentiment that excluded me. Their embrace told all. They were saying that the details could be discussed; all that mattered now was the feeling. Lesley had come to Pimlico, not for advice or rescue, but to be congratulated, to be told that her madcap nuptials were a triumph of common sense. I had totally lacked grace, not to say warmth. I had skipped round her plight with the mocking insensitivity of a schoolboy.

And then the awesome truth dawned on me. That despite everything, no, because of it, it was more than possible to love Archie – after all, I loved him. Also that age and absurdity had far less weight in the argument than the mystery of the man – or than his dignity. And that any judgment one made about the emotional condition of others, even those one knew well, was doomed to error.

I held out my hand to them.

'I'm extremely sorry, Lesley,' I said, with a glowing sense of struggling back to a path from which my ego had led me astray. 'It was most thoughtless of me. Put it down to the shock.'

Lesley took my hand. Joanna, moving slightly away from their intimacy, pretended to be tidying her hair.

'I'm glad that you wish to marry again,' I said, 'and I hope you'll be very happy. I'm devoted to the old rogue, and Joanna won't mind my saying that I love you very much. Thanks partly to Archie, I'm now saying things which I mean, and saying them as simply as possible, whereas a few weeks ago I couldn't have said them at all, let alone with anything to match this degree of sincerity and joy.'

'Isn't he a pompous old sod?' said Joanna equably.

'Is he going to marry you?' Lesley said. 'Look, why couldn't we have a double wedding? After all,' she added with a show of logic, 'I was the one who introduced him to Archie.' And she had the nerve to giggle.

'And Patrick was the one to introduce me to you,' said Joanna, sharing in the sudden fun.

'Exactly. But how did you two meet?'

'It's not very romantic.'

'Everything is.'

'He advertised for a female person between twenty and thirty with a lively interest in the arts.'

'What, in *Time Out*?'

'No, *The Times*.'

'How boring. But at least you didn't have to send him a photograph.'

'No, he insisted on seeing me in person.'

'The first time he saw me in person,' Lesley said, recovering her wits with every second of this daft dialogue, 'he asked me out to dinner.'

'I was only his secretary, so I had to wait.'

'But why are we waiting now?'

They both turned to me with the same sort of lopsided grin, their brands of coyness interchangeable as well as unspeakable, and before I had time to wonder whether my personal trap was always falling for a similar type of woman, and my private failure taking as a joke the twists and turns of feminine emotion, and my lot to be cast as a ponderous half-wit by the opposite sex, I said, 'All right, I'll take you out to dinner – mind you, I've always wanted you both to meet – on the sole condition that Lesley tells me as honestly as she can all she knows about Archie Aitken.'

'I'll tell you everything,' said Lesley. 'When haven't I?'

We dined at a so-called bistro round the corner with a blackboard on which yesterday's left-overs were chalked up as specialities and a proprietor who bridled at every request; he seemed to take eating at his establishment as a personal affront. Both women were facially enhanced by candlelight, Lesley's unadmitted grey hairs glittering like tinsel, Joanna's fair skin deepening peachily in tone. I had the almost erotic illusion of ruling a sultanate in the middle of Pimlico, in fact of being as bored as a sheikh by too much of the feminine. I had had enough for one night of their quaint collusion.

Not for the first time Lesley talked throughout the meal, but at least I had asked for it. Doughy swallows of onion soup now and then muffled her flow, as Aitken's efforts to shorten the Great War were mentioned with keen approval. For a while the challenge of spaghetti tied her discourse – of Dr Crippen's being brought to book – up in knots. Her helping of cheese sharpened the flavour of the petty larceny that had sent the *Titanic* on her way. Joanna and I listened rapt. We heard about Aitken's skill in ushering in an age more worldly than wise by prompting Lawrence to write *Lady Chatterley's Lover*. We gathered that he had rocked the throne by producing Mrs Simpson at the wrong moment.

One or two novelties, punctuated by the crack of her biscuits, crept into Lesley's testimony. I hadn't known, for instance, that the General Strike in 1926 had been initially caused by Aitken's reaction to a coal-miner who, having formed the habit of eking out the family pot by poaching game from the Aitken preserves, had been surprised one night by the fat silhouette of a capitalist bearing down on him out of the bushes and beating him off with a stick or cane. The grimy interloper, alas, had died of cardiac arrest, which according to Archie might just as easily have struck him when lying hungry in bed. But this microcosm of the class war was taken up with sullen aggression by the man's union, and a few months later the country was at a standstill, apart from Archie and a few friends driving trains to make sure London didn't run out of essential supplies like pheasants. No one knew all this.

Well, as told by Lesley, it was just possible. Her engagement had certainly improved her authority of tone, as if she now owned Archie's secrets as well as his person. Equally on the cards was another useful addition to the canon in the shape of an insight into the private motivation of Anthony Eden – or Harry Wharton, as Archie still called him. In the mid-fifties, for some reason down on his luck, Archie had the opportunity to blackmail Eden over the desirability of divulging his schoolboy past as the wet handsome hero of many a ruse or riot at Greyfriars. This had produced or contributed to that access of temper that had spilt over into international affairs and ended biliously in the chaos of Suez.

Blackmail? I quizzed Lesley about the propriety of this accusation over the third bottle of wine, ordered from the glum slouch at her request, but she refused to be drawn on detail. The Suez crisis, she said, was the turning point in Archie's life too, when he realised that every event he influenced went sour, and it might be far better for our times if he bowed out of them.

'What about Churchill?' I asked.

Lesley looked more solemn than ever, as if already at the altar. 'I think Archie should tell you himself,' she said. 'It was his finest hour.'

But of none of this, from Crippen to Churchill, was he

remotely proud, Lesley went on. He viewed it all as a record
of failure second only to what might have happened without his
interventions. Indeed Archie was now considering what steps
he might take to repair the damage, perhaps by emerging dis-
creetly from retirement and applying his influence to the current
scene. That, Lesley indicated, was why he had insisted on seeking me out, as a man in his prime with the power to give him
back a say in things. And also why he had demanded Lesley's
hand: to give him back his youth as well, to put him in touch
with the trends of modern thought. Here Lesley had the grace
to eye me and utter a short laugh. Self-deprecation was never
her strong point.

I sat back. I felt suitably sceptical; Lesley's love-life had
taught me to believe only the worst. But, taking an overall view,
it seemed incontrovertible that a sufficient number of the
occurrences of the twentieth century had sprung from Aitken's
timely presence for me to reflect, if not assume, that they could
and would have been otherwise, if he hadn't been scarred in his
schooldays by Frank Richards's presumption in turning him
into Billy Bunter. The nuances in this stroke of humour were
peculiarly English. Aitken had been taken at once seriously and
as a joke, by plenty of influential people who had a soft spot
for Greyfriars, not because he actually was Billy Bunter, but
because he looked like him, and behaved uncannily as those
topnotchers might expect Bunter to conduct himself, had he
only grown up. The nice quirk was that Aitken, retarded by all
that publicity, forced into other people's view of his image,
hadn't grown up. The boy had merely lived on in adult
form.

'By the way,' Lesley said, on the liqueurs, 'I think he wants
you to be his best man.'

'How can I be best man and give away the bride?'

'Stretch yourself,' suggested Joanna.

'I can't stand on both sides of the aisle at the same time.'

'Of course you can do it,' said Lesley, wrapping it up. 'You'll be sitting on the fence as per usual. Anyway he hasn't got any friends left. They're all dead.'

'What about Edgar?'

'Oh, heavens, no, that won't do at all. He's not telling Edgar about us.'

'Not telling him?'

'It's all part of the joke,' said Lesley ominously.

The next day I caught a train to Chichester with a copy of A. J. P. Taylor's *English History 1914–1945* in an overnight bag. It was to be an adventure on my own, though after last night the prospect of solitude appalled me. I simply felt unable to confront Archie once more until I had checked the events of his life against recorded fact. I must decide for myself what significance his patchwork of surprises held for me and how accordingly I would have to change my own life to accommodate them. Only then could I accuse him of misleading me. Or accept his fantasy as truth.

Not since 1940 had I visited the Sussex village where my father had sent me to avoid the expected bombardment of London. That timeless spring, before the skies were invaded by the smoke trails, had been tipped by the threat of war into a golden age. I had often ached to return. Now and then I had thought of renting a weekend cottage under the downs of the paradise which as a lad I had created for myself out of the revelations of sunlight coining the floors of woods, of birds breaking from a hedge in fear, of lazy schoolrooms where bullies lurked, of page after page of *The Magnet* in the warm air. These were my first hours of conscious pleasure. In that place, if anywhere, I had taken root.

Avoiding the commonplace luxury of the hotel opposite the cathedral, I found a bus to convey me westward along a road that was once sylvan. Now, forty years later, a suburb straggled amid dead elms. I should have guessed. If the centre of the village, the pub where I put up for the night, the tiny school, were all recognisable enough, though reduced in size by the shrinkage of memory, the fields that lapped them had long gone. Crescents linked the dozens of bungalows, the gardens banked with maturing shrubs. Time had destroyed space.

But, in the meadow where I had sighted an owl by daylight on my way to another dose of Greyfriars, the intervening years had unearthed the mosaic pavement of a Roman villa.

This, in perfect condition, was now enclosed within a long shed of brick and concrete to protect it from theft and weather. It was a beauty. Stunned, beyond orientation, I wandered about a once familiar place, trying to fathom the curious emotion prompted by a picture of my boyhood self unwittingly walking day after day across that hidden pavement, that pattern of history inches below my feet.

Wasn't it a bit too much like Aitken for comfort? I had pursued my affairs for almost half a century, ignorant of his existence, believing all I was told by newspaper or book or wireless about those years, while all along Aitken's influence had been working on events behind my back, so as now to put them beyond recognition. The village I thought I knew had vanished irrecoverably; so had the century I thought I knew.

As a good tourist I looked over the mosaic pavement above which my own past was buried in thin air. Obediently I parsed the inscriptions in the stone. I again thought of my feet in shilling sandals treading the solid earth that then covered these secrets. I strolled through the middle-class estate that now concealed for ever my discovery of nature. I sat down against a wall that had once been a hedge and, closing my eyes, imagined reading a scene where Bunter brought the house down by challenging the staff's assumptions as to law and order, the rules of the game of life. Bunter had always won, if by the most immoral of means, and he had always taken due punishment for it. If spared, he would win again, and for his sins he was now marrying Lesley. I laughed aloud, to find a thin man gazing at me from the narrow window of a potting-shed.

Then suddenly, as I cast around for other landmarks, it was no longer a matter of whether Aitken's confidences to me were true, but of how I was going to accept the fact that, even if I didn't favour his version, if I regretted one man's ability to make so cataclysmic a difference to the fates of so many others without their knowing, I was the kind of man – impressionably reading *The Magnet* in time of war, afflicted by an unconscious urge not to take human activities at face value, believing nobody had sole access to the truth – who longed for things to be different, for the simple reason that as they stood they were intolerable.

I moved back towards the pub. Opening time crooked a finger. Aitken had singled me out. He had trusted me. He had given me an alternative lifetime, a more comical and less conceited twentieth century than the one through which I had staggered on the fringe of boredom. Aitken had recognised, before I did, the rebel in me. Perhaps he had exploited that rebel. But at least he had brought it openly into being. I had needed the ludicrous combination of a fat man of ninety and an equally fat boy of fourteen, both apparently ageless, both beset by sin and saddled with a magnificent frailty, to show me a way forward out of a civilisation that was running backward.

In the snug I took a large gin and tonic and some crisps into a corner. I opened A. J. P. Taylor. I tried to begin reading. It was impossible. My mind resisted the printed facts, convinced that either they were false or they left too much unsaid. Behind such passages as I forced my brain to ingest towered the spectral figure of Bunter. Bunter was at once mocking the little men who jostled on the highways of society for fame, wealth, power, and edging them towards the disasters which their public efforts all too often produced for the rest of us. Even the lead-up to war in 1939 now seemed so absurd as to bear the hallmark of Bunter, and I could no longer dissociate Aitken from Churchill's jack-in-the-box emergence from the wilderness at the moment destiny required him. His pop-up into the politics of

1940 had a distinctly Bunterish air of coincidence about it, as soon as one peered between the lines of Mr Taylor's narrative. Churchill had made history, while making a dunce of it. And it all mattered far less than the mosaic.

Another gin and tonic, while I tried not to think: no longer difficult, for it now struck me that my particular brain hadn't really been made for thinking. Instead I let the joy of the mosaic, as I sat in that warm bar downing the tots and crunching the crisps, hover somewhere in the centre of my head. How beautiful it was. The mosaic appeared to suggest that, ever since making my superficial discoveries in the air above it, I had been mistaken. I had lived at all only by allowing every element in my life to be slightly wrong.

My pattern of failure stared at me. For years I had uttered opinions devoid of value – the crude fodder of the dinner table, the roughage of marital tiffs – springing as they had from a personality that diminished in vision as it increased in articulacy. I had so misjudged a woman or myself as to marry her. I had slithered into jobs or projects only if they seemed at the time to lead to better ones. I had dug my heels into the *status quo*. I had lived too long in certain houses or overstayed my welcome with certain women, just to avoid moving into an undefined future that struck terror into my soul.

As for truth, as Aitken had proved and A. J. P. Taylor confirmed, you could never gather enough facts to suppose yourself anywhere near it. Q.E.D.

I sipped a last drink as the bar emptied. Loud opinions drained out into the car-park. The landlord began mopping up. My mind, having thrown out thought as useless, was now sodden enough to come up with any definition of truth, and it so happened that it was this: that the only truth worth having was a blazing fraction of it, like the mosaic, such as the first glimpse of Bunter on a faded page of *The Magnet*, like Joanna's body naked on the carpet that one time, such as Aitken's arrest of Dr Crippen or inspiration of D. H. Lawrence, like this last-orders moment of being in tune with myself for once, yes, just a tiny bit of the truth, which flashed into the spirit, illuminating the entire world in a rather garish way, a glimpse of the sheer heaven of what life might have been meant to be. Wasn't. But never mind.

I tottered up a narrow stair to bed, glad to be drunk. I had escaped the watch I usually kept on myself. I no longer cared whether I could find anyone else to feel that all Aitken had said had a veracity far beyond the details I could see around me or, still less, read in the textbooks. The only thing that counted was that I felt better. I had got rid of my own lies, supported by the sense and silliness of my relations with the monstrous Archibald Aitken.

8

When in high spirits I reached the office at lunch-time the next day, hoping Joanna would be free for a bite in the wine-bar where I had first heard about Billy Bunter from Lesley, the girl at the switchboard told me in a gust of conspiracy that my secretary had slipped out to Fenwick's to buy a wedding dress. For a split-second I panicked. Surely my declaration hadn't been interpreted as a proposal? But I knew Joanna and Joanna knew her work-mates. Since the other girls snootily thought her a cut above them, she had been using demotic code for a spree in the Burlington Arcade to render her more worthy of attending my ex-wife's nuptials. I should have felt relief blossoming at a narrow escape from commitment. Instead a moment of excitement withered.

The ceremony in question had evidently been maturing in my brief absence. Two messages invited me to telephone Lesley and one to call Aitken. In addition a scribbled note from Lesley formally asked me to give her away on a date three weeks hence at a church that was for the moment a secret, and to abide by my promise not to breathe a word to anyone, least of all Edgar, from whom other people's happiness, it seemed, was to come as a surprise. I doubted the wisdom of this, but had no say – and actually, in my reformed state, no opinion.

Also on my desk was a memo from the Minister enquiring, without direct reference to our talks during the visit to our old school, whether I could indicate when he might expect a draft of my report. As always he was available, if needed for consultation.

It was then, still alone in the spaces of my office, that I noticed how crisp all the decisions could be. They had made themselves behind my back. Sitting briefly at Dornford Yates's desk, I resigned. In one sentence I wrote to Rickie a note conveying my sense that the task for which I had been appointed was, like so much of the graft of government, not worth doing, at least by me. The note sounded, also like government, portentous, but never mind what they thought of me; the opinions of others were as void as my own.

As I folded the letter, I gazed round at the enclave of culture – Conan Doyle's books, the Henry Moore, a flourish of the eighteenth century in the moulding, an oil of the twentieth on the wall – which I had falsely supposed was second home. But it was just the past, decoratively dead. My need of it, as a device to lock me into the present, had gone. I rubbed my fist on the envelope.

Saving up Lesley for later, I then telephoned her betrothed.

'He's in bed,' said Edgar dully.

'Who with?'

'Don't overstep the mark.'

'Haven't you been looking through the keyhole?'

'You sound as though you've been having lunch with your secretary,' Edgar said. 'If she hasn't told you what I told her when she gave me all that wine, then don't believe her when she does. Archie's money didn't come from Italy, and anyway it's all spent.'

'From Germany perhaps?'

'So she's told you. Well, Archie likes to think he started Mosley off, but if Archie did Archie changed his mind, because in fact he put a stop to him. He got all his school chums together and they whipped off to the Albert Hall in a body and shouted the place down. Haven't you seen that bump on the back of your hero's head?'

'Not recently.'

'He intercepted a rubber cosh. But it was worth it, he always says. It woke up the British people to a jackal in their midst.'

'But I thought,' I said lightly, 'that Archie had recommended Sir Oswald to his chap in Jermyn Street – you know, for the uniform.'

'That's as may be,' Edgar said. 'An evening shirt of unconventional design is a bit different from the whole country being overrun by a gang of upstarts.'

'Where did he get his money then, Edgar?'

'He hasn't got any. I should know. I look after it.'

'You mean, there's none left?' I asked, already anxious about the high cost of weddings.

Sounds of a scuffle came on to the line, a squeak bitten back, then a grunt, as of someone being coshed. 'Oh, do stop it, Archie . . .' There followed a seemly pause.

'Patrick,' said Aitken, 'I'm not equal to speaking on this confounded instrument.'

He sounded querulous. Perhaps Smedley, already suspecting that domestic changes were on their way, was being tiresome.

'Didn't you want to talk to me?'

'A little bird informs me that you won't rest until you know all about Winston. Well, this is just to say that I can tell you nothing on the telephone.'

'Could I come to see you?'

'Is that the most hilarious plan you can devise? I thought you had more spunk than that. Isn't there a convenient point to which Soames could bring me? He needs an outing. If his peaked cap isn't going at sixty miles an hour on some intriguing excursion, he starts moping and muttering threats. It'd be a kindness to a retainer.'

'What about the old school?' I proposed mischievously.

'Greyfriars?' expostulated Aitken. 'By now you should have cottoned on to the fact that it will never exist unless I found it. Frank Richards made it up – by selective theft! A wall or two from Eton, a cloister snaffled from Rugby, a pinch of Winchester snobbery, a mixed bag of classrooms as miserable as he could find, and I dare say my own school provided a few splashes of local colour. But you surely don't mean . . .?'

'It was my school too, Archie.'

A pause thronged the line with static. 'There are some things I tell nobody and expect nobody to know.' His voice went weaker, almost fearful; then it sharpened. 'Ah, well. How do you intend to use this information against me, even supposing it to be true?'

'I just thought we might visit the old place together,' I said. 'It's packed with fans of yours. They've never stopped talking about your winning the History Prize. The headmaster quivers with pride every time the great name is mentioned. He might even give us lunch.'

'Lunch?' Aitken said. 'It was always thin stew in my time. No treacle puddings or sausages or stuff like that. My father used to try claiming back a proportion of the fees because I ate so much in the hols.'

'All has changed,' I lied. 'They want to put up a memorial to you.'

'But I'm not dead as far as I know.'

'Well, a plaque then.'

'That will please Lesley. Hooray, I'll tell her tonight when everyone's gone to bed. What do you say to tomorrow?'

'I'll try for it.'

The implications of this scheme had no time to reach me before Joanna swanned into the office with her normal togs in a plastic bag. 'Dressed to kill!' she said, swirling on the carpet woven by a pupil of Burne-Jones. Her dress, boldly patterned, bore a disconcerting resemblance to a mosaic. Her manner, equally bold, suggested that since Lesley's announcement our relations had passed to a new level, perhaps a higher one. With an effort I stopped thinking and peered for a proper reaction into the recently discovered areas where I thought my feelings were. Joanna looked quite beautiful. I believed her to be very nice. We had much in common, including or apart from Bunter.

'You look as if you're about to ask me to marry you,' said Joanna.

'I might at that.'

'I would have to say no,' she said. 'There being three conditions which you can't meet.'

'Name those conditions.'

'You'd have to throw in this stuffy job.'

I flipped the envelope at her. 'Next?'

'You couldn't go on living in that awful house.'

'It's my wedding present to my ex-wife. She'll need a base in London. Not even someone I once married could be expected to spend her whole time with Archie. The third?'

Joanna frowned. 'You have to find a way of telling more people about Billy Bunter, and that's the worst of the lot, because for ages nobody'll believe you, and not being believed, having twits laugh up their sleeves at you, being recognised on the street as an old crank with a bee in your bonnet so big that no wonder you've got a swollen head, will mean that you won't survive at all without the help of someone who loves you as much as I do, and I'm only your secretary.'

I looked at her. She was crying. Her mosaic already looked familiar, almost second-hand. It had taken the shape of her body, somehow revealing the self beneath it. All this sentiment felt slippery.

'I suppose I could try to write a book,' I said as evenly as possible. 'It would be better than a report on the state of culture, because it would, in fact, be culture. Anyway, in your flat, there's no room to do much more than sit hunched over a small sheet of paper.'

'As in the lav,' she said, gurgling in an effort to drown tears.

'Well, then, I accept your proposal,' I said hurriedly. 'Now, Miss Feathers, let's get down to it. There's a lot of clearing up to be done here before we attend the wedding.'

All night I affected to regret my scheme to get Bunter back to school, while secretly relishing it. It had possibilities more explosive than any earlier act of mine except getting married, or any future one except marrying again. I had alerted Dr Trench to our visit without mentioning names, for I expected recognition to be immediate. It was not. Our visit hung fire. The headmaster concealed his bafflement by conducting a post-mortem on the Minister's speech, which he saw as a much-needed fillip for the morale of the school. Meanwhile Archie, showing his senility, sank into a chair and drained his inch of Amontillado at a gulp. I awaited the promised arrival of Pocock to put matters right.

Throughout lunch at the top table Archie hardly spoke. The week's stew seemed thinner than ever. There was no sign of Pocock. The boys rudely ignored the staff and the staff politely ignored Aitken. I had somehow left it too late to make a persuasive announcement. It must have been a saddening moment for a man who had not only won a prize, but achieved a proxy notoriety merely by attending this school. But why was I being so feeble? And Aitken too? Was it simply because we had been educated in these glum environs that neither of us could own up to his being Bunter?

Then a voice shouted, 'Here I am at last, why won't you laddies learn how to avoid detention, so that I won't be always bloody late for my mess of pottage?' and Pocock shambled up the dining-hall, waving a hand to his favourites, and took his seat on an ample section of bench next to Aitken.

While I continued to give ear to the headmaster's admiration for Rickie Rathbone, the geography master slurped stew into the middle of his beard and snatched the final slice of bread which Aitken was eyeing. Pasting a glob of marge on it, he

folded it without finesse and forced it into his system with his
fist. Then he turned to his neighbour.

'What did you say your name was?' he said.

'What?' snapped Aitken.

'I only asked you who you were.'

'Do you want the truth or the lie?'

'Try me on the lie,' said Pocock. 'It stands a chance of being
more interesting.'

'I'm Billy Bunter,' said Aitken.

Pocock swivelled on the bench and with a burning hostility
inspected the impostor at his side. It was evident that he thought
sacrilege had been committed. His eyes slowly took in the steel-
rimmed glasses, the jowls and chins and cheeks that generously
concealed the structure of Aitken's face, the small eyes that
were now prickling with pent-up annoyance, the squiff of hair
that licked off the bald dome. Without hurrying, as if deceler-
ated by shock, Pocock lowered his gaze to the oddly brief chest
that prepared the way for the stomach below it, the rotundity
that swelled against the edge of the table and curved down into
the vast waistband of Aitken's trousers. He peered at legs that
looked more like torsos than limbs. And then he said, 'Christ!'

'Not exactly,' said Aitken.

From Pocock's earlier loud evidence I knew that he thought
Bunter was the man for him, but perhaps only because he didn't
exist. Here was a schoolmaster of flesh and blood facing a myth,
a glutton meeting his god. For a moment Pocock sat stunned
in front of his pupils, mouthing his amazement without a word.
The whole of geography vanished into the void. He could deny
no longer the reality of a legend that had enraptured him only
when it wasn't literal. His life had fed on fiction. He wanted no
fact. Pocock stood up with his hand to his head, the bench
squeaked under him, a boy drew near with a plate bearing a
few portions of rapidly cooling jam sponge, and he said, 'Well,
cripes, I don't know what's wrong, but by my book you've
snuffed it, when was it, 1957, so I suppose your clever friend

there' – looking fiercely at me – 'can come up with the answer.'

'I doubt it, because I'm the only answer,' Aitken said. 'Here I am. Fairly pleased to be back here, if you'd only pipe down for a moment. I never did claim that History Prize, you know. A guinea in those days, or a book. Who'd want the book? That guinea, taking inflation into account, must be worth a lot more than this lunch. I've never eaten worse, except when I was here. You can't learn history on rations like these. What the boys need isn't a fat fake, but a square meal.'

'Who's calling who names?' demanded Pocock, swelling visibly.

'A man who was on good terms with Mr Churchill hardly needs the patronage of the staff of his old school.'

Aitken had raised his voice. The remark had been heard without undue interest by a forward section of the boys. The headmaster rose passively to intervene.

'A correction,' he said. 'Mr Churchill wasn't here, I think. He went to Harrow, as I understand.'

'And none too hot on the academic stakes,' said Pocock belligerently.

Sensing a touch of dissension on the platform, the school had quietened. Sticky cutlery being cleared away faded into the background. Pocock uttered a brutal laugh.

'Tell them about Churchill, Archie,' I said, fearing that this might be my one chance of winkling the story out of him.

'This caveman thinks he knows the text,' Aitken said.

'What text?' said Pocock, bridling.

'*The Magnet*, is there another?'

'God, I know it backwards.'

'Who was Snoop? Inform your ignorant pupils who Snoop was.'

'Sidney James Snoop,' said Pocock, even more on his mettle after the veiled insults, 'was a lazy aggressive lad, but cowardly, always trying to cash in on the fame of his superiors while – like the rest of the pack at Greyfriars – asserting his own superiority.'

'Just so,' said Aitken in a whisper, then loudly, his cross voice echoing down the hall: 'Randolph Churchill. A sneak if ever there was one, who somehow got hold of the rumour in the late thirties – heaven knows how, because I was the last person to want exposure on any account – that I was a power behind the throne, a king-maker or breaker, who might know where and how to put in a good word for his venerable pa, who was as far out in the wilderness as I always myself wanted to be. Anyway Randolph routed me out, said with some pride that he was Snoop and congratulated me on being Bunter – drunk, of course, but never mind, some of the world's greatest decisions have depended on taking too much of what we're not supposed to have at all. And would I help his father get back into harness, implying with a leer of conspiracy that this would be my special way of winning the war which had just broken out. That's all that happened.'

'Never met Churchill at all, did you?' queried Pocock cockily.

'I didn't say that. Of course Randolph wheeled me into the presence. It was evident from the first not only that Winston knew all about Bunter, but that we had a lot in common. We stared, as it were, into the mirror of each other. He put on weight at the very sight of me. But the trouble was that he had for-gotten his values. In the misery of being out of power Harrow had died in his bones. He hadn't remembered what Greyfriars taught us – that we privileged few were the backbone of our island race, the protectors of its long heritage, the guardians of our culture, and also that the way of bringing the best out of the rest of the British was to treat them as dirt to patronise them with lofty oratory, to crush them with the knowledge that you needed their help.

'It was a moment of total understanding. If in a different way, I was as famous as he was. A household name. There was a certain rivalry. But he actually wanted to be a hero, while my only desire was to deflect other people's interest in turning me into one. It felt at that electric moment that I was passing power into his hands. My very presence in his room, introduced by his only son, stirred the man to eloquence and the will to do battle. At a time of despair Churchill saw reflected in me all the good things, the things worth fighting for, which for so long had lain low in our people – their grandeur of vision, their love of food and drink, the nobility of their aspirations, their urge to explore beyond the known world, their blood, toil, tears and sweat, if you like – and he had the wit to respond to the challenge. Of course, I had nothing to do with the actual politics that enabled him suddenly to erupt upon the front bench of life itself. But I gave him his moment – yes, thanks to the dreadful Snoop, I gave him his moment. And he snatched it. He wallowed in it. He excelled himself, he surpassed everyone else, he broke every record of altruistic egoism. And he never saw me again. You may be forgiven for thinking it hardly a coincidence that *The Magnet*, from no shortage of readers, ceased publication in 1940, the very year of Churchill's most potent influence. He had it suppressed, of course. I had served my turn. Men are never grateful to those who help them. As for Randolph, he later vanished of his own free will into a butt of malmsey.'

It was a moving and modest testament, as credible as any to which Aitken had given voice in my presence. The fact that rage and affront had prompted so public a declaration of one of his secrets lent it more verisimilitude than perhaps it deserved. But the hush which the story produced was colossal. Even the boys seemed to sense that matters of moment were afoot onstage. Their usual racket sounded as faraway as an echo of Greyfriars on best behaviour.

'I never heard the likes of this,' said Pocock in a deflated whisper.

'It's certainly a most interesting gloss,' murmured Dr Trench.

With a snort Aitken stood sharply up, rocking the bench on which sat several members of staff, their brains still struggling to correct his essay in the surreal. Pocock, his eyes now gleam-

ing with the gratitude of a convert, hurried to help him, but
Aitken waved all assistance aside and made off. 'Home, Patrick,'
he cried, as he sped down the corridors looking for exits.
Pocock followed at an eager trot. The headmaster danced at-
tendance at his heels, with invitations to address the school on
any subject of his choice, select any book for his history prize,
allow a memorial to be erected to his fictional past. But the
moment had gone. Bustling out, thrusting aside the blandishments of men who had seen the light too late, Aitken had turned
against his Alma Mater. He bulged with increasing majesty at
every step. With more dignity and less haste than yesterday the
Minister had brought to his departure, the old man swept out
of the school with a grizzled farewell and tumbled into the old
grey Wolseley, where Soames, a sandwich curling in his hand,
had nodded off at the wheel. 'Home, Soames,' said Aitken. He
awoke with a gurgle, slapped on his cap, and skidding off spat
gravel at the party on the steps.

Aitken relaxed, half closing his eyes. It was an unfair moment
for me to strike. 'Were you really living on Hitler's money in
those days?' I asked.

'Oh, you've been listening to Edgar. Well, he has an entirely
different version of events. Most people do. And don't forget
he was a small boy at the time.'

'So was I.'

'Well then,' said Aitken comfortably, 'you don't know either
then, do you? I don't suppose anyone ever will.'

I let a suburb pass. Then I said, 'I liked your Churchill story
very much.'

'Yes, wasn't it a stroke of luck?'

'Are you suggesting yet again that without your influence
events might have panned out otherwise?'

'It always comes down to one man in the end,' Aitken said.
'It didn't have to be me. It so happens that it was Winston. I
merely gave all the help I could, as did the entire nation.'

'But it was the spirit of Greyfriars that won the war?'

'I did have to remind him of the standards that made it worth fighting.'

'I might not be here, then, if it weren't for you?'

'Nor might I.'

'But . . .'

We were through another suburb and moving into more central districts.

'Don't worry, old son,' said Aitken, his eyes closed. 'I wouldn't have objected to being your father, if only I could have found someone decent to marry.'

9

The wedding was fixed for three weeks hence and I imagined that Aitken, having cast me as his scribe, might wish to entertain the remnants of his bachelorhood by plugging the lacunae in my knowledge of his effect on our times or, rather, of his deception of history, so that he could enter upon married bliss with a clear conscience. He would want to clinch his story.

My resignation, brusquely accepted by the Minister, was now morally in force, even if in theory I had a month to work. I therefore had few qualms over making my time available, though rather more about using up my savings on train journeys to Ashford or, worse, on further trips to the continent. I had discovered at least one thing about the truth: it cost as much money as effort to arrive at it. Thus, while in the office Joanna and I began to sift the masses of paper, which perhaps like marriage led to nothing while being hard to ditch, I awaited the call from The Dunes. And felt a juvenile panic about the prospect, as if Aitken were now my only chance of making good.

On the third day my tailor, whose concept of respect for a customer had caused him never to ring me, telephoned to say that, as requested, he had visited Littlestone-on-Sea to measure Mr A. Aitken for the suit I had asked him to accept, and would it now be in order to commence cutting the cloth? My heart sank, as would my resources. But there was no choice. Archie's whim was law.

The next morning brought a letter from Fortnum & Mason, not signed by the Greyfriars old boy who had made 226 not out but with a commercial scribble, confirming their pleasure in supplying the order which Mr Aitken had placed on my behalf for a wedding breakfast for one hundred guests. This, as they understood the commission, was to be delivered to Littlestone-on-Sea, Kent, with the utmost discretion on the date specified, as the party was to be a surprise for persons unnamed. It was certainly a surprise to me, forcing me at once to take the rare risk of contacting my bank manager before replying to the effect that I would let them know the number of guests later, but it might be as few as twenty. Who could Archie possibly ask? As Lesley had sepulchrally pointed out, all his chums were dead.

However, these intrusions gave me the excuse for a call to The Dunes, to demand if not an explanation at least an audience. I steeled my nerve for the usual battle of wits with Edgar, but after a long interval suggesting demise, in which case I would be in pocket, Soames picked up and pretended, amiably enough, not to know who I was. There was nobody there, he said, disproving this fact by that very statement. All right, then, Soames went on, he was in sole charge, with orders not to admit anyone to the house or say more than he had said already.

In the nick of time I recalled an earlier exchange between this vassal and his employer. 'Come on, Soames,' I said, 'don't forget your cut in the proceeds – where is everybody?' He then grudgingly admitted that he had seen off a party of three at Gatwick Airport only this morning and they weren't due back for a fortnight. At once, as Joanna tore up a further batch of muddled evidence intended for my now abandoned report, I telephoned Lesley, whose answering service informed me that she had gone abroad.

I contemplated, indeed discussed with Joanna, a night raid

on The Dunes, if only to rescue the papers from the heavy hand of Soames. Until then I hadn't realised how keen I was to get at the documentary proof which Aitken had promised me: it might prove nothing, of course, except that forgery was an art, but I thought of it as my birthright. I positively didn't want it guarded by the indolence of Soames in order to be doctored by Aitken's bride-to-be when she tottered back from her pre-marital honeymoon. In any case there was a complete collection of *The Magnet* to be saved. It might, properly sold, foot some of my bills. Joanna, however, unsportingly considered these pro-posals unethical. They were the sort of thing Bunter might do. 'But you're not Bunter, are you?' she said possessively, tossing a pamphlet on avant-garde poetry into the wastepaper basket. 'You're my Patrick.'

By the second post, none too soon, arrived a letter from Aitken posted in the Canary Islands. He offered no explanation of his presence in tourist territory, no excuse for not explaining it or for leaving me in the lurch, and no clue to the company he was keeping. His scribble was merely a set of instructions hidden behind a code so crude that I hoped Edgar hadn't taken it anywhere near a boiling kettle on the way to the letter-box. A brown spot on the paper, which in that climate could hardly be rain, suggested it had been penned in the environs of sherry. So did the tone. I was to see to it that the occasion of which we had spoken would shame neither him nor the other interested party. He hoped I would seek the advice of the fellow in charge of the ecclesiastical edifice we had avoided on our way to lunch abroad, who was in the know and had the best interests at heart of yours truly, Archibald Aitken. The letter had all the signs of a good dinner in it, even on it. The envelope was yellowed by paella.

At this point I gave up resisting. There was again no choice. If I cared for Lesley, still more if I loved Aitken, I had to pursue the arrangements for their wedding to the last moment when the bridegroom fingered the ring out of a waistcoat pocket

paid for by me and the bride materialised dreamlike in a Gothic
porch belonging temporally to a cleric whom I had been urged
in schoolboy circumlocution to meet. If I were the victim of a
conspiracy masterminded from foreign parts, Joanna proved
unmistakably that she was a homely part of it by the scale of
her laughter at my predicament. One graceless complaint at the
way I was being manipulated, and she accused me of being
against the marriage. One tiny protest at their absence, and she
berated me for denying how happy happiness could be. They
were having a good time; I envied them: that was the received
wisdom in the office, as Joanna ripped up paragraphs that had
taken me nights to draft.

But Archie's word was my bond, so I went alone on that
pilgrimage by train and bus to confront the vicar. I should have
guessed he wouldn't be at the vicarage; nobody these days was
in his rightful place. With an air of pity his wife directed me to
the church next door ('you can't miss it') and there at the altar,
engaged in silent prayer, knelt the man himself. Rising at last
to his feet, he was a lofty vague figure who seemed to levitate
along the flags in his cassock towards a distant vision – perhaps
of Archie, to judge by the light in his eyes when I mentioned
the name. He beckoned me into the vestry.

'Mr Aitken has been for so long devoted to the welfare of this
church,' he said to my astonishment, 'that, on grounds of his
age, I have made an exception in wedding him to a divorced
woman. In any case the lady tells me that her former marriage
meant so little to her that it would be wrong to recognise it.
So you're the best man, Mr Weymouth?'

'The best man doesn't always win,' I said, with an itch both
to tease the vicar and to deal with Lesley later, 'I'm also my
ex-wife's father, as it were. I shall be giving her away. Is that
irregular?'

'In our eyes Mr Aitken can do no wrong,' he said. 'You're a
friend. Have you heard him reading the lesson? It's so fresh
that he might just have made it up. A revelation.'

'He has certainly been a revelation to me.'

'And so free with his fortune. I'm sure that you as a friend have plenty of reason to commend his generosity.'

'Not a great deal.'

'No, you wouldn't,' said the vicar. 'He prefers it not to be known. Thanks embarrass him. That's why we can't often persuade him to join us in worship. My dear wife naturally has no money. We live on the precious little I earn. Our luxuries are all due to Mr Aitken. Richly given, piously enjoyed. Had she known, my wife would have asked you to tea.'

All this sounded oddly cold, with more than enough undertones to set me thinking. I wondered if it was to experience these subterranean tremors of yet another of his selves that Archie had sent me to the vicar. There was no doubt that they shifted yet again my view of the old scoundrel, now apparently a saint. 'Well, he's an unusual man,' I said, in the hope of peering further into Archie's spiritual depths.

'Indeed,' said the vicar. 'Not many people know that he once had a premonition of the second coming, and that's not as blasphemous as it sounds.' He lowered his voice, as if the divine ear had access to the vestry. 'It was Mr Aitken, you know, who inspired the then Archbishop of Canterbury, Dr Lang, to compel King Edward VIII to abdicate. Mr Aitken said that for him it was a matter of conscience . . .' I waited for the news that Archie had felt his usual species of innocent guilt over the trick he had played on society by conjuring forth Mrs Simpson. 'Rightly so,' the vicar went on. 'His Majesty wanted to marry a divorced woman.'

This was too much. 'Sauce for the goose?' I said, to point the inconsistency.

The vicar stared at me with remote intelligence. 'Mr Aitken always gives us a goose for Christmas,' he replied. 'A finer flavour than turkey, he claims. There's a good deal of fat on it, though.'

'Like him.'

'Who cannot like him? I prefer only to marry people I like.'

'Like your wife.' The urge to deflate this parson, and Archie's stories, and Lesley's betrayal, was not to be resisted.

'Have you met my dear wife?'

'She told me where to find you.'

'We must repair that omission,' said the vicar. 'Let me ask you to tea.'

Over tea, to my shock, I heard more of Aitken's sterling work for the church. We ate fish-paste sandwiches which the vicar's wife coyly stated were dressed crab, a recent gift from Aitken. We cut into a madeira cake which Soames had baked that morning on kindly instructions from his master, who was abroad on business; printed scraps of the confectioner's paper still adhered to its crumby crust. But these were small fibs. The truth was larger. Aitken had paid for the belfry to be restored. He had endowed a choir-stall. His generosity had enabled a group of youngsters – actually from Mr Smedley's youth club in Folkestone – to take the ferry and compare home-grown religion with the more garish product across the Channel. On Mr Aitken's behalf – he was ill, poor soul, much of the time – Mr Smedley often tested out the reconditioned bells by ringing them and sat in the choir-stall to sing its praises. It was a pity that Mr Aitken himself was rarely able to enjoy the outward show of his beneficence.

As I listened to these sweet-natured reflections on the unholy use to which Smedley had been putting his employer's possibly ill-gotten resources, I debated how much Aitken was gravitating to marriage only to order his finances (no, keep his money) and to rid his last moments of life of the hangers-on (no, just Edgar) who had bedevilled it for years. Was Lesley the woman to bring him a modicum of peace? Hardly. But at least she knew how to be in love with someone, especially if he were down. Archie hadn't long to go. So, with a man of just on ninety, she would want to create time for him, expand opportunity for him, live daily on the edge of risk.

I knew her so well. I knew the extreme of optimism which she brought to love. Having decided it for herself, she would make a new man of Archie at his last gasp, reform the old lag, hustle him into breaking every record of longevity, force him to redound to her credit, bring him his merited fame as the artist whose canvas was life, the politician who governed us all by never going into politics, the legislator it was now time to acknowledge, the rebel who held the stage from behind the scenes, the puppet-master we would love if only we knew who was pulling the strings, the ultimate scamp.

Oh, yes, oh, yes – that, of course, was why Lesley had leapt at this terminal challenge. It was to ensure that only she would be in a position to say, at a party that lacked life, when an occasion needed humour, if our century came up at table for dissection, when hope ran out and everyone was quarrelling and nobody knew where next to turn for relief or a joke or some new fad to believe in, that she was married to Billy Bunter. Collapse of party.

Yet I returned to London with a hazy sense that for the past quarter of a century, after whatever disaster had struck him silent at the time of Suez, Aitken had turned for help to the values of the spirit. He had lived off the fat of his conscience. He had opted out of reality into the supernatural. That was an area unknown to me. It would need to be discussed, if he ever dragged his pampered bones out of the fleshpots of the Canary Islands.

In the event Aitken failed to return until the eve of his wedding, by which time I was as nervous as a bridegroom. I at once dashed down to The Dunes in the hope of luring him into the sozzled indiscretions of a stag party, even if it had to include Edgar, but the mood in the house was as alien to revelation as it was hostile to festivity. Aitken was in tetchy spirits, Smedley at his most protective. Perhaps the little man's intuitions already feared loss. Anyway he declined to bring up some wine from the cellar on the grounds that there was nothing to celebrate. It became painfully evident that he wasn't in the know.

'There must be a drink in the house, Edgar,' I said.

'What for?'

'I'm thirsty.'

'You're addicted, you mean,' Edgar said. 'Soames will be serving you quite enough water with your supper.'

To this no answer sprang to mind. Nor was there a positive response to my suggestion that this might be a quiet moment for me to cast a glance at the archive, wherever it was.

'Of course I know where it is,' Edgar said. 'It's behind all the old *Magnet*s in the study. All locked up, for obvious reasons. Tight security here.' He glanced at me smugly. 'It so happens I've mislaid the key.'

'Oh, butter-fingers,' Soames said, bringing in a plate of cheese-straws that looked disconcertingly like the left-overs from a wedding.

Without a word Aitken began to wolf them. Now and then his mouth shaped a capacious yawn as though he had already been married several years. It was probably a ruse with a hidden purpose. Once indeed, from the corner of my eye, I caught what I thought was a wink. Talk, even at supper which consisted of a flan tasting of fish-paste and gooseberries that resembled stewed eyeballs, kept coming to a standstill. Nobody seemed anxious to reminisce about their sojourn in the tropics. More than once, to keep my end up, I regretted Edgar's loss of the key, and only when he slipped out with ill grace to pretend to search for it did Aitken briefly perk up and whisper, 'Bear with me if I appear to have a stroke at the psychological moment. I've got ghastly nerves about tomorrow, and it's my only way of putting him off the scent.'

When it came, Aitken's seizure was a non-vintage affair, carried off so poorly that for a few seconds he seemed really ill. Eyes rolled, throat choked, hands fluttered in a cartoon of demise, as Soames with sullen indifference bore him away in the wheelchair. As usual, no one reappeared to clear the table or entertain the guest. Wondering how on earth, with what further absurdity, we would all manage to struggle through the next twenty-four hours, I tried the study door – locked – and felt my way to bed.

The day of the nuptials dawned bleak and wet. A species of breakfast was served. Nowhere on view were the platefuls of sizzling protest described by Lesley. Edgar busied himself about the house, perhaps searching for keys. Soames roamed the drab rooms with a dustpan and brush. I brooded over the secrets I was missing behind the locked door and awaited with anxiety the morning's first horror, the arrival of a Fortnum's van stuffed with victuals, the harbinger of married bliss, herald of despair for Edgar and penury for me. I wondered if Archie, who now waddled downstairs looking falsely convalescent, had yet sampled Lesley's cuisine. She cooked as she made love: lots of it, you could say, but too much effort chasing too little savour.

When the van drew up in a squall shortly before eleven, Edgar began without protest or even question to help the well-spoken youth unload the hampers. I waited jumpily for the penny to drop or for Aitken to drop it with a clang. But no banns were published. Aitken merely said, with a timid show of bravado, what fun it was to be once again giving luncheon parties for his friends – and all thanks to me! Edgar, flapping the arms of his suit round a case of claret, looked daggers at the hurrying sky, while I pondered my unenviable role as founder of the feast. It seemed almost fair to be so cast; after all, I had already paid a handsome deposit after allowing my parsimony to make a few changes in the proposed menu. But the point I had failed to realise was that as general benefactor, furnishing both the food and the wife, I was expected to convey to Edgar how these two forms of sustenance were linked. Every time I squeezed past Aitken in the passage he hissed such unnerving asides as 'Have you done it yet?' and 'Does he know?'

I felt badly let down. It seemed more reasonable that the

man who had popped the question should provide the answer, however explosive the effect on Smedley. I began to dislike Edgar for not knowing, then to avoid him so that he wouldn't know. His presence grew in my mind as threateningly large as his suits. Yet he spoke not a word. He gazed funereally at the baked meats heaped on huge platters, the pyramids of prawn vol-au-vents, the smoked salmon overlapping the dishes in garish swathes, taking every surprise in his stride as the type of behaviour to be expected of Archie at his worst. He showed no interest in what guests would be attending this costly feast. He behaved with the impeccable manners of someone who wasn't there at all.

Noon came and went. Archie vanished heavily upstairs. Rain lightly fell. The young man from Fortnum's, as urbane as he was urban, made comments on the weather ('It's a lovely day for it, sir') that had the inaccuracy of a forecast. Edgar nodded. The young man ventured a remark on country life, as if dictating a nature note. Edgar nodded again. Even Soames, also presumably in the dark, seemed to have lost the will to survive in the midst of an inexplicable banquet not prepared by him for guests who never appeared. Silver glittered leadenly on the table. Plates gaped like yawns. We were all at a loss, awaiting an event for which I was being held responsible.

Within a few minutes, whether I spoke or not, a number of arrivals would precipitate that event. Cars would start wondering where to park. Lesley, driving cross-country from Haslemere, was due at any moment, if not delayed by her temperament. Joanna, at my further expense, had promised to take a taxi from Ashford. A cassock must soon bustle down the drive to give the game away. Yet as we stood there at odds surveying with mute distaste the plunder of farm and ocean, only Edgar Smedley seemed to matter. He stood hurt and fidgety, his fingers twiddling at the table edge as though critical of its craftsmanship, with the air of a still small boy who had devoted his life to anticipating the tragedy about to befall him. And I simply couldn't tell him the news. I felt too much of his pain.

I thought I heard the first car, then a knock at the front door, but – grumbling down the stairs, tapping his stick – it was only Aitken making his sluggish way through the house towards us. He must say something now, I decided. He would have to speak out. I willed it. Edgar, statuesque in his ridiculous wraps, a stone-cold version of his never very warm self, tensed. And into the room, shuffling, his face distorted in equal measure by age and embarrassment, gazing for a response out of the tiny eyes behind the magnifying gleam of the glasses, stepped Billy Bunter.

He halted inside the door, arms hanging loose, small feet tight together, showing off his suit. It was the suit he had tricked me into buying. The jacket was single-breasted and black and it fitted at a stretch over a waistcoat that bulged into the room. The trousers had lost their creases by the mere act of his putting them on. Encasing his thighs and narrowing to the ankles, they were of a singularly loud black and white check, a pattern in which few would choose to get married or, for that matter, attend school. A bow-tie of some flamboyance jutted almost unseen beneath the folds of his chin. He was supporting this huge caricature on Sir Oswald Mosley's stick. In every sartorial detail, in his pride, in his perplexed but still hopeful stance, expectation of approval mingling with conviction that his gesture would fail, in the air of mischief he conveyed, in his eager attempt to be himself, the man was the image of Bunter. No, more, the apotheosis of Bunter. Indeed a character passing well beyond Bunter into realms of his own.

With a flashy smile the youth from Fortnum's, recognising size rather than identity, wished this phenomenon good morning. I stared at my very old friend, unspeakably moved by his silliness. And with a whimper Edgar, losing control of his legs, shifted as if to assault the bridegroom, somehow dodged him, brushing past by a whisker, and left the room. A spasmodic choke, almost a cough, could be heard at odd intervals hastening upstairs.

Without more ado the party broke over us. So did the weather. Rain sluiced into the garden. Cars swished to the front door blinded by water. I gazed out for the dripping figure of A. J. P. Taylor or a Trevor-Roper soaked to the skin, both invited by me, both absent from the scene; history, so obviously in the making, no longer mattered to them. The rooftops drummed and tingled. I hurried out to rescue the half-drowned vicar who had got a golosh sunk in the lawn. Entangled in an umbrella blown inside-out, the headmaster of our old school crunched up the drive, wetly followed by Terry Pocock in a plastic mac. Not far away the sound of the sea pounded on the shore beneath the hustle of rain.

I kept an eye open for the who's who of noted widows I had also asked, in the hope that the quality of the champagne would induce them to confirm Archie's influence with their late husbands. No Lady Mosley stepped with elegance out of a cab, the Countess of Avon had forgotten the date, Mrs T. S. Eliot was otherwise engaged, but here was my former rival Sholto Pritchard dashing out of the weather, much as he had entered my married life, to pour cold water over me, and behind him, to my surprise, Cyril Venner plodded with the same amiable indifference to the heavens opening as he brought to the welfare of his pupils. A dozen members of a Billy Bunter fan-club I had run down clamoured for their waterproofs in a hired coach. To boost the numbers Witherby, the shrink who had vouched for Aitken's sanity, had driven down a few of the members of my club who had recognised Aitken as his fictional self. Having paused at pubs, they now roistered into the house in search of refreshment.

Aitken's big hall had begun to look small with guests. The young man from Fortnum's was instantly generous with his firm's wine. Perhaps he didn't know who was paying for it. On the windows the storm rattled like the gossip within. I sipped my own overpriced fizz. There was no sign of Edgar, and by now I was really anxious to see him; to enjoy not his agony or rage, but the familiarity of his presence. There was no sign of Joanna either. Her absence emptied the faces of the guests into futile gaiety. A glimpse of her would make the fun cohere, the happiness arrive. In my suit Aitken was politely focused on the ludicrous Pritchard, as though seeking last-minute advice on human relationships. Very soon, if Lesley didn't appear, this veteran suitor would be conjuring snaps of the past out of his back pocket. Mouths closed over my prawns. Lips lapped up my bank account. The persistent truancy of the women, at well after one o'clock, was now mounting into a massive protest against male assumptions. A great occasion had teetered to the brink of low farce.

I might have guessed that on this of all days fate would decree an entrance, stagier than good taste might allow. Their coming was announced by a screech from outside, gathering everyone at the windows to witness it. The picture was of two women dancing in the rain. Out there, bobbing wetly up and down in white against the uniform grey of the weather swirling in from the sea, the two quite unrecognisable people I knew best were executing an attempt to fight their way through the downpour, arm in arm, their nicely shod legs jumping in and out of the puddles on the drive, with no more than an academic effort to reach the cover of the house, where they must have known we were all sick to death of waiting for them. They were enjoying every second of their own slow motion; for them time was stopping, as if to photograph their antics. It was, despite my irritation, a view of happiness which, standing stock still alone among the guests, I would be unlikely to forget or share.

To raucous cheers Aitken hugged his bride. I kissed Joanna unnoticed. As the smoked salmon slipped down and teeth were rinsed in champagne, everyone wanted to know the story. Lesley's car had broken down a short while before Joanna's taxi took the same lane through the marsh, hence the rescue, and the cab driver had refused to risk the floods at the gate, thus the dance up the drive. It made sense. But it had still been un-shareable, that sight, a moment almost more solemn than the one soon to come in the church.

Smedley did not appear before we tumbled into anyone's old car and made off up the road. There was little dignity in our approach to this solemn occasion. To escape the rain the guests jammed the south door, then fanned out within the church, shaking their outdoor clothes over the font. Looking back to glimpse Lesley waiting alone under the drips of a yew, I realised that I had the ring in my pocket. This produced an exquisite dilemma; my loyalties, like my duty, lay both outside and in. I had to make a choice between alternatives not yet united. Blinded by the rain I stumbled over the tussocky grass of the graves to Lesley and kissed her.

'Why aren't we getting married?' she whispered.

At the organ the vicar's wife launched the opening number and the show began. As Archie stood in his outfit dwarfing Lesley in her chaste white, the absence of any chorus of relatives seated formidably on opposite sides of the aisle struck me as touching. They were both alone in the world; there was nobody left to expect too much of them. Now and then, during a sparkling account of 'God moves in a mysterious way' by the club deputation and the body of fans, Archie looked in brief concern over his shoulder as if anticipating arrest, but Edgar was still sulking somewhere by himself. I held Joanna's hand; her grip tightened as the vows deepened.

At the most unctuous moment of the service, when the vicar was bent laboriously over the couple and Archie was doing his best to force the ring on to Lesley's finger while memorising the next phrase to repeat, an iron clack from the south door echoed in the vault. I resisted the temptation to turn. I knew what I would see. Resentment had been overpowered by curiosity. Edgar was here.

The ritual moved on, compelling the usual sort of reflection of the nature of marriage: how the need for it stalked one with animal cunning, then pounced; how it seemed, also like a wild beast, both pointless and powerful – there was no call to succumb, yet marriage sprang from an atavistic desire to hide away from life, while masquerading as a challenge; how tender an institution the words of the service made it sound, whereas all it provided was a decent home for one's aggressions; how, when it came to it, marriage was an event, perhaps *the* event unless you happened to be Aitken, in a life on which all too few events obtruded. By now my hand, trapped by Joanna, felt hot and numb, and it was then, intensifying the effect of theatre, just as the vicar was closing the doors on Archie's ninety years of freedom with the words 'Those whom God hath joined together let no man put asunder', that one bell tolled in the tower behind us. It had an odd irregular rhythm. A second or two thrilled between each stroke. Then after a few notes of doom, as if a trick of time had overlapped the wedding with a funeral, an almost strangled single clang hung thinly in the air.

The vicar's face, unwilling to interrupt the spell he was casting, trembled for a moment, perplexed, then, as the bell expired on a soft reverberation, nodded sharply to his wife at the organ. She slid along the stool, swung her sturdy legs over it with gymnastic speed and hastened to the west of the church, where a baize curtain screened from view the chamber beneath the belfry. As it fell stagily back into place behind her, not a scream but a moan of fright arose from the base of the tower, muffled by fabric settling into its folds. And in mid-sentence, the committal words cut short by his wife's alarm, the vicar, surplice swirling, pushing without ceremony between the almost lawfully wedded couple, strode to the back of the nave, Archie hobbling behind him on his stick, and tore back the curtain on its runners.

The scene thus revealed was one of inefficient tragedy that only in retrospect verged on the comic. Edgar Smedley was lazily swinging in mid-air with the bell-rope knotted round his neck. His legs twitched. He seemed to be suspended in a sack, but it was only his suit, a particularly large one which I had last seen Aitken wearing over luncheon in France. The chair on which he had perched to arrange his suicide was kicked away; it looked untidily out of character with the man. A prayer-book which had been lodged on its shelf lay face down on the stone. The whole spectacle sent a shiver of horror through the congregation. The only trouble was that Edgar had signally failed to bring off his protest. The voluminous collar of the suit had saved him. His eyes were popping out, but only in mute appeal to be released from his embarrassing mistake. His face was flushed, but less in death than in rage. His arms fluttered convulsively, but rigor (if not timor) mortis was a long way off.

An open-mouthed tableau formed under the sway of the gibbet. The vicar's wife lay sobbing on a tombstone, still showing too much leg. And then Aitken moved, Aitken alone, proving in one action the probable truth of escapades in which no number of his words had been quite enough to make me believe. 'You silly bugger,' he cried, taking Sir Oswald's stick firmly in both hands.

There was a flash of steel. Not quite like greased lightning, retarded by his age, the blade of the swordstick curved into the air above Edgar's head and sliced into the rope. It failed to cut clean through, but the force of the impact caused Aitken to stagger back a yard or two, thus giving him the run-up required for a second assault. The sword swished. This time the strands almost parted, with the odd side-effect of tightening the noose round Edgar's neck. His legs thrashed in panic, and then a twist of his shoulders, a wriggle that sent a shudder down the suit, freed him from the rope, which shot upwards to produce a final clang from the bell, as Edgar writhed on the stones in the arms of the vicar's wife, who let out a cry even more shocked than her last. And at that moment, from far away, getting nearer, passing the church, then receding, other bells clamoured,

diverting attention briefly from the present drama. But it was
only a fire engine dashing through New Romney to probably
another false alarm.

Pocock now entered the action. With surprising tenderness
he picked Edgar up, and muttering words of comfort that
sounded as muffled as curses, he carried the little man's loose
shape, trousers flapping in the breeze of their progress, to the
vestry, where he laid him out on top of the opened register
which we had been soon meant to sign. Edgar at once rolled
off the desk on to his feet, wanly feeling his neck, meeting no
eye, and with an arrogant snort gazed with hatred at Aitken
and simply ran off before anyone could stop him. His feet
clattered down the nave. As we made a belated effort to close in,
he was tugging at the south door, then it slammed behind him,
the noise lurching down the church.

Before anyone could give chase, Archie said with quiet
authority, 'Let him be', and we were left with a ritual uncom-
pleted, a couple almost wed, a maniac at large, and a collective
sense that death had been averted at a moment when life had
hardly started. For some minutes the occasion risked descending
into an anticlimax of stupendous proportions.

The vicar, concerned only to succour his wife, seemed feebly
inclined to cancel the rest of the marriage. There were whispered
consultations at the rail. Meanwhile Venner drifted up and
down the aisle in silence as if invigilating an exam. The middle-
aged Bunter fans sat in their pews looking with polite amazement
at Archie, whose huge arm rested on Lesley's shoulders like a
yoke. With the self-conscious mien of a self-made hero Terry
Pocock mused over a memorial tablet. Joanna, still trembling,
tightened the vice on my hand. It was touch and go whether
our lungs would be allowed to expand into 'Glorious things of
thee are spoken'.

Then Lesley said, 'Look, what's all this? I want it all, Bunter,
I won't be cheated, you can't let me down now. Why should
we let that silly man, who's been blackmailing you for years,

spoil the one time in your life when you're doing something he wouldn't like? It's a moment of truth.'

'Are you suggesting,' Aitken asked with asperity, 'that Edgar was putting it on?'

'Not at all.'

'Is that true?'

'What do you mean?'

They stood in tense tandem on the steps of the altar on the brink of a quarrel. Aitken's face looked energetic and grumpy, Lesley wore that air of combative obstinacy which had shadowed her earlier marriage. In a trice the congregation turned into an audience. The fan-club was all ears. Only in the nick of time, with a sigh, did the vicar begin just where he had left off. 'Forasmuch,' he intoned, 'as Archibald and Lesley have consented together in holy matrimony', and with slight disappointment we settled on to the pitchpine and found our places in the prayer-book. Lesley had won. Archie was to be well and truly married. Edgar and all just impediments were put to rout.

For me this was indeed a moment of truth, which might even lead to more and more of that elusive product. With Lesley's help, with access to the archive, I would soon know for sure whether Crippen might have escaped justice or the *Titanic* sailed triumphantly into New York, if the Great War could have been abbreviated, whether Edward VIII might still be on the throne or Oswald Mosley elevated to the peerage after an unbroken spell as Prime Minister. I would find out whether Churchill should have sunk without trace in the wilderness or Montgomery remained an officer unfamed by victory in the desert. The papers would prove whether T. S. Eliot or D. H. Lawrence could have been prevented from impressing their drab or lascivious genius on my century or if Anthony Eden had lost his temper at the time of Suez because he feared exposure as the Greyfriars boy he was, and at last whether history itself had been as wax in the chubby hands of this entirely splendid character on whom Billy Bunter was said to have been based.

Lesley would watch over my interests, as over his comfort. We
would all chuckle over the implications. I would soon know it
all. As the service drew peacefully to its close and we sang the
hymn and the light darkened in the church, the secrets of the
twentieth century were suddenly at my command, to present
them as I would, to tell their truth as I saw it.

The sun had come out. From the windows, at the last minute,
splodges of purple and smears of colour as garish as blood
abruptly suffused the faces of guests as they drifted down the
nave. Outside on the steps we were ambushed by a chatty
photographer, arranged, and forgotten, by me. After some argument from Aitken, whose habit of anonymity was mistaken for
modesty, we formed up. I stood behind Lesley looking vaguely
proud. Joanna towered over Aitken with a set smile. We
surreptitiously held hands like understudies of the stars of the
occasion.

'You,' hissed Joanna, 'are responsible for all this.'

'No, no.'

'Oh, yes. The very first time she mentioned him to you, you
know, at that wine-bar, you began to feel unreal, didn't you?'
she said out of the corner of her mouth. 'Like fiction, you said.'

'Suppose I did?'

'Now do please smile, all of you,' said the photographer with
a grin.

'Well, then,' said Joanna, 'how does it feel to have been
writing a story all along? Made up out of your childhood,
invented by your youth, spun out of your distinct failure to live
an adult life, wouldn't you put it like that?'

She sounded angry. The photographer elongated his grin
under the camera that hid his eyes.

'Do please behave yourself, Joanna.'

'Come on, folks,' said the photographer, 'this is supposed to
be a happy occasion.'

'No, the point is,' Joanna whispered, 'that you've come out
a changed man. I mean, I'm impressed. You got rid of a job

you couldn't stick. And you're going to marry me, isn't that right? You've made a commitment.'

'I suppose I have.'

'You might sound more enthusiastic.'

'It's difficult when you're smirking for posterity.'

'Just one more,' cried the photographer. 'All together now, hold it!'

Joanna gazed out at the graveyard without a trace of humour. 'You actually have changed, Patrick,' she said. 'You've passed out of fiction into fact.'

'Do you really think so?'

'Facts have to be faced.' She turned to me, grinning at her own jest.

'Thank you, one and all,' said the photographer with a click. 'That's it!'

Archie insisted that we both travel back to The Dunes in the old grey Wolseley, as if afraid of being alone with his wife. Joanna was in front. Lesley sat between Archie and me in the back, holding both our hands. My hand was becoming rather tired of being held. So was my mind. The wedding had severed like a bell-rope the thread of interest that had tied me to Bunter, and I now wanted to escape, as Edgar had, and pursue my own life, preferably in the front seat with Joanna.

Soames drove on. I felt squeezed, if not squashed, and also curiously stirred by illicit desire as Lesley's thigh garbed in silk moved inadvertently against my trousers. Beyond the rolled-up windows a landscape of bungalows, love-nests, dirty weekends muffled by shrubbery, passed at speed as Soames conveyed us towards the next move in the game. What was supposed to happen to us now? A cup of tea? Fond farewells? I recognised my feeling: the anticlimax I had noted earlier, mingled with a fear of never eluding the toils of this now united couple who had dominated me for so long. Lesley had worsened the best years of my life. Aitken had thrown my manhood into disarray by forcing me back to infancy.

I tried to rally. 'When are you proposing to tell me the rest, Archie?' I asked.

'I'll be dealing with that in future,' Lesley said, patting my hand; she sounded uncommonly like Edgar. 'Archie's going to need rest before the balloon goes up. He's a famous man. He's not just yours, Patrick, he belongs to the world. I have to protect him from the vultures. A few TV spots, some write-ups, what-have-you, I'm working on that. I can tell you right now that yours won't be the only book about him. There's far more to say than you could imagine in your wildest dreams.'

'I suppose we could permit him to sift through the papers before anyone else,' Aitken said weakly. 'After all, he's almost family.'

'Who wants proof, darling? Patrick doesn't want it. He believes you. Isn't that enough?' They were talking about me as if I didn't exist. 'I shall be looking after the archive from now on. I'm your curator, put it like that. You ought to be delighted that Edgar's now thoroughly discredited. At least I opened your eyes to his capers.'

'You did well,' murmured Archie. 'You did very well. That man was beginning to own me. It is bad enough that the house belongs to him.'

A silence fell as we bowled along a shopping parade. Lesley's hand went limp in mine.

'The house belongs to him,' she repeated as if learning a foreign language.

'I do think,' said Aitken, 'that I signed a document to that effect.'

In front of us a child zigzagged across the road with a bucket and spade.

'But where are we going to live?'

'I rather thought in your estimable residence – in Surrey, isn't it?'

'But that belongs to Patrick,' said Lesley, aghast.

'In that case,' Aitken said in relaxed tones, 'I can try not to take up too much space. I'm certain Patrick won't mind if you establish my sepulchre in his grounds when you complete your design for it. Hurry along, though. Marrying a beautiful woman was my one remaining ambition and I appear to have achieved it. Death is now the only challenge left. I shall endeavour to embrace it with all due speed, since you evidently feel I shall be in the way.'

With care Soames skirted a pram on a zebra crossing.

'We must buy another place, of course,' said Lesley.

'Why not? If Edgar, now happily surviving, agrees to lend us the money I made over to him in a thoughtless moment.'

With more care Soames turned a corner.

'What that Hitler's money, Archie?' I enquired as casually as possible.

'Good grief, no,' he said. 'I spent all that. It only lasted about twenty years. Since then I've been living off a whip-round. All my old school-chums stood by me, you know.'

A glimpse of the sea yawned in front of us. I thought of Anthony Eden plunging us into the muddle of Suez while fighting off his exposure as Harry Wharton, of Churchill out of gratitude contributing to a fund, of J. B. Priestley eschewing his royalties in Aitken's favour for fear of being pilloried as the plump prototype of Johnny Bull. It seemed unlikely that these men had combined to ease Aitken's passage through life, even less probable that Aitken had entrusted Edgar with the use of the money, but Archie had been defying plausibility for a lifetime, and one never knew. Never.

'Well, I must say,' snapped Lesley, and irresponsibly Aitken huddled into his corner grinning.

This second tiff of their marriage was now interrupted by a thud of brakes as Soames swung into the drive. My head banged into Joanna's seat. Lesley shot woodenly forward like a puppet. The drive, it seemed, was jammed with vehicles. Even through shut windows I could smell smoke, which made sense of the fire engine which stood, motors rumbling, outside the front

door. Various guests had taken up attitudes of shock on the
lawn to stare at the house, from the entrance to which a lot of
frothy runnels of water trickled. Around the back of the
Fortnum's van a number of sodden cardboard boxes were
littered. The young man who had served us, brandishing a pair
of empty bottles, was deep in explanation with two firemen. As
I raced to the scene, a last papery puff of smoke caught my
nostrils from one of the windows, all open, and a fireman
appeared on the roof waving an axe. 'All clear,' he cried, as if
a war had been won.

In due course Aitken, forcibly accommodated in the wheelchair by Soames, was permitted to enter his former home which
seemingly now belonged to Edgar. The floor of the hall, where
we had celebrated the marriage in advance, was awash with
bubbles, a lagoon of grubby champagne lapping at our feet. The
study door was for once unlocked, the scars of axe-blows visible
around the keyhole. The walls were browned by smoke, and as
we peered in from the passage a petrol can which had been
lolling on the tide came to rest against a damp dictionary, as the
water drained through the floorboards. The shelves, from which
on that first night long ago I had read of this or that ruse foisted
by Bunter on his unsuspecting masters, were now empty. But
the carpet was a mess of charred paper, in which a complete
collection of *The Magnet* could be inferred only from the un-
burnt scraps. Nothing but a date, a title or a few lines of
adventure had survived.

It was at once evident that the fire had been started in this
room; that it was no accident; that the archive at the back of
the shelves, if it had existed at all, did so no longer; and that
Edgar, if indeed he owned the property, would be unlikely to
have any valid claim to the insurance. His gesture in burning
the house down was as effective as the suicide.

Without expression Aitken sat in the wheelchair in the door-
way gazing at the ruins of his boyhood, the holocaust of a
fictional self that had retarded us all. It was as though an old

England had gone for good, destroyed by the fires of envy, reduced to ashes by Edgar's resentment that his old mentor had tried to change the present, instead of being content to brood on his past. No slow tears rolled down Aitken's fat cheeks. He didn't manufacture a fit to blind himself to the evidence. He took it slowly in. Was he thinking, bitterly or not, of Edgar, his betrayal – his love, if you could call it that? I had no idea. I suspected only that some virtue that had sustained Aitken through the thick and thin of his lies and his honesty had now drifted away on an ebb and flow of water and champagne. He wouldn't be the same man again.

Nor would I. For it emerged, as we retreated from the mess, that the only way the fire had been held at bay, while the youth from Fortnum & Mason alone in the threatened house waited for the hastily summoned fire brigade, was by bursting open one bottle after another of the reserve wine and shooting it into the flames that licked in ever higher clouds of smoke around that priceless collection of *The Magnet*. I wondered if I was insured for the drink thus used to dowse the fire. Yet plainly the house had been saved by my hospitality. Three or four dozen bottles of champagne had whizzed their corks into the conflagration, to celebrate it, whooshed what little was left of my bank account into a vain effort to preserve what solid detail I needed to translate myth into truth, to give Bunter the reality he had always deserved, to make fantasy fact.

Now I would never do it, any more than Aitken would ever fully come clean, or Lesley be straightforward with herself, or Joanna add up to a rounded human being, or Venner alter the way he educated children, or Edgar Smedley be more than a small boy born without the gift for growing up. We would all survive, no doubt. But we wouldn't have done what we wanted to do, and we would die with charred copies of our aspirations swilling round our ankles. That was the bad news.

The good news arrived only just in time. The fumes and guests were still dispersing when a squat burly figure waddled up the drive, as if coming in ninth wicket down to save the side. Behind him drifted a youngish blonde in suburban finery who bore a disquieting resemblance to Joanna. Seeing Gerry Feathers for the first time since boyhood – he had been delayed by a signal failure – was for me the afternoon's final bonus: here was a man with stories to tell, triumphs to recount, a past to overawe the anticlimax of the present. I might even discover why he had never played for England. Joanna introduced us with becoming nerves. We shook hands like old friends, as the firemen cleared up the detritus of a vanished life.

'Is the show over?' he whispered.

'Good heavens, no,' I replied, and within a few moments we were waving Archie and Lesley off to their heavily subsidised honeymoon at the Ritz, with the intention ourselves of repairing to the best dinner in the district. It might even turn out to be in France.

Archibald Aitken died of natural causes on 9th June 1984, a few days after his wedding, a week before his ninetieth birthday. Apart from proper grief, I was relieved to have no further need for dealings with the Secretary of the Athenaeum, A. J. P. Taylor, Soames, the Minister for the Arts, Terry Pocock or the truth.

Risking bad taste in the wake of a funeral, I married Joanna Feathers a bare week later. Her father not only gave her away, but opened the batting at a cricket match in our honour and insisted on Debbie undertaking a small dinner party at his hotel. Both of them made ducks.

Edgar Smedley wasn't sent to prison for arson, embezzlement, attempted suicide or any other of his crimes against humanity. To cure his mental disorder or just to improve his game, he started going five times a week to Dr Witherby shortly after my wedding. Where the money comes from and what the result will be are questions that now and then drive me to distraction.

Archie Aitken had given his love to my ex-wife. He had placed his trust in me. In our memories was his posthumous fate secure. He could safely go down in history as a man who had concealed the twentieth century from itself until the last minute. I have done my bit. Meanwhile we all await Lesley's memorial to him with the bated breath it will no doubt deserve.

Sometimes, as I lie in bed and the rain dashes on the window and half-dreams hang about the shadows of the room, I wonder if Billy Bunter is still alive, and pressing my paunch more comfortably into the hollows of Joanna's back, I have no doubt at all of the answer and I fall asleep with the deepest gratitude, looking forward to the next day.

LANCASHIRE LIBRARY